# DANNY PLATTEN

# ROSIE

BLACK TREE
PUBLISHING

Design and Production by Black Tree Publishing, Hull
Gemini House, Lee Smith Street Hull HU9 1SD
Telephone: 01482 328677

Printed by: Fisk Printers, Hull

# CONTENTS

# 1
# Rosie Moves On

Rosie Lambert was brought up in the small town of Chesterfield. Her family would be regarded by most as middle class social climbers who had worked for their success. Her father was well educated but his family, although well off, were not would you could call rich. Rosie's mother hailed from a working class background. Having tried her hardest over the years to fit in with her husband's friends she grew to know that she would never fit in with the crowd.

Her parents had their differences, then. Rosie had sensed all this in her early teens; her father and mother were arguing more and more, Rosie could not stand the disagreements and the relentless shouting. Once she started college she felt her parents were never going to change, and all Rosie wanted was to get to Leeds University, where she could be out of the way. Her mother was drinking more and more and her father was spending more time away from home, supposedly working late at his small business.

The problems at home were also affecting Rosie's exams at the college. However, she had tried to get through all this because she desperately wanted to go to university. Her father had tried to reassure her that things would still be the same with Rosie and himself, whatever happened between her mother and him. He told her that he would always be there for her, no matter what.

Rosie was, bit-by-bit, becoming a different person, going out more now and drinking more than she had done in the past. She was trying to shut herself out from all the problems at home.

She was looking forward to starting university and getting away from all the bickering she had endured, which was becoming worse by the day. Recently she had heard her father and mother shouting at one another; something about her father seeing a younger woman. Rosie also heard her father tell her mother it was finished between them and that he wanted a divorce.

As things became more unbearable for Rosie, her friends noticed the change in her. She was going home with a few different young men from the clubs. Her girlfriends would boast about their sexual exploits but Rosie was not impressed. She thought she had something wrong with her because they talked of the excitement they had experienced when being touched by some young man.

Rosie had not experienced that same excitement. In fact, she was pleased when it had all finished. It was as though she thought it would just happen, this wonderful feeling that they all spoke about. Unfortunately it had not. Not yet. Rosie was a good-looking girl and a lot of the young men fancied her. Sadly, for them at least, the feelings were not mutual.

Rosie thought about the accusations her mother was throwing at her father. This affair was with a girl somewhat younger than him. She had overheard her father say that, if it had not been for Rosie, he would have left a long time ago.

This upset Rosie a lot. She thought back to the days when her parents would shower her with affection and take her everywhere with them. Now, they rarely sat down for a meal together. Rosie was beginning to feel lost and she longed for all the bickering to stop.

Fortunately she passed her exams and had managed to get herself an offer from Leeds. Her father was so pleased for her that he told her if there was anything she wanted she should tell him immediately. Her mother, on the other hand, had lost her way. The drink had taken over her life and little else mattered to her as long as she had a drink. When Rosie repeatedly told her she must stop drinking all she got was a negative response, her mother mumbling something about not drinking that much.

Her father told her he was going to leave her mother

and move in with a young woman called Mandy. That when she left for uni things would be sorted out regarding her mother, the house, the money and everything else. Rosie was now accepting the situation and was prepared to go her own way, stop worrying about her parents, and looking forward to her own future.

By the time Rosie sets off for Leeds with her father she has already said the necessary goodbyes to her mother. Her father apologises to Rosie. He's noticed the change in her over the past few months. Now, his words are echoing around her head as he reiterates that he will always be there for her. As they arrive at the flats where she will be staying Rosie feels free. No more arguing, no more shouting; she can get on with her own life and who knows what the future will bring?

Quickly, once at uni, she meets a girl called May Johnson who just happened to be looking for a roommate. Rosie didn't fancy the halls of residence and, as they got on well together at first meeting, she wasted no time in moving into May's flat. May, who has no scruples and calls a spade a spade, makes Rosie laugh with her antics. Like many, if not all of their fellow students, they enjoy themselves, having a few parties, meeting new girlfriends and, of course, plenty of the opposite sex.

Rosie's sexual experiences with young men to date had not really lived up to expectations; she was looking for the deep and fulfilling sexual experience that many of the girls talked about. And then, out of the blue, along came Danny. She met Danny at Leeds Uni and fancied him as soon as she saw him.

# 2
# Playing The Game

A good-looking man in his mid-twenties, Danny has dark curly hair and dark, doe-like eyes. And, she thinks, a body to die for. Rosie could not resist his charming chat up line when they happened to meet in a queue inside the university restaurant; she saw him looking at her, and then he approached her and just came out with it.

"What's your name?" he asked.

"Rosie," she said, feeling her face flush up.

He looked down at her, pushing his dark curly hair back with his hand.

"Rosie, could you please write this number down for me? I have a problem with my right hand."

With the pen and piece of paper he gave her, she wrote the number down for him, and then he looked at her and said, smiling.

"Keep it. Ring me."

He laughed as he walked away, she watched him as he turned and gave her a wink. Rosie gave him a little smile back. She also noticed other girls showing a lot of interested in him.

She looked at then pen and paper knowing, without even a second thought, that she would definitely telephone him.

Today, thinking back, she realises she knows nothing about him. Is he a student, a lecturer or just visiting?

She tells her flat mate May, who likes the boys a lot.

"You are going to telephone him, aren't you? I know you're going to," smiles May.

"I have been thinking about ringing him all day. I can't wait any longer."

Rosie fumbles with her mobile phone. She looks at the phone and then at May. She needs some reassurance.

"Shall I? What do you think?"

"Go on, telephone him Rosie," says May, encouraging her to make the call.

Rosie looks at her. May is watching her and sees Rosie is still very nervous. Finding the courage she dials the number. His number. It's not long before a sexy voice is heard on the phone. For once Rosie is lost for words. She bites her lip.

"You... you gave me your number to ring you. I'm Rosie, from the university."

There is a long pause.

"Rosie? Oh yes, Rosie. I remember. Of course I do. It's nice of you to telephone me."

There is a slight pause again.

"I was wondering if we could meet up sometime, Rosie?"

Rosie giggles and then, putting her hand over the phone, she whispers to May.

"He wants to meet up."

May whispers to Rosie, giggling and unable to wait and see what happens.

"Go on! Tell him yes."

Rosie sits up, shuffling around with excitement. She puts the phone to her ear and tells him.

"Yes, that would be nice. I would like that."

She is getting more excited by the minute.

Danny asks in a low husky voice, "Do you like playing games, Rosie?"

A little confused she asks, "Games? What kind of games? What do you mean?"

Danny does not elaborate on the question he has asked. He tells her, "Maybe we can talk about that later. Have you a pen?"

She motions to May to hand her a pen. May searches frantically through her bag. Finally she finds a pen and hands it to Rosie along with a piece of paper.

"Yes, okay. Go ahead."

"Tomorrow night at eight o'clock take a taxi to Portland

Villas, Hendon Square. Come to apartment 109. Just ring the bell in the hallway then come up in the lift."

Rosie is having doubts now but still finds all this very exciting.

"I've got all that. Apartment 109, yes."

"Good. Don't be late Rosie. I'm sure you will enjoy our meeting."

"I won't be late," she says, then wishes she hadn't said it. He puts the phone down. May, unable to wait for Rosie to tell her, asks, "Well, come on, what did he say?"

With a curious look on her face she says, "He asked me a strange question. Then he asked me to go to his apartment in Hendon Square. At eight o'clock tomorrow night."

"What was the strange question? Bloody hell, Rosie, he must be loaded. You need a lot of money to live there."

She smiles thinking she won't tell May too much about what Danny said.

"To get a good looking man is good enough, but to get one with money is bloody marvellous. I can't wait for tomorrow night. I'll have to find something nice to put on, if you know what I mean?"

"You're not telling me what question he asked. Anyway, black underwear. All men like black underwear," May laughs.

"It might not get that far," she says again, blushing.

May laughs out loud at that one. "You're joking! Might not get that far! I bet they'll be off faster than you can say Rosie Lambert."

They both start laughing. Rosie pushes May over on the sofa and jumps on her playfully.

All the next day Rosie is thinking about what he will be like when they do meet up. She is unable to study anything. Once back in the flat she fusses around looking through her small wardrobe trying to pick some suitable clothes, and underwear. She picks through her small box of different pieces of costume jewellery, deciding on the best earrings to put on. Later that evening she gets undressed. Once naked, she looks at herself in the mirror, lifting her breasts with her hands, pouting her lips before smiling at herself. She gets into the bath, lays back and closes her eyes thinking of what lies ahead.

When she has bathed and made herself up she is a good-looking girl and does not really need a lot of makeup. She has managed to find some nearly new underwear, and some black stockings just on the off chance that things might, just might, hot up a little. She chooses a small black dress, tying her lovely long black hair back to expose her beautiful face.

"God this man doesn't know what he is getting. Don't forget to get your taxi money from him," May tells her.

Rosie laughs thinking *'May is joking'*.

"So when we meet I'll just say to him, 'Give me my taxi money?' Like hell I will. You have to speculate to accumulate my girl."

They both laugh. Rosie picks up her bag then turns to May.

"Wish me luck."

"With that body you do not need luck. Go to it girl." She gives Rosie a wink.

The taxi is waiting. Rosie tells the driver where to go.

"You did say Hendon Square, miss?" the taxi driver asks.

"That's right. You know where it is, don't you?" she says, feeling rather posh.

"Yes miss, I know."

They arrive at the apartments. Rosie pays him, and as she gets out of the cab she looks up at the building and is very impressed. She enters the entrance hall. Everything is in different shades of marble and is spotlessly clean. She is a little nervous now, as she presses the button for apartment 109. She seems to be waiting a long time before someone answers.

"Yes?"

"It's me, Rosie."

"Please come up Rosie. Just come straight in and go into the lounge and wait for me."

Rosie is a little confused as to what is going on but decides to do what he said; he may have a surprise for her. She enters the very large apartment. It is beautiful, the lights are low with some background music playing. As she walks through to the lounge her eyes are everywhere, so this is how the other half live? She stands still, waiting for Danny to come to her. Suddenly arms come around her from the back, he kisses her neck and, at the same time, he puts a mask over her eyes. She makes a move to take it off but he whispers in her ear.

"No, my darling, don't be afraid. It's the game."

She stands there feeling his hands on her, touching her. Slowly he undoes her zip on the back of her dress. He is kissing her back and then up to her neck. She can smell his aftershave. He has a very gentle touch as he undoes her bra and slides it over her shoulders. Rosie is trembling with excitement as he takes her hands and places them on his now bare chest; she cannot control herself as she explores his body.

The black dress falls to the floor. Rosie feels it fall and steps out of it. He leads her to the bedroom. She wants to see him, to see his face but she does like the excitement of not seeing. As they get to the bed he puts her onto her knees at the end of the bed, gently putting her face down on the bed while she is still kneeling on the floor. Then he spreads her arms on the bed. He kneels behind her, pushing himself closer to her. She feels his fingers gently touching her most intimate places and then she gives out a little scream as he enters her. Her body is burning with desire as he moves slowly but precisely, as though he knows every sensitive part of her body. She moves with him, slowly taking every bit of his pleasure that she can. He withdraws then lays her on the bed. His hands are everywhere and, at the same time, he starts to kiss her breasts and then he moves down to her stomach. As he goes further down she arches her back to meet him. Never has she felt anything so intense; she can hardly bear the pleasure. Then he lays beside her. For the first time she is able to hold him and is soon on top of him and, straddling him, she puts him inside of her.

They are both perspiring as they begin to reach the peak of pleasure. Rosie's body shakes as she releases her orgasm. She has never experienced something so wonderful like this before and it seems to last forever.

She still has her eyes covered. He whispers to her not to take off the mask, and after more sex she falls asleep exhausted.

When she wakes she feels around for Danny in the bed. He isn't there. She wonders what to do until, after a short time, she decides to slowly remove the mask. She rubs her eyes, gets off the bed naked and looks around the room. There is no one to be seen. She calls out his name.

"Danny, Danny, are you there?"

There is no answer. She checks each room. She finds the bathroom and decides to take a shower, thinking he may be back soon. But after her shower no one comes so she dresses, thinking, *'How strange.'*

She realises that she liked what happened. She dresses and decides to leave, as Danny is nowhere to be found. Before she goes she notices a note on the table with some money. She picks up the note, which just reads *'We will meet again Rosie. Take the money and buy something special for our next encounter.'*

The money on the table is more than she has ever had in her life. She is a little mad thinking he is paying her for the sex, but has more than enjoyed what just happened. She walks towards the door then opening it, pauses and turns, looking across at the money on the table again. Then she goes back, picks it up, leaves the apartment looking at the money, smiling to herself as she thinks, *'Buy something nice? Well, why not?'*

She arrives back at the flat. May has just got out of bed.

"Bloody hell Rosie you must have had a good night. Tell me all about it."

Rosie takes the money out of her pocket and shows May.

"Oh! Come on Rosie you didn't? Not for money?"

She has a smile on her face as she tells May, "I never saw him at all."

"If you never saw him where the hell have you been and where is the money from?" May asks, looking puzzled.

She laughs, "I've been with him."

"You never saw him, but you've been with him? Come on Rosie, you're talking in riddles."

Rosie giggles as she explains.

"I went into his apartment. He was there. I don't want to tell you everything that happened. All I can say is wow, wow, wow. All the time I was there I never knew sex could be such an adventure. We were at it all night. And later when I went to sleep

he must have left. He just left the note and the money."
May is now very interested.

"What did the note say?"

"I had to buy something nice for next time."

"So you did it and he liked it, then?" May is thinking this is getting better by the minute.

"You could say that. I have never ever experienced anything like what happened last night."

"If it was that good can you put in a word in for me? Then I won't have to go with these bloody juveniles we are surrounded with," May says, laughing.

"I can tell you this. It was definitely a night to remember. No more questions now, I'm tired." Rosie goes to bed telling May, "If anyone asks about me tell them I am in bed with a cold."

Over the next few days Rosie is impatient and continuously waiting for a call from Danny. Having tried to phone him a couple of times she only gets his answerphone. She dare not leave a message. Every time she has gone for a meal in the uni restaurant she is looking for him. Unfortunately he is nowhere to be seen. She has been out and bought some very nice, sexy underwear ready for him. Prepared, then, if he does telephone her and asks to meet up again.

After a few days she comes to the conclusion he is not going to phone. Life at the university gets back to normal. May asks Rosie to go out with her and a few of their friends at the weekend, and, with nothing else on offer, she agrees.

The lads who they usually go around with are good for a laugh but none of them are what Rosie views as worthy of getting serious with. They are not what you would call sophisticated enough and most of them are always skint. May and a couple of their friends are getting ready for their night out. It's all short dresses and plenty of makeup.

"Have you seen that good looking Norwegian lad? His name is Kjell?" May asks Rosie.

"Yes I have seen him." She is really not interested.

"Well he is joining us tonight."

One of the other girls, called Sue, is laughing and shouts across.

"First there, first served."

"You mean serviced don't you?" May says, laughing.

Soon they are already for the off. Handbags at the ready they go to join the lads. The taxi is outside and everyone tries to get in. The lads are enjoying themselves already; as the girls squeeze in as best they can there are arms and legs everywhere and more than a few wandering hands. The girls really don't bother too much. Sue calls out to one of the lads.

"Get your hands off my crown jewels."

Everyone laughs and soon they are on the way to the club. As they enter the club the music is blaring out and there is hardly any room to move. After some time and quite a few drinks they are rather intoxicated. Kjell has had his eye on Rosie for some time and approaches her to dance. Rosie has had a few drinks now and thinks he is a good-looking lad and decides to dance with him before the other girls get their hands on him.

Kjell doesn't take his eyes off her body as she is dancing; she has her eyes closed as if in another place. Rosie, who has a very tight skirt on and a silky see-through top that shows off her very lovely figure, is swinging her hips from side to side. Kjell pulls her towards him, making her open her eyes.

She looks at him and smiles. She pushes her body up towards him. They are dancing close now and he is kissing her but Rosie has only one person on her mind and that's Danny. She is thinking of the things they did and this makes her feel sexier.

Unfortunately Kjell thinks it is him that is making her look the way she is. The night soon passes. A couple of the other girls have managed to get themselves a man to take them home, including May. There are a couple that are stoned and out of their heads. Kjell asks to take Rosie home and she agrees. They take a taxi back to Rosie's flat; inside the cab Kjell is anxious to feel as much of Rosie as he can, and having had quite a lot to drink she doesn't bother to stop him - but she is not responding too much to his advances.

They arrive at the flat, he pays for the cab and then they make their way in. Once inside, he kisses her and soon they are on the sofa. He fumbles around trying to undo her bra, not saying anything. She just lays there wondering what he is doing. Finally, he undoes the bra then makes a grab for her breasts. After fumbling around he attempts to have sex with her. He lays on top of her, and before he gets anywhere near to have sex he cries out.

"What's wrong?" Rosie asks looking at him.

He looks at her rather embarrassed.

"Sorry, I couldn't wait any longer."

"Wait any longer? Sodding hell, any longer? One minute."

Rosie pushes him off her and goes to the bathroom.

"I think you can go now," she calls from the bathroom.

When she comes out he has gone. Soon May comes in with a young man.

"Where's Kjell?" May asks, looking round.

"Gone home to clean his trousers. He has made a mess on them."

"What mess, Rosie?" May says looking rather puzzled

She whispers to her.

"Put it this way, he came and went very fast."

"Was he a virgin?" May asks, laughing.

"A very fast virgin. I'm going to bed. Hope yours lasts a little longer than Kjell did."

The lad with May calls out for her.

"Come on then, May."


Rosie is feeling a little let down by Danny. He built her hopes up, and now she feels he has led her on a bit. Most of her friends from last night have bad heads and are not feeling too good, May is no different; her boyfriend didn't leave until nearly daylight. May told her he was not much good in bed either.

Rosie sees Kjell later. He is very embarrassed about the short sexual experience with her. As he sees her he puts his head down and looks away. She laughs to herself, thinking he was not the first to do what he did and probably he won't be the last. After a few more experiences he may last a little longer which, after her experience with him, wouldn't have to take much.

# 3
# Enjoy Yourself

Rosie is in touch with her family now and again. When her parents were together she had often noticed just how embarrassed her father had been at times with her mother. More so when they had friends visiting the house, probably because he came from a better-off family, and had a very good education. Since he left Rosie's mother's behaviour seems to have got progressively worse.

Her father seems to be in a good relationship with Mandy despite the age difference. He is proud of Rosie going to university, and does see her regularly. Her mother is inclined to drink too much, and there have been rumours she takes drugs. She is unable to manage very well on the money her father gives her.

Although she loves her mother Rosie is not proud of her. Every time she sees her she looks worse than she remembers. Her mother visits Rosie at her flat, arriving in a drunken state. Rosie is not happy. She looks at her mother, not hiding her anger.

"Mum, just look at you. I hope no one saw you come here."

Her mother stands and sways, as she looks back at Rosie.

"Why... what's... wrong? That bloody father of yours won't help me. I can't manage on the bloody pittance he gives me each month. You couldn't help me out Rosie could you? I'm bloody desperate. I'm skint."

Rosie knows where the money will go if she gives her anything. But looking at the state of her she takes some of the money she has left from the funds Danny gave her.

"Here, mum. Don't spend it all on booze. I haven't anything else until I get my allowance from dad."

"Thanks Rosie... I have... an appointment... I'll see you... sometime next week."

Rosie sees her out, thinking her mother will never change. In fact, she knows she is getting worse.

Not having heard anything from Danny after another couple of days she takes out her phone thinking she will give him a call but expecting to get his answerphone again. She looks at the phone again then plucks up the courage to dial the number. She is scared and is about to end the call when the answerphone briefly clicks before a voice comes on the phone.

"Hello Rosie."

Rosie is taken aback. "I hope you don't mind me telephoning you Danny. How did you know it was me?"

"I have your number from the last time you phoned me. I have been away a while. Maybe you would like to meet up again tomorrow night? "

Rosie can feel her body getting warm just talking to him.

"Yes I would like to meet up," she says, trying to sound casual.

There is a silence then Danny tells her, "I will send a car for you tomorrow night, eight o'clock outside your flat."

Rosie is getting more excited as she shudders again remembering their first encounter.

"I'll be there."

"Hope you managed to buy something nice, maybe suspenders and stockings? A lovely loose dress would be appropriate. Oh! And Rosie, be ready to play the game. Just do what my driver tells you."

Again Rosie pauses. She gets lost for a while, wondering what will happen. And then, finally, she answers.

"Yes, I will."

She is desperate to tell May about the call but decides not to tell her about what he has suggested she wear. May comes in to the flat, looking at Rosie.

"Okay, what are you smiling about?"

Rosie does a little dance. "I'm meeting Danny tomorrow night.

He is sending his car for me."

Rosie is very excited and is not concealing it.

"Rosie, you seem to have got yourself some rich bastard. He must have some friends. Could you put in a word for me please?"

May might be laughing but she isn't joking. She really does hope that Rosie will put in a word for her.

Rosie tries to play her big date down a bit.

"It isn't as though it's a serious relationship. It's just a date."

They both sit talking before Rosie starts selecting her clothes for the following night.

Next day at uni she is like a cat on hot bricks, just like she was the last time before meeting Danny. Unable to concentrate on anything, Rosie thinks about her last date with him and it is making her feel more excited by the minute.

She arrives home to get herself ready. After bathing she is very careful with her choice of make up. Rosie is that beautiful that she would look good without it. In the bedroom she has her underwear laid on the bed and, as she pulls herself into it, May enters the flat.

"Where are you, Rosie?" she calls.

"I'm in here May," Rosie calls from the bedroom.

"Bloody hell Rosie, that's nice. I fancy you myself seeing you in that," May says.

They laugh as Rosie finishes putting her underwear on, smoothing her stockings up her legs then fastening the suspenders. May is sat on the bed watching her.

"Rosie whatever you do please try not to be, how shall I put it, easy meat. You know what I mean, don't you?"

She looks at May with a big grin on her face.

"Easy? I don't know when I haven't been easy."

"I'm the same. Any time anything gets between my legs it's like a key to open the safe. My legs fly open," she says, giggling.

They are both giggling now. Rosie is just about ready and is looking at the clock. She picks up her bag and looks in the mirror; turning to look at the back of her dress and smoothing it round the contour of her bottom. She hopes Danny likes what he sees. She is already infatuated with him, happy to do all that he wants. All she cares about is making him want her.

"Yes, I think that will do."

She walks to the window, pulling the curtains to one side as she looks through the window.

Then, rather excited, she shouts, "May, come have a look at this."

May runs to look through the window and, when she gets there, sees a very large black stretch limousine.

"That thing is big enough to carry an army."

With one last look Rosie calls out to her friend.

"May, I'm off."

Once outside she walks up to the stretch limo. The chauffeur is stood with the back door open. He has a small box under his arm. As she approaches him, he greets her.

"Good evening Miss Lambert. Please make yourself comfortable." She gets into the limo and, once comfortable, the chauffeur hands her the box then closes the door. She looks around. There are drinks in the centre of the seats in a specially made rack. Music is playing. Rosie has never seen anything like it.

She opens the box and, looking inside, sees a smaller box, and then underneath that there is a black frilly mask and a note. She opens the small box. What she sees makes her smile and she cannot hold back her excitement as she takes a pair of beautiful earrings from the box.

She reads the note. It says, *'Rosie, the game has started. Put on the mask. Please sit back and make yourself comfortable. And Rosie...'*

He has her full attention now.

*'...enjoy it.'*

She takes the earrings first and puts them on. Then, smiling, she is about to put the mask on. She sees the chauffeur smiling, looking at her through the rear view mirror. Then he realises that she sees him looking at her. He closes the shaded window behind him. She puts on the mask then sits back in anticipation, waiting for something to happen.

After some time Rosie feels the limo coming to a stop. There is no sound aside from the music. She hears the door open then someone sits besides her, not saying a word. She can smell a lovely perfume. The door is closed and then, to her surprise, the other side door opens and someone else is sat next to her. She is wondering what is happening, and is about to take the mask off when the limo starts to move.

A hand squeezes her hand, which is somehow reassuring. She is sat rigid until his lips touch hers. She knows the smell of his aftershave and this relaxes her. His hands undo her top. His hands are soon feeling her breasts. He is kissing her neck. Then she feels hands in between her legs. She can smell the perfume, and then someone breathing very close to her. As lips meet a tongue enters her mouth. She is getting very excited now with everything that is happening. She senses it is a woman kissing her but she cannot help herself, as other hands are undressing her and touching her. He is kissing her breasts as he takes her hand and places it on his now erect penis. Her other hand is now placed in between the woman's legs. At first she tries to resist but then relaxes and goes along with what is happening. All her sexual senses have been awakened and are now in full flow as she lets herself go. This is Rosie's own utopia. She is torn and, not knowing which way to turn, she feels hands all over her body as she is made to lay across the seats. He is soon on top of her and as he enters her she can feel the other woman is very excited, and is kissing her on other parts of her body.

"Oh! Yes, yes." She cries out as she reaches her climax. It seems that all this excitement has been going on for hours. Soon all of her body stiffens then shudders. As before, she pulls his hair and digs her nails into his back as the moment of complete satisfaction passes through her body. The limo is still moving. She feels so exhausted as she lay still, waiting for something else to happen. She is about to talk when he just says to her, "Sshhh."

She does not move until the limo stops. The door opens and all is quiet. When it starts to move again she waits for some time before she decides to remove the mask. She sits up, putting her clothes on. She notices the chauffeur watching her dress through the rear mirror. He is not showing any embarrassment at her spotting him watching her. Looking around she sees a woman's panties on the floor. She thinks, *'What am I doing here? Never again.'*

Rosie is soon dressed. She just sits there thinking, what just happened? After some time the limo comes to a stop, the back door opens and the chauffeur speaks.

"Everything okay miss?"

He says this smiling, looking at her rather nonchalantly. She picks up her bag, he helps her out of the limo, and she makes her way to her flat. She opens her bag looking for her keys and she cannot believe it. There is a lot of money in her bag. She takes the money out; she thinks she must be dreaming as she holds a roll of £50 notes. Before she enters her flat she looks at the money again. She smiles to herself; she knows she was lying to herself. She really enjoyed every minute of what happened this evening. She goes into the flat. May is sat waiting to hear what happened.

"Oh! Rosie, come now and tell me what you have been up to?"

May leans forward waiting the answer. Rosie is teasing her.

"Can't tell you May, sorry. I'm off to my room," she turns and smiles at May. "Night, night."

Rosie calls to May and gives her a little wave and a smile as she closes her bedroom door.

May flops back on the sofa disappointed. She didn't get to know what Rosie had been up to.

Rosie feels exhausted; she takes the money from her bag and thrown it all over the bed. She lays down on the bed smiling with all the money around her. She closes her eyes, wondering what her next adventure will be. Then she has an overwhelming feeling of regret; how come all this can be happening to her, when will it end, will it end? She thinks, *'Will it all end in disaster?'* She soon falls to sleep.

# 4
# Another Bit Of Business

On the occasions when Rosie can get to the restaurant at the university she looks for Danny but up to now, has not seen him. Some time has passed since her last adventure. She is sat in the restaurant when she sees a group of girls speaking to a man. She stands up to see him more clearly and realises that they are all laughing. She cannot believe it. She is sure it is Danny.

She is trying to push her way through some of the people who are queuing for food. Unfortunately, by the time she gets to where he was, he has gone. She goes to one of the girls and asks if she knew who it was the girls were speaking to. The girl looks at her.

"What do you want to know for?"
She is not looking too happy with Rosie asking her questions.

"I thought it was someone I know. His name is Danny."
Rosie waits anxiously for an answer.
The girl shakes her head.

"No, you're mistaken. His name is Paul. He sometimes visits. Why, I don't know, he always attracts a lot of attention. Still, looking at him you can understand why."

Rosie thanks her and goes looking around to try to find him. She thinks he did look so much like Danny. She kicks herself that she didn't see him more clearly.

Once again Rosie has given up any hope of seeing Danny. She cannot stop thinking about what has happened to her on the last couple of meetings with him.

She is sat in her flat when her mother pays her another visit.

"Hello darling... I thought I would... pay you a visit. I don't know what to do. I am paying one bill after another. You couldn't help me darling could you?"

Rosie's mother staggers to the chair and falls in to it. Rosie is reluctant to let her know she as any money otherwise she will never get rid of her. As her mother sits down Rosie can see she has been at the drink again and suspects she has probably been taking drugs.

"I can only manage £20 max."

She knows if she gives her any more she will just spend it on drink.

"Bloody hell Rosie, can't you manage a little more than that?"

Her hands are shaking as she pulls her coat closed.

"No mother, that is it. I have my bills to pay as well you know."

Her mother shakes her shoulders and grimaces.

"Have you anything... to drink? Wine, cider... anything?"

"No, nothing," Rosie tells her as she goes to get the money.

Her mother is watching her take the money from the bag, noticing that Rosie has a fair bit of cash.

"Come on Rosie. You can let your mother have a bit more than £20."

She stands up to get a closer look into the bag. Rosie sees her looking and closes the bag, giving her mother the cash. Her mother snatches the money and, not looking too happy, she heads for the door

She mutters, "If you see that bloody father of yours, and his floozy, tell him he's a greedy bastard."

She leaves slamming the door.

Rosie is concerned about her mother, and is thinking about ways she could help her. If she tells her father she knows he will not want to know, and will not help her mother. Since they parted his favourite saying is, *'She made her bed now let her lie in it.'*

He has no interest in her mother's problems. May comes into the flat.

"Hi Rosie, any news yet on your Mr Wonderful?"

"Nothing, although I thought I saw him. Well, it looked like him in the restaurant speaking to some girls but by the time I got through the crowd he had gone. One of the girls said that his name is Paul, not Danny."

Rosie looks so disappointed; May tries to make her feel better.

"You must have been mistaken. You're that bloody infatuated, and desperate to see him again."

"I don't think I will hear from him again. Anyway, it was nice while it lasted. Short but very sweet."

"We'll probably both finish up with two poor bastards; have two or three kids and then finish up old and bloody haggard."

"Sodding hell May. You might but I can assure you I won't."

They are both laughing.

Rosie is laid on her bed reading when her phone rings.

"Hello!"

"Rosie, Rosie how are you?"

She recognises the smooth talking voice. It is Danny on the phone.

"I'm fine. I am surprised to hear from you. I thought you had forgotten me."

"Rosie, how could I forget you? I wondered if you are ready for another game?"

"Another game? I'm not going to be blindfolded again am I? Could we just have a normal date?"

There is a silence. She is waiting for what seems like ages and about to ask if he is still there when he gives a little laugh.

"Rosie, it wouldn't be the same. Maybe later we could think about that. So, you're not happy with the game so far and all the generous benefits?"

"Yes, but I was hoping to have a kind of normal date with you," she says, sounding sad.

Again, there is a silence, "Rosie if you don't want to do what we have been doing or what we'll be doing then it's okay with me. We can call it a day and you can look for... what did you say? A normal date?"

She thinks she has put her foot in it and Danny won't want see her any more.

"Danny, I have enjoyed our meetings, and I would like to see you again. I am prepared to wait so I will do as you say."

"Yes. That's my girl. I would like you to go to the Imperial Hotel at around nine o'clock tomorrow night. I will send my car for you. Go to room 71, ask for the key at the reception, just go inside Rosie and wait there. Do what you want when you get there, take a bath, have a drink, watch TV, anything you like. Just stay there until I arrive."

She thinks she will have to please him, and is looking forward to meeting him again.

She tries to sound really enthusiastic, which isn't far from the truth. "Yes, I'll be there."

"Rosie, be a little adventurous. Wear something very, very special just for me."

She laughs, before saying, "A little adventurous? Yes, okay."

"Bye for now Rosie. Until we meet again."

She is about to ask him if he had been at the university when Danny puts the phone down.

Danny is stood in his apartment. When he puts the phone down on Rosie he turns to speak to a young man who looks very much like himself. He has been listening to the conversation between Rosie and Danny.

"Well, brother, seems we have another bit of business taken care of. Our little new recruit is ready for another meeting. By the way, Paul, make sure everything is ready at the hotel before she gets there."

Paul smiles at Danny.

"Don't worry I will see to everything. Jayne is going with me. Do you think they will know one another?"

"Rosie won't be in a state to recognise anyone by the time we arrive. You make sure Jayne is the same."

"Must be off. See you later," says Paul. "You let the clients know everything is ready for tomorrow night," he says, finishing his drink.

"Will do. I'll take the payment too."

Paul leaves, leaving Danny alone. He picks up the phone to speak to the people they have lined up for tomorrow night.

When Rosie puts the phone down she goes to her bedroom, closes the bedroom door and takes the bag she has with the money in it. She takes the money out, smiles and daydreams.

"Something a bit adventurous? Okay, Danny, let's see what we can do."

May arrives. Rosie smiles at her. May guesses she has something to tell her.

"Come on girl, what's happened? You have that wanting look on your face."

"Wanting look? What do you mean? I have had a call from... guess who?"

"Yes, Rosie. Easy. It's Mr Wonderful isn't it? Tell me what he said, I can't wait."

"Tomorrow night at the Imperial Hotel. He is sending his car for me."

"Imperial Hotel? That bloody place costs a fortune for one night. I couldn't afford a cup of tea there it's that bloody expensive."

"I'm not coming in to uni. I'll give it a miss today. I have a couple of important things to take care of."

"You lucky sod Rosie. Don't forget to ask if he has any friends for me? They would wonder what had hit them if they got a bit of me," May says, showing a little envy.

"I will May. If an opportunity arises I will try to get you fixed up."

"To be honest Rosie I don't give a shit how old he is as long has he has lots of dough."

They both laugh.

The next evening Rosie is ready. She puts the money she has in her bag, and then puts it in her wardrobe. She is really looking nice. She does not know what to expect but this makes it more thrilling. She waits for the car to arrive. May is getting ready too - she is going out with friends and she looks at Rosie.

"You enjoy yourself girl. I'll see you tomorrow. I will probably finish up getting laid by some scrawny juvenile."

Rosie sees the car waiting. Laughing as she leaves she

tells May, "Wish me luck? Bye."

May sits there envious of Rosie and wishing it were her going. She has left and May is just about to leave herself when Rosie's mother comes into the flat.

"Hello Mrs Lambert. Rosie has gone out."

Rosie's mother looks at May.

"I left my bag in Rosie's room. I'll just go and get it."

She goes into the bedroom and closes the door behind her. She searches around for the bag that she has seen Rosie take the money from. She looks in several places then, opening the wardrobe door, she sees it. There it is. She grabs hold of it to look inside, smiling to herself. She cannot believe how much money is in the bag. She takes a couple of £50 notes, then shakes her head and takes some more money. As she is taking the money May opens the door.

"Okay Mrs Lambert, I'm going now. I have to lock the door."

Rosie's mother turns so she cannot see what she is doing.

"I'm going now. I must be mistaken," she says. "I probably left my bag in my house somewhere."

She throws the bag back in the wardrobe and joins May after stuffing the notes into her pocket. They both leave the flat. Once outside, Rosie's mother hurries off down the road.

Rosie arrives at the hotel. She leaves the car and, the doorman opening the door for her, she heads inside.

"Evening madam," the smart doorman says after her.

Rosie turns and smiles at him. She looks around. She is in a beautiful foyer. She proceeds to the reception desk, where a young man comes to her.

"Can I help madam?"

"Room 71." Rosie tells him.

"Just take the lift to the first floor."

She takes the key card.

"Turn left when you exit the lift."

She goes to the lift and, soon after, she is outside the room. Rosie hesitantly opens the door. Once inside she looks around. What a beautiful place she thinks to herself. There are two large sofas, and on a large glass table there is a bottle of Champagne on ice. Strangely, it has been opened. Again a note lies nearby. *'Feel free to enjoy the Champagne. I will be joining you soon.'*

She sits down and takes a glass and pours herself a drink, laying back into the lovely plush sofa. She loves the taste of the very nice Champagne and, after a couple of glasses, she feels good. Very good indeed. She goes to put some music on and as she gets up she stumbles a bit.

"Ooops," she says, feeling rather light headed.

The music is playing as she investigates the other rooms. Staggering, she holds on to a door. Her vision is a little blurred as she tries to focus on where the sofas are in order to get back and sit down. She somehow manages to get back and falls back on the sofa. The music sounds strange in her ears, as though it is echoing, and getting further away. Her mouth is very dry so she tries to reach for the Champagne just to get a drink of something. After taking another drink she feels very dizzy. She is laid back, her eyes are closed, the room seems to be spinning around, and slowly she begins to lose consciousness.

Danny and Paul enter the room. They see Rosie laid on the settee. Danny looks at Paul.

"It's okay. Bring Jayne up now if you can manage her and I'll see to Rosie?"

"Yes no problem," Paul says as he leaves the room.

Rosie can vaguely hear voices, and as she tries to open her eyes she can just see a man's face close to hers. He is talking to her. She can hear her name and tries to sit up but is still unable to see clearly. She still feels very light headed.

Danny walks towards Rosie and starts to pick her up.

"Come on my sweet, let's have you on the bed."

Her eyes are half open now and she is looking at him. She has a faint smile on her face. She knows someone is picking her up but is unable to resist.

"Yes, Rosie I know you are feeling good aren't you? No blindfold for you tonight my sweet," he says laughing.

She is laid on the bed. Danny looks at her thinking what a good-looking girl she is. He brushes her hair back,

"You are a beauty. I'll have to look after you."

He goes back into the other room as Paul brings in the other girl. She looks as though she has had a lot to drink. They take her to the bedroom where Rosie is, and lay her down alongside Rosie.

"Well brother, shall we do it then?" Paul asks.

"Yes, get the hypodermic needles," Danny says, smiling. Paul is soon back with a tray with the needles on. Danny takes one of the needles and fills it with something from a small bottle.

"Here, put that on her arm."

He gives him a strap, which Paul places around the top of Rosie's arm. Then Danny taps the needle, holding it up in the air, letting a little of the substance out. Then, finding a vein in Rosie's arm, injects her with heroin.

They do the same with the other girl, Jayne. When they have finished they both go back into the other room.

"Give them an hour. The people should be here by then. Shift that Champagne bottle or we could be in the shit if the clients drink that. Empty it out Paul."

Danny goes to the bar and takes a whiskey while Paul empties the bottle of Champagne that contains Rohypnol; the drug that has rendered both the girls unconscious and, along with a little dose of heroin, unable to resist anything that anyone is doing to them. He empties the Champagne down the sink in the bathroom.

After half an hour or so Danny and Paul go to get the girls. They are both helped back into the other room, and sat on the settee. Rosie is now awake but all her movements feel strange. She starts to giggle; Danny moves close to her.

"Hi! Rosie, how do you feel?"

She tries to speak but her words just don't seem to come out properly. She now feels very nice as though she is floating in space. Danny kisses her. Rosie responds putting her arms round him.

"Like that, don't you Rosie?"

Danny feels that he has her where he wants her. She nods her head. Then Jayne is awake, and Paul is talking to her trying to put her dress on properly. The dress is rather small to say the least.

The doorbell rings. Danny goes to the door.

"Come on in gentlemen, ladies."

They all come into the room. There are two elderly men with two women alongside them. The men are dressed in evening suits, the women in long dresses. As they enter the room they walk across to where the girls are sat. One of the men looks at Rosie and says, "Very nice."

Paul introduces the girls, who do not really know what is happening.

Everyone has drinks and the music is playing. One of the men pulls Rosie up. She manages to stand as he puts his arms around her. Her head just flops onto his shoulder. Nevertheless, she is smiling. While he is dancing, just staying in the same place swaying to the music, his hands are feeling her bottom. He pulls Rosie closer to him.

The other man is sat on the settee with Jayne and the women are sat with them. He is feeling as much as he can of Jayne while the women watch on. Then, one of the women goes up to Danny. She puts her arms around him and is kissing him. Danny just lets her - he wants to please her. She wants him to dance and he does as she asks; she moves her hand down to his crotch and squeezes him.

Paul is sat close to the other woman. She just seems to like to observe. The man with Rosie has taken his coat off now and starts to lead her to the bedroom. She just goes with him. She can see a face close to hers but who it is she does not know, and at this moment she does not really care. She feels very relaxed now.

The man lays her on the bed and starts to remove her dress. She just lets him do what he wants. Her dress is now off, the man removes his clothes not taking his eyes off Rosie. The woman he was with is now stood in the doorway with a glass of wine in her hand watching him. She walks slowly over to the bed.

"How beautiful she is," she says.

The man just smiles as he begins to explore Rosie's body. Rosie can feel him touching her, but is not really responding. He takes her hand and guides it where he wants it. She holds him tight and is just doing what he wants.

The woman standing close to the bed unzips her dress,

pulls it over her shoulders, and just lets it drop to the floor. She slowly gets on to the bed. She is now feeling Rosie; she lays alongside her, and kisses her while the man watches. Rosie is now laid between them. All she can feel is hands all over her. She is completely overwhelmed by what they are doing. Her body is now moving in response to the hands touching her most intimate places. The man starts to have full sex with her, while the woman is kissing Rosie's back and feeling her breasts. Rosie is in a dream. In her mind she is experiencing a replay of what happened in the limo. She throws her head back and cries out in pleasure. She is so light headed now she feels she is separated from her body. She can see other figures in the room, and the voices are now becoming a lot clearer but not clear enough to make out what they are saying properly.

Jayne has been experiencing the same thing with the others, and is now laid on the same bed as Rosie. They are completely naked. There is a lot more going on between all of the people and this goes on for a long time. It is very late when the people leave and Rosie and Jayne fall asleep. Danny tells Paul he will see to the girls. He tells Paul to leave, as it is nearly daybreak. Danny sits in a chair and falls to sleep.


It is around lunchtime before Rosie and the other girl wake. They are both feeling as though their heads will burst at any moment. They look at one another; Rosie can remember some bits of what had happened last night but not all. She realises she has no clothes on and covers her body with a sheet as she sits up.

"Where are we?" asks Jayne.
She is looking around the room and then Rosie remembers the hotel's name.

"We are in the Imperial Hotel."
She is wondering who the girl is.

"How did I get here?" Jayne asks Rosie.
She shakes her head.

"I don't know how you got here."
As they are speaking Danny comes into the room.

"Good morning ladies. How are you feeling?"
They both look at him then both try to pull on the sheet to cover

themselves.

"My head is throbbing," Rosie tells him.

"Come on girls, you're not going to be shy are you? We'll get you something for that headache before you go."

He gives them a cup of coffee.

Jayne asks him, "Where is Paul?"

"He'll be coming back soon," Danny says, reassuring her.

Rosie cannot remember if it was Danny who had had sex with her. She looks at him rather embarrassed,

"I must have had too much to drink last night," she says.

He looks down at her as she is sat on the bed and smiles.

"Yes Rosie, a little too much. I think you both had too much."

He reaches out and helps Rosie up.

"Would you both like to freshen up?"

He leads Rosie gently to the bathroom. As she holds on to the sheet wrapped around her, more or less pulling it off Jayne, Jayne has to grab another sheet to cover herself. Jayne gets up, and follows them to the bathroom.

They are both in the bathroom. Jayne looks at Rosie.

"I think I know you, don't I?"

"Do you, have we met before?" Rosie asks.

"University? You're at the uni aren't you?" Jayne asks Rosie.

"Yes, how do you know Danny?" Rosie asks, trying to piece things together.

"Danny? No, I don't really know him. I know Paul." The girl is looking rather puzzled now.

Rosie remembers in the restaurant when she thought it was Danny. This is the girl that said his name was Paul.

"Where is Paul? What's his second name, do you know?" asks Rosie.

"Don't know where he went but I think that him and Danny are brothers. I think their second name is something like Franklin-Smith. Yes, that's it, a double-barrelled name. Paul Franklin-Smith, yes definitely. I remember now."

Now Rosie gets it. They are brothers who look very

much like one another. But why are they always at the university, she wonders.

Rosie is in the shower letting the warm water run on her face. She washes her body, and as she is rubbing soap on her arm she notices a bit of a bruise on the inside of her arm. She touches the bruise part and it hurts. She tries to remember what has been happening to her but is unable to remember all that happened last night.

As she goes back from the bathroom she just has a bathrobe on that she found in there. Both Danny and Paul are sat talking on the settee. They both look at Rosie. She cannot believe how alike they are. She just stares at them.

"This is my brother Paul, Rosie." Danny says, looking at Rosie who is unable to take her eyes off the brothers.
He walks across to her, putting his hand slightly into her robe as he smiles at her.

"Get yourself dressed Rosie. Has Jayne finished in there? Tell her to hurry and get herself dressed?"
She does not say anything. She just goes to the bathroom and tells Jayne to get dressed then goes to the bedroom to get dressed herself.

The girls don't say anything to one another while dressing apart from complaining again about the bad headache they both have. They are both dressed now and go to join Danny and Paul. Danny is stood watching them enter the room. He has two envelopes in his hand. He walks across to them and hands them one envelope each. They both take them from him, not saying anything.

"Enjoy yourselves. We'll meet again soon," Danny says as he walks across to pick up the telephone.
Rosie does not know what to say. Paul walks across to them, puts his arm around both of them and leads them to the door, where he kisses both of them on the cheek.

"If you take a couple of these they will get rid of that terrible headache you said you had."
He puts a box with white tablets in their hands. Rosie recognises the aftershave Danny uses is the same Paul wears. She wonders if he has been involved with her exploits in the past.

"Well my sweets a car is waiting for you downstairs. Off you go. We'll be in touch."

He kisses them again as they leave the room to go to the car.

Once in the car Jayne tells the driver her address, which is in the same block of student flats where Rosie lives. Rosie looks at Jayne.

"Same place," she tells the driver

She asks Jayne, trying not to be too nosy, "Have you been on any other, shall we say, dates, with Paul?"

Jayne answers as though she is embarrassed to admit it.

"Yes, a couple of times. I must tell you, I never expected what happened on those dates."

Rosie finds it difficult not to ask more,

"What didn't you expect? Being blindfolded?"

"How do you know that?" Jayne asks looking at Rosie.

"Because the same happened to me."

While Rosie is talking she undoes the envelope and takes out the money. Jayne sees what she is doing and opens hers. Rosie sits looking at the money. Jayne now knows what has been happening.

"Do you think it has only happened to us?"

"I don't know. I thought it was just Danny being interested in me but now I think maybe not."

"Will you go again if he asks Rosie? Or will you stop seeing him?"

"I will have to think about that."

She doesn't want to tell Jayne that she has got to like what has been happening to her. And the money is very nice too.

When they arrive at the flats Jayne and Rosie tell each other where they live, and exchange their telephone numbers before arranging to meet sometime soon.

Rosie makes her way to her flat. She feels she needs another tablet. She takes a pill out and swallows it. Her head is still pounding. Once inside the flat she knows May will be at some lecture so she will be alone. Inside the flat she decides to go to her bedroom. She takes a drink of water with her and the tablets. She sits on the bed. Putting her bag on the bed she leans forward and puts her hands to her head, holding it; she is going through everything that she can remember happened. She guesses she is being used but even knowing that she is still prepared to carry on. If Danny asks her, that is.

She walks to the wardrobe and opens the door. Her bag with the money in is laid just inside the door. She picks it up and opens it. She can see some of the money has gone. She is thinking. Surely May hasn't taken it? She counts it, puts the other money she has just received from Danny in the bag, and puts it in what she thinks will be a safer place.

Exhausted, she goes to her bed and lays down, just pulling the cover over her. It is not too long before she is sound asleep.

First thing she hears is May calling her. Not good for a headache.

"Rosie, Rosie! Are you awake?"

"My head. Don't shout. Bloody hell May my head's about to drop off," says Rosie.

She takes another tablet from the box that Paul gave her and takes it with a sip of water from the glass on the table alongside of the bed.

"Girl, it must have been some date. What time did you get back? You look like shit! What have you been drinking?"

Rosie, who looks very pale and not her usual self, gets up from the bed and points to the door. May turns and goes to the other room, with Rosie following her.

"Want a cup of coffee? Looking at you I would think you do."

May is getting the cups ready; Rosie looks across at her.

"May, have you been in my room while I have been out?"

"Why would I go in your room?" May says, looking confused.

"Someone has been in my bag. Some money has gone."

May looks straight at Rosie.

She asks, "Are you saying I took the money? Bloody hell Rosie I thought you knew me better than that."

Then May remembers Rosie's mother going in her room,

"Wait a minute. Your mother came just after you left.

She went in your room saying she had left something there. Her bag or something I seem to remember."

Rosie now regrets asking May if she had taken it.

"No, I know you wouldn't take it. I can guess where it has gone now, sorry May."

May just shakes her head enough to say what does she think she is, accusing her of taking money from her bag? May remembers Rosie's mother trying to hide something from her when she looked in Rosie's room to tell her she was leaving.

"Rosie, if you have anything that is valuable you best make sure it is safe in the future. Okay?"

"Yes May, I will. Don't be mad at me, I am really sorry." Rosie just smiles. "Yes okay, forget it. Here, drink your sodding coffee." May is not too pleased.

She does not want to tell May too much but does tell her that Danny has a brother who is so much like him and that he was there with another girl from uni.

"Bloody hell Rosie there's a chance for me yet if they like uni girls," laughs May.

"Maybe, we'll see."

Rosie doesn't elaborate on the events of the previous night.

# 5

# Champagne Girls

The two brothers have a flat in a nice area of Leeds. None of the properties Rosie has visited so far belonged to the brothers; the venues were all organised for their clients. They travel to London regularly, where their parents live. Both brothers were in the banking business, dealing in shares, but got more and more involved in the sex trade. They have, on occasion, been involved in the grooming of teenage girls and also bringing in girls from Eastern Europe.

Danny is the oldest brother and seems to be the brains, recruiting girls specifically for rich clients who pay a lot of money for what they refer to as 'fresh meat', otherwise known as girls new to the sex industry. They also have other people in different towns grooming girls.

As he's telling Paul, Danny is organising a couple of girls for two clients for the weekend.

"Paul, we will give Rosie and Jayne the job rather than bringing someone up from London. We may still have to string them both along a bit but I think they will oblige."

Paul agrees, asking, "Do you think they will need some of the persuaders again?"

"If they do we best have some of the you-know-what ready. These two clients are very important. They like the best, and the more girls we can get locally the better. I'm working on a couple of others at the moment."

"I have a very nice young thing nearly ready," Paul says.

"I will find out just what the clients want and where they would like to see the girls. I'll give the girls a ring a little later just to test the water and see if they are coming along but there won't be any problems," Danny says.

"See you later then bro. I'm off to see my new girl Jade," says Paul, leaving.

Danny smiles at Paul.

"Hope Jade is a good looker. Could do with another one like Rosie."

Paul goes to the car park for the flats and gets into his flash sports car, wheel spinning before speeding off down the road.


Rosie is in the flat when her mother turns up.

"Hi darling. I thought I would pop in to see you. You don't look well, have you been poorly?"

"Okay mum, where is the money you took from me? Have you spent it on booze?" she asks.

"Money, what money?" Her mother is trying to look innocent.

"Look mum, I know you took it, just admit it. Don't come into my room anymore if I am not here."

Her mother knows it is pointless trying to deny taking the money.

"I was desperate love. I'm sorry. Where did you get all that money? Not your dad?"

"Dad didn't give me it. It's not your business where I got it. I hope you are not asking for money again?"

Her mother walks towards her, asking, "Would you just help me out this last time? I am flat broke. I'm desperate?" She puts her arm around her.

"No. And I mean no. Just get yourself sorted out mum. I am not going to give you anything. Anyway, I only have a little cash left."

Rosie's mother keeps trying but Rosie is adamant. She does not give her anything. Her mother leaves the flat cursing; she is not very happy that Rosie will not help her.

Rosie has made arrangements to meet Jayne. She is hoping Jayne will have some tablets left. She has used all the tablets that Paul gave her and they made her feel better for a while but she realises it is not just the headaches. She is so irritable without them and she knows that after a couple of hours or so she needs to take another tablet.

They meet in the restaurant and sit talking about the night they met.

Rosie asks, "Jayne, have you any of the pills Paul gave us?"

Jayne can see she looks desperate.

"I was going to ask you the same. I have none left."

"Have you heard from either Danny or Paul?" she asks Jayne, hoping she says yes.

"No. I was thinking of ringing him. What do you think we should do?"

"I was thinking the same. Shall we?"

She says this with a desperate look on her face. Jayne takes her mobile out and telephones Paul. The phone keeps going straight through to answerphone. Jayne shakes her head.

"No answer."

"I'll try Danny's number."

Rosie waits. The phone is ringing. Danny answers.

"Rosie, I was about to telephone you. We have something on this weekend if you are game?"

She looks across at Jayne.

"Danny, Jayne is with me."

There is a silence and then Danny tells her.

"Ask Jayne if she is interested? Would she like to join us? It is going to be something special with some very nice rewards."

Rosie puts her hand over the phone and tells Jayne what Danny has said. Jayne motions to her that she will go.

"Yes Danny, Jayne will go."

"Okay my two lovelies. We'll send the car to pick you up on Saturday evening. Usual time, eight o'clock."

Danny laughs to himself.

Rosie asks Danny, "The pills Paul gave us... any chance of getting any more?"

"The pills, oh! Yes, you can wait another day can't you?" Danny thinks that's good, it will make it easier for the next part of their plans they have for the girls.

"Okay Rosie take care, see you soon." He ends the conversation.

Jayne looks across at Rosie.

"Are we doing the right thing?"

"I can't answer that for you. I know I'm going."

"Okay, me too. My roommate has quit uni and I'm looking for a new roomie now. Good job I had a bit of extra cash."

"Yes, got to admit it is nice to have a bit of money and not having to struggle. We may get a little boost to our finances." After they make arrangements to meet, Jayne leaves telling Rosie she will see her soon.


Rosie's father, who she has not seen for a while, telephones her.

"Rosie my darling, how are you doing? I haven't seen you for a long time. I have been so very busy. Do you need anything? And have you seen that mother of yours? Is she still at the drink?"

She is surprised to hear from her dad.

"No, I'm okay dad. I am managing all right for the moment. I have seen mum. She wasn't drunk. Well maybe she was a little. She said she was a bit short of cash."

"Don't tell me she was hard up again?"

Her father knows that the wife he abandoned likes her drink. Rosie thinks that she better not tell him everything.

"Yes, she was asking for money and was a bit drunk."

"A bloody little bit drunk? She can't help herself. She will kill herself with drink the way she is going. I will come and see you next week. Mandy will come with me too. Are you sure you are okay for money for now? How are you doing at uni?"

"I'm fine dad. Uni is okay, no problems as yet."

"Anything else to tell me darling before I go? I will see you soon. Love you. Oh, and by the way, Mandy sends her love."

"Thank Mandy for me. Bye dad, see you, love you."

Rosie is thankful she has a good dad. She cannot blame him for going for a younger girl. She now thinks she understands a man's desires after her short experiences she has had with them.

May is back in the flat now and she has been a little concerned about Rosie, who has been rather irritable. Rosie just gives her a bit of a smile when she sees her. May cannot help herself from asking Rosie questions.

"Rosie, what's been going on? You just have not been yourself since you went out that night."

She is reluctant to tell her anything.

"Look, nothing has been going on. I have not been feeling very well but I'm feeling a lot better now. I have seen Jayne, the girl who is at uni who lives in these flats. We are going out at the weekend with Danny and his brother."

"Where are you going? Anywhere nice?"

May wishes she were going too.

"Don't know. He is sending a car for us."

Rosie is looking forward to seeing Danny, and is wondering what he has in store for them. When she has gone on one of the adventures she hates to admit to herself how much she has enjoyed the different experiences she has had.


Saturday night arrives. May has already gone out without saying very much to Rosie. May has been uptight, and there has not been the usual banter between them. Rosie looks out of the window and sees the car arriving. She takes one last look in the mirror, straightens her very revealing dress and then leaves her flat.

The driver smiles at her and opens the door. Jayne is sat smiling as she gets in.

"You look great Rosie."

"Thanks. You look very nice yourself."

They are getting close to their destination. Jayne looks rather worried so Rosie takes her hand.

"Come on Jayne let's enjoy ourselves. What do you say?"

Jayne smiles and nods her head. The driver opens the door. They are outside a very large house, which looks to be in its own grounds; they walk towards the large door and ring the bell. Danny opens the door,

"Come on in girls. Wow. You both look fab."

They follow him, looking round at the beautiful oil paintings in the hallway and large stairway then head into a room which has a very large fireplace with a fire blazing away. There are quite a few people stood around drinking and talking. As they enter the room they all go quiet and are looking at the girls.

The men are not young but are very smart and the couple of women with them are not so young either but looking very nice in their long evening gowns.

Danny walks over to Paul, who is with a couple of men.

Paul takes hold of Jayne's hand.

"This is Jayne." Then he takes hold of Rosie's hand.

"And gentlemen, this is the beautiful Rosie."

The men smile at them both as Danny goes for some drinks. They both feel a bit out of place Paul leads them away so he is able to talk to them.

"Enjoy yourselves girls, don't be shy."

Danny arrives with the drinks.

"Champagne, girls."

They take the glasses off him. Danny puts his arm around Rosie; every time he is anywhere near her she is so infatuated with him. She longs for his touch and for his hands to caress her. His hand slides down to her bottom. Rosie just looks at him, the music is playing, there is an assortment of food and drink laid out and some people are taking the food. Danny asks the girls if they are hungry. He takes Rosie's hand then places a couple of pills in her palm and whispers to her.

"Take them Rosie. They will make you feel good."

Paul also gives some to Jayne. She just stands looking at them with her hand open; Paul takes them and puts his finger up to open Jayne's mouth and puts them in.

"Swallow. Come on Jayne, don't spoil the party."

Jayne takes a drink, swallowing the pills. The brothers take the girls and are dancing with them along with another couple dancing.

Rosie is now feeling light headed but very relaxed. She is holding on to Danny and, looking around, she sees an old man with greying hair. He is sat in a large chair close to the fire and looking at her. One of the men takes him a drink. He takes the drink from him still not taking his eyes off Rosie. He calls the same man over to him and whispers in his ear. The man looks at Rosie and nods his head.

Paul takes Jayne and sits her down. He takes some white

powder from a small container. One of the women comes over as he tips some of the powder on to the glass table and, credit card in hand, he cuts the powder - cocaine - into three lines. The woman bends down at the same time as she is looking at Jayne, and, with a rolled up note, and one finger closing a nostril, hoovers up a line. Jayne is feeling good now that she sees Paul looking at her.

"Try it, Jayne."

He moves her head down to the powder. She picks up the rolled note, discarded by the woman. She is looking up at him as she does the same as the woman.

"That's my girl," Paul says. Jayne lies back in the chair, smiling.

Danny is watching Paul and leads Rosie over to the table. He looks at her.

"Would you like to try a little Rosie?"

Paul gets up from his chair and Danny sits down, pulling Rosie onto his knee then putting some more cocaine on the table.

"Just sniff it up one nostril, with the note. Like they do in films."

She does what Danny asks her and soon all the powder has gone. The man in the chair in front of the fire has not taken his eyes off Rosie since she entered the room. He has seen her taking the cocaine. The man he talked to comes across to Danny and taps him on the shoulder. Danny looks at him, nods his head towards the old man and walks away.

Both Jayne and Rosie are now giggling and staggering about with drinks in their hands. They start dancing together with the men in the room watching them.

Danny gets in between them, and is dancing with them. He undoes the back of Rosie's dress. She is not bothered; the men are now all calling together.

"Take them off."

They are all laughing. Rosie's eyes are half closed as she lets the dress fall, exposing her black underwear and beautiful body. She just carries on dancing. Paul slides Jayne's dress over her shoulders and one of the older women comes up to her and helps her remove the dress. When the dress is on the floor she pulls Jayne towards her and puts her arms around her, undoing Jayne's bra. Jayne just looks at the woman, trying to focus on her.

The man waves to Danny. He takes Rosie, still dancing and giggling, over to him. She is only in her small panties and bra. Danny stands Rosie in front of him. He takes her hand and kisses it; he pulls her closer to him, feeling her body. Some of the men are now stood around Jayne, taking their turn in dancing with her. She just lets them do what they want; she is now naked, the men and the couple of women are also in a state of undress. They are soon all in a frenzy of sexual activity.

The old man takes Rosie into another room, and closes the door. He cannot stop touching and feeling her. She is now laid on a thick rug on the floor, her eyes closed. Her whole body seems as though it is floating away. She senses that she is being touched in her most intimate parts but does nothing to resist. It is as though she has not been touched before; her back is arched, wanting more and she does not care who, or what, is doing it. Never has she felt like she does now.

The old man lays on top of her. She cannot see his face. She grabs hold of the rug with her hands either side of her and at the same time she is biting her lip as he enters her. The room begins to spin round, her body is moving up and down, then faster as she reaches a climax and then lays still.

Danny sees the old man come back into the room. He walks back to his chair, sits down and is now watching the others. Danny goes and collects Rosie. He brings her back in the room and she is soon lost in a crowd of naked bodies.

By the early hours of the morning some of the people are laid around asleep and some have gone to the bedrooms. Paul and Danny try to rouse Jayne and Rosie, who seem to be under the influence of drugs.

"Let's get them dressed."

Rosie is now coming round a little as Danny is dressing her. She puts her arms around him. Her head flops around as he manages to get the dress on her. Paul is doing the same with Jayne, who has still not come round at all.

"Shit, Dan, this one is really out."

"Don't worry. She'll be with us shortly. Get some coffee."

Danny finishes dressing Rosie.

Paul leaves Jayne laid out on the settee while he gets the coffee. He is soon back and they get Jayne sat up and, tapping her face, she partly opens her eyes. They force the coffee down her, some inevitably dribbling down her chin. They do the same with Rosie who is coming round a lot faster.


After some time both women are just about conscious and Danny and Paul help them to their car. Once inside the car Danny tells Paul to drive. Danny gives Rosie and Jayne some of the tablets they had asked for along with a couple of packets of their favourite white powder. Rosie looks at it and then at Danny.

"Take it if you need it," he tells her.

He kisses her forehead; Jayne can just about understand what is going on.

"Take this and share it. We will be in touch."

She takes the envelope and pushes it in her bag.

"This is the place isn't it?" Paul asks Jayne as they arrive at their flats.

She just nods her head when the car stops. The girls both get out and Jayne is still very unsteady on her feet. Rosie supports her as the car speeds away.

Rosie helps Jayne up to her flat as she is still staggering a little. Once inside the flat Jayne flops out on the settee. Rosie sits alongside her, opens her bag and takes out the cash.

"I'll share this money, Jayne."

Rosie notices there is not the usual large amount. She gives Jayne her share and then takes the pills she was given, gets a glass of water from the kitchen and pops a couple in her mouth.

Jayne is now laid back asleep with her money in her hand. Rosie just looks at her and sits down, feeling she has very little energy.

She takes the couple of small satchels of powder from her bag. She sits looking at them, and a tear runs down her face as she recollects some of what happened through the night. In her mind she knows she is losing control. She helps Jayne as best she can to the bedroom and goes back to the settee and lays down. Soon she is fast asleep.

Jayne wakes up. It is late afternoon. She gets out of bed holding her head.

"Shit, shit," she says as she walks from the bedroom into the small lounge. She sees Rosie laid on the settee.

"Rosie wake up... Rosie."

She opens her eyes. She sees Jayne, not knowing for a moment where she is.

"What time is it?"

"Sodding hell, I don't know what day it is never mind the time. I need a drink. Do you want a coffee?"

Jayne runs her hand through her blonde hair as she walks into the small kitchen.

Rosie sits up, and trying to straighten her dress she walks over to the mirror. She just stares at herself thinking, *'I look like I've been run over by a bus.'* She sits down, opens her bag and takes out the tablets as Jayne walks back with the coffee.

"I could do with a couple. I've got the bloody shakes," Jayne says as she hands Rosie the coffee. She takes the coffee and tells Jayne, "I put your money on the small table in the bedroom; you have the other stuff don't you?"

"Other stuff? Oh, you mean the uppers Paul and Danny gave us?" Jayne asks.

Rosie, not wanting to say cocaine, answers, "And the small satchels."

Jayne picks up her bag and opens it, taking out the satchels, "You mean this?"

She sits down next to Rosie, still holding the satchels. She looks at Rosie, and is about to say something when Rosie says, "Don't feel bad. We have done what we have done. I think we better hold on to this stuff. We may need it."

Jayne looks at her, smiles then asks, "Will you move in with me?" She likes the idea, thinking May won't be asking questions all the time.

"I will think about it. I will have to tell May, my roommate. I know she won't be pleased."

"I think it would be great if you will Rosie," she says as she downs another of the uppers.

Rosie remains at Jayne's flat until nearly dark and then leaves for her own flat. She knows she will get a barrage of questions from May so she is prepared as she enters the flat. May is sat watching the television.

"Well, well, look who's here. Where have you been girl, you're looking a bit rough. You haven't slept on the street all night have you? You look as though you have."

Rosie walks past May on the way to her bedroom.

"Don't talk stupid. I slept at Jayne's flat because we got back late."

Before May can ask her anything else she shuts her bedroom door. May calls out to her.

"Why are you so bloody mad at me? I haven't done anything."

Rosie does not answer but undresses, puts her robe on and sits on the bed. She is not feeling too good. She takes a small satchel and sits for a while, looking at it before opening it. She pours a little of the powder on the table. She looks round then picks up a nail file, and runs the powder into a line, and bending down she takes a deep breath, holds her nostril and sniffs up, closing her eyes and holding her head back for a moment or two. Her eyes begin to water as she falls back on to the bed feeling wired but in a way, relaxed. A smile comes over her face. Later, she takes the edge off the night by popping a couple of downers and falls into a deep sleep.

Monday morning and Rosie wakes up shuddering a little as she climbs out of bed. She has to go through the lounge before she can go to the bathroom. She opens her bedroom door. May is sat drinking her coffee and just looks at her without saying anything. Rosie walks past her en route to the bathroom. She takes a shower, letting the water run onto her face, and, as she is soaping her body, she thinks of the very few things she can remember. Did Danny go with her? She vaguely remembers having sex with someone. She can remember naked bodies. Not much else. She shakes her head, giving up trying to remember what happened. When showered she goes back through the lounge, stopping in front of May.

"I have to tell you May, I'm moving in with Jayne. I just

want to tell you it is nothing to do with you."

May is mad at this news. She looks back at Rosie, not hiding her displeasure, "I can't believe you, I thought we were friends. It's since you have been messing around with that bloody Danny. I don't know what you are doing but you're turning into another person. If you want to move out do it, but I think you better take a long look at yourself Rosie."

She is now mad at May for the tone of her voice and this telling off.

"Look at myself? You want to look at your bloody self. You're no picture."

May is nice looking but a little on the big side with big breasts. Rosie walks off into her bedroom. She decides she is not going into uni today. She is getting dressed as she sees the small box on the bedside table with the uppers in. She picks it up, takes two out and takes them.

She takes the money from last night out, putting it with the other cash in her bag. She has accumulated quite a bit of cash, and, putting it in her bag, decides to keep it with her while she knows what she is doing. She soon makes up her mind that she will move in with Jayne. She telephones Jayne hoping she is still in her flat. Jayne answers the phone.

"Hello."

"It's me Rosie, I can move in with you today Jayne if you want? I will get my belongings together and come round. Are you going into uni today?"

"I was but if you're coming this morning I will come to your place and help you."

While they are talking on the phone Rosie hears the front door bang shut. She opens her bedroom door and sees that May has gone.

"It's May. She's just left. She is not very happy, we had a bit of a row."

"I'm so sorry Rosie. Is it my fault for asking you to move in with me?"

"No, things have been a bit strained between us. Anyway get your arse over here and help me move," she says, trying to laugh it off.

Jayne joins Rosie. They collect all of her things, and get everything ready to move to her place; she wants to make sure she has not got anything of May's. As they leave Rosie takes some money, and places it on the table. As she locks the door she pops the keys she has through the letterbox.

Rosie is soon settled in; as the day passes they have been having an occasional glass of wine. They both feel a little more relaxed now; with taking the tablets they feel as though they are on one continuous high. She asks Jayne if she wants some of the cocaine. They both agree. Rosie gets it ready. They both look at one another, laughing as Jayne goes down to take the first snort of the white powder. She lifts her head up, revealing the white powder on the end of her nose. Rosie wipes it off laughing then goes down to take hers, again with a quick sniff along the line of powder, which is all gone save for some slight traces. Jayne puts her arm around Rosie, kissing her on the cheek. "I think we will get along together fine Rosie."

"Me too. To you and me, Jayne girl." Rosie drinks the remainder of the wine in her glass and then falls back on the settee laughing.

## 6
# Meeting Ramon

Danny and Paul are talking about last night.

"Things went okay last night. I must say I expected a little more resistance from the girls," Danny tells Paul.

"Me too but I think they will be game for anything now. The stuff we gave them is doing the trick; they're hoovering it up big time. Oh yes, Danny, the other girl I told you about, she has been on a couple of our games and has seemed to like it. I will give her another one of our specials the limo. I have a couple that are keen to have the experience. Wealthy and into anything in the swinging club."

Paul laughs. He is enjoying the quick and easy money along with other benefits from the wealthy people they are providing the girls for.

"Paul, I think we should let the girls sweat for a while. You know, let them get a bit desperate for the white stuff then we will really have them."

Danny is smiling now, and Paul looks back at him. "We will have to bring a couple of the girls up from London. Maybe the new girls Ramon has, he says they look very nice. Those Latvians of his will fit the bill."

"Yes, they should be the bee's knees, I agree. I will go and bring them. You see to everything here. Don't answer Rosie or Jayne if they telephone for a week or so. Or at least until I come back."

Rosie and Jayne have missed a lot of uni due to their antics but have pulled themselves around enough to get into a lecture or two. Rosie finds it hard not to take some drugs to help her concentrate. She needs to take a lot more now. Jayne and her have been dabbling more with the cocaine too; that is going down very fast.

Rosie is in the uni restaurant with Jayne. She sees May coming towards her. She has tried to avoid her but May comes to their table.

"Can I sit down Rosie?" She gives her a funny look, ignoring Jayne.

"Yes, if you want," Rosie says, not looking at Jayne.

"Your mother came to my flat. You haven't told her you've moved have you?"

Rosie thinks to herself, *'Shit, I forgot to tell her and my father.'*

"To be honest I didn't. I will give her a ring and let her know."

"Rosie, you do not look yourself. If you want to talk to me I am always here, you know that. I'll see you then." May walks away and joins a couple of the other students who are looking across at them.

Jayne looks at Rosie sheepishly, feeling a bit embarrassed and knowing that she is partly to blame for Rosie moving in with her.

"You better let your parents know that you have moved, otherwise they will be worrying about you."

"Yes, I'm going to but you will see how my mother can be a bit of a nuisance. If she ever comes round and I am out don't let her in. She is usually a bit pissed."

Rosie telephones her father and tells him she has moved, making an excuse as to why she decided to share with Jayne. He makes arrangements to meet up with her the following week at a restaurant nearby. She tries to call her mother but is unable to contact her.

Over the next few days she gets a little worried. She has been trying to telephone her mother on both her mobile and the landline but has not been able to make contact. She has her own problems now. She has very little cocaine or anything else left. She has tried to call Danny, and Jayne has tried to call Paul without success as they are not answering their calls or responding to the many messages left. Rosie and Jayne are now feeling very bad and getting cold sweats and the shivers. A lot of this is psychological, granted, but their habits have certainly spiralled out of control quickly.

"Do you know anyone we can buy anything from?" Rosie asks Jayne.

She thinks for a moment.

"I think I do. A few of the students get their smokes from an Asian guy. I think he deals in anything so maybe we could buy something from him if I can find out how to contact him? I'll check with someone who I know."

Rosie didn't smoke cigarettes but she is now puffing away on one, holding a glass of wine in her other hand.

"Try now, Jayne."

She is getting rather desperate. Jayne, who also feels the same, tells her, "I will, I'll try now."

They do manage to get a supply going but it is now getting expensive and they know they will have to pay what the dealer asks otherwise they are going to suffer. Rosie knows this but is like everyone who gets into drugs, convincing herself that she can stop at anytime, or she could if she wanted to.


Danny stops his car outside a very nice house in the leafy suburbs of London. The house is surrounded by trees and is quite private. There are cameras placed all around the property and, as he approaches the door, it is opened by a very large chap with a flat nose and a couple of scars on his cheek, dressed in a t-shirt which looks too small because it is stretched to its maximum over his muscular body, his large arms covered in tattoos.

"Victor, how are you?" Danny asks, smiling at him.

"Good, come," he says in a very gruff voice. Danny follows him. Danny is well built but compared to Victor he is a dwarf.

As they enter the room a man with lots of gold on his fingers and round his neck, dressed in fine clothes with long black hair down to his shoulders, is sat in a chair with a very nice looking girl sat on the arm of the chair next to him. He has his arm around her and holds his hand out to Danny.

"Danny Franklin-Smith. Nice to see you again. How is your brother, good?" he says with a strong accent in broken English.

Danny goes across to him and shakes his hand, at the same time smiling at the girl.

"Paul is fine Ramon. Everything is going good in Leeds, and our people in Manchester are doing very well also."

"Good, Danny. Business good for you business good for me. We have two very nice girls for you. Slovakian nice, and fresh and all ready to start work. Go get Danny a drink," says Ramon to the girl sat with him. He smacks her bottom as she gets up to go for the drinks; she turns, and giggles.

They sit talking for a while, the patio doors open. Ramon looks across to the doors, and Danny also looks across.

"Hi, Danny. This is one of the girls. For you. Natalia. Isn't she lovely?"

She is stood in the doorway, with the light behind her making her small white dress transparent and leaving very little to the imagination. She has very large breasts, long blonde hair and a beautiful figure. She is stood with her hand on her hips, smiling at the two men.

Ramon calls her across; as she gets to him she leans across and kisses him at the same time as looking at Danny. Danny is very impressed.

"Ramon you amaze me. Keep up the good work."

Ramon pushes Natalia towards Danny. She sits on his knee. She smells very nice and he can feel her body, so smooth through the flimsy dress. She wriggles her bottom as she sits on his knee.

Ramon is laughing, "Danny, Danny you must stay the night. We have party. Go back tomorrow."

"I can't say no," Danny says, as another girl enters the room. A tall girl with dark eyes and flowing blonde hair.

"This is your other girl Danny. Her name is Monika."

Again Danny shows his approval he walks across to Ramon.

"Oh yes Ramon. You'll be wanting this - it's the amount we agreed." He hands him an envelope. Ramon takes it and looks inside, nodding his head in approval.

"Let Natalia show you to your room. We eat and drink

around seven. Maybe you busy, yes?" says Ramon, throwing his head back and laughing.

Natalia takes Danny's hand and leads him to his room.

Once in the room Danny lays on the bed, takes out his mobile and can see he has had numerous calls from Rosie. He smiles, knowing that they must be desperate. He calls Paul as Natalia lays down beside him, undoing his shirt and stroking his chest while he is dialling the number.

Paul answers the phone, "Hi brother. How did it go?"

"Paul, everything is fine. The two new Slovakian girls are very nice, business will boom with these along with the three new girls. I have had numerous calls from Rosie; they are ripe for picking now and I know what they want. It seems that they are very desperate for some chemicals too. Even asking for smack, whatever we've got."

"Looking forward to seeing the Slovakian girls," Paul laughs. "What you said about Rosie, well Jayne has been telephoning me every bloody ten minutes. We'll let them sweat a bit more and then we can provide them with what they require. I'll see you when you get back. I've got a bit of business tonight with Jade who is more than willing to oblige now."

"Okay Paul, see you soon."

Danny looks at Natalia, running his hands through her hair and then down her body. She stands up and lets her dress fall to the floor. Now stood in very flimsy underwear, she starts to undress him as he just lays and lets her. She walks across to put some music on, with Danny watching her bottom. As she walks, her breasts seem to move in slow motion. She looks as though she is tiptoeing with her body movements; she is so light on her feet. Then she walks back to him, very slowly, knowing she is teasing him. She is soon touching his body. Danny is so aroused he takes her hand and as she straddles him she wastes no time in moving slowly, as though to the music.

Danny is more than happy to let Natalia do what she is doing. Her head is moving from side to side as she lifts up and down. She controls him, not letting him finish the love making until she is ready. Then Danny pulls her to him, kissing her. She smiles at him and in a very sexy voice asks him, "You like?"

"Oh yes, I like," he says as she lays beside him.

A couple of hours soon pass. Natalia has left him so he gets ready to join the others. He is soon ready and goes downstairs. A few more people have arrived; some nouveau riche with no class, the type of people who have used their money in a very crude way, which has impacted on their dress sense and manners. Danny walks across to Ramon who is stood with two of these characters. Both seem to be eastern European.

"Danny, you have nice relax with Natalia?"

"Yes Ramon, you could say that." Danny is laughing as Ramon slaps him on the back and gives out a big roar of laughter.

"These are my friends. We have got five Romanian girls. You interested Danny? Price not too high?"

"Yes, I am interested. A couple for Manchester, and the other three for Brighton. You can deliver? I will take the two Slovaks with me to Leeds tomorrow."

Ramon leans close to Danny.

"Romanian girls only good for massage parlour or peepshow booth. Not very good for special people, but cheap price."

Danny agrees to take them but only at a good price.

Ramon tells the men in Romanian what Danny said, then he tells Danny. "No problem. They will make price good, and deliver. They cannot speak English so I will explain our procedures for the money, and delivery."

Danny shakes hands with the two men, and tells Ramon, "We will move three English girls here to London in a couple of weeks or so when we think they are ready. Then possibly they could go to the Emirates. I am sure they will be enjoyed by our Arab friends."

"Nice young English girls always good business."

Ramon is more than pleased knowing Danny is impressed. Danny thanks him, then spends the rest of the night drinking and enjoying the girls.


Rosie and Jayne have managed to get their hands on some crack cocaine and some pills, which the dealer guarantees are the best uppers on the market. They believe him as he deals with many of the students. They have also purchased some heroin, in order to numb their experience, although they don't intend to make a habit of it.

Back in their flat, Rosie is preparing to take some of the H. Jayne is sat alongside her, unable to wait.

"I need this so bad," Rosie says as she heats up the heroin on some foil and takes a draw. As soon as Rosie lifts her head, Jayne snorts two lines of coke, her preferred drug. Then they both lay back relieved. They are soon delirious; Rosie can feel herself go into a place where all her problems have gone away. She smiles as she lays against Jayne, who puts her arm around her as though protecting her, and they eventually both go to sleep dreaming of pleasant things.

Over the next few days they head back to uni, doing their work. Both still take the tablets and work their way through the rest of the drugs and would have to admit that they've both let themselves go a bit. Rosie and Jayne have been ringing Danny and Paul; the money they had has gone down fast as they have had to visit the dealer a few times and the price of the smack has gradually increased with each purchase.

Rosie has to telephone her father to tell him she cannot meet him as she has other commitments. They agree to make other arrangements for a later date. Neither she nor her father has heard from her mother, which is unusual. Her father is not overly concerned but Rosie is, convincing herself that her mother must be okay. Rosie has a lot of other things on her mind.

Danny has arrived back with the girls who have been set up in a small flat. Danny and Paul have got them working and they do their work with enthusiasm that pleases Danny. The money they give them is a pittance but they are happy enough with the set up. Ramon always says that if there are any problems with any of the girls he will sort them out.

Danny gets a call from a very wealthy politician who needs a few girls for a bit of a party for a minister and a few of his friends. Danny tells him no problem and makes the arrangements with the MP regarding where and when.

Danny thinks they should now get Rosie, Jayne and Jade

to work, so Danny tells Paul he will ring them and get them to be a part of this one. He telephones Rosie, who answers the phone sounding as though she has just fallen out of bed.

"Hello."

"Rosie, it's me Danny. You sound a little different. Is everything okay?"

Rosie sits up and tries to clear her voice.

"Hi. I tried to telephone you. We thought you had finished with us."

"Finished with you? Why would I do that? Listen, Rosie, I have some very important friends who are having a party. Would you and Jayne like to come? You will be well rewarded as they are very wealthy, very important friends."

She is quiet for a short time before asking, "Will you be there?"

"Yes of course I'll be there and I'll have something special for you," Danny says knowing he can do what he likes with them now.

"I'll tell Jayne. Where do we have to go?" She is feeling better knowing he has contacted her.

"We will send a car for you. Just get yourselves looking great and I'll see you there, okay? At eight o'clock Saturday night Rosie."

"Eight o'clock Saturday, okay Danny." She is thinking that, with important people there, there should be a generous pay out. At lease she hopes that's the case.


Jayne arrives back at the flat and Rosie tells her what Danny has said. It's come at the right time.

"I have nothing left, my cash has gone. Have you anything Jayne?"

She looks at her hoping she will say yes so that they can get some new clothes for the Saturday evening.

"No I haven't got anything. We'll just have to make do with what we have got."

"I suppose I can rake up something to wear."

They both agree. Rosie takes out her comforters, and offers a couple of pills to Jayne. She takes them without hesitation.

They are ready for the Saturday evening. Rosie is still

excited at seeing Danny again, the car arrives for them with a chauffeur, and Jayne does not look too good at all.

"Come on Jayne, buck yourself up."

Rosie tries to straighten Jayne's dress, and then pushes her hair back.

"There we are, you look a lot better. Come on, give us a smile." Jayne tries to smile but her heart's clearly not in it.

Rosie knows Danny will not be happy if Jayne is not looking her best. The car stops to pick up Jade. The three girls know each other but not on a really personal level. They chat before the car stops.

They arrive at a large house and when they get out the chauffeur walks with them to the door, opens it and heads inside with them all. They go in and can hear voices and music.

The chauffeur leads them to another door and opens it, motioning for them to go in. Rosie sees Danny among the crowd. He sees the girls, and walks across to them, kissing them on their cheeks then takes them all to get drinks. A few of the men are talking to the girls that are already there. Paul takes Jade to one of the men and Danny tells Rosie and Jayne to mix. Rosie feels a little disappointed that Danny has not shown her too much attention. He looks at Jayne.

"Are you okay?" he asks Jayne, frowning.

"Yes I'm fine." Jayne is a little frightened now.

A young man who looks rather distinguished and has never stopped looking at her since she came in approaches Rosie.

"My name is Julian, what's yours?"

She likes the look of him. She can tell he comes from a good background and he speaks rather well.

"I'm Rosie," she says, smiling at him.

"Oh yes, Danny has told me all about you."

Julian stands talking to her. The other girls are mingling with the other guests; Natalia is looking nice, is getting a lot of attention from the males, is showing her confidence, and has a relaxed attitude dancing around, and enticing the men to touch her. Jayne on the other hand is on her own standing away from the guests and Danny is watching her. A small fat man who has had a lot to drink approaches her and is trying to touch her, then, as he moves to kiss her, she pushes him away. He is getting very annoyed and starts to shout at her. Danny goes over to them, telling the man he will sort her out, and takes her to another room where there are no people. He grabs her and pushes her up against the wall.

"Listen, you do not refuse the clients anything, you do as you're told. Do you understand?"

He puts his hand round her throat; he is not the person she thought he was. He releases her and, instantly, his whole attitude changes again. He smiles as he says, "Now, you take these."

He gives her some pills. Jayne is afraid and takes them while he stands watching her.

"You stay here." He says as he leaves the room. He calls the small fat man over to him and whispers in the man's ear. The fat man smiles then shakes hands with Danny, and heads for the room where Jayne is.

Everyone is getting in the mood. The drugs are being taken openly, Julian is still with Rosie, and has put some coke on the table. He takes some, then Rosie does the same. She is relaxed and enjoying his company. She asks to be excused, and goes to the bathroom. While she is tidying herself up Natalia comes into the bathroom laughing with Monika. She sees Rosie and smiles.

"You English?" she asks.

"Yes, where are you from?" Rosie responds.

"Me Natalia, this girl Monika. She knows very little English. We Slovak. What your name?"

"I am Rosie."

Natalia puts her arm around her and smiling tells her, "We will be friends Rosie. We go now, enjoy ourselves, get some nice rich man's money."

They leave the bathroom. Julian is waiting for Rosie with drinks in his hand. He gives Rosie a glass then he takes her hand.

"Come Rosie."

She does as he asks.

They are in a bedroom with a very large bed. He takes her drink from her hand and puts it with his on the table. He puts his arms around her, kissing her. She just stands and when he begins to undress her she starts to respond. She has taken a few drugs, and drink, but is still able to enjoy what he is doing to her. She is now laid on the bed fully naked. He is kissing her body. She loves every minute of it as he continues to explore every part of her.

"Oh yes, yes," she cries, as Julian presses his naked body up to her.

She reaches for him. His whole body stiffens as she rolls over on top of him. She looks down at him, seeing that he is enjoying her every move and she starts to move with him. Feeling him inside of her makes her body respond even more.

He soon manoeuvres himself on top of her, she opens her legs to let him enter her then her legs wrap around him like a vice. He is not tender; he is rough with her while they are having sex and she likes it. She is scratching his back, digging her nails into him. He grabs hold of her shoulders, and pulls her up to meet him while forcing himself further into her. She screams out but this makes him even rougher. They are both perspiring as they continue to enjoy the sex until both them cry out as they simultaneously climax. Julian collapses on top of her. Exhausted, they both lay there.

"Can you manage a bit more of that?" Julian asks.

She just smiles and nods her head. Then when they're ready they get back to more lovemaking.


Julian gets up and dresses as she lay watching him. When he is fully dressed he looks at her, smiles then leaves the room. Rosie gets up and is soon dressed and following him. As she leaves the room Natalia and Monika are coming into the bedroom with two elderly men. They all laughing. Natalia winks at Rosie as she passes her.

Rosie looks around for Jayne as she enters the room but she can't see her. Danny comes across.

"Everything okay?" he asks.

She knows now what is expected of her, and as before she suspects that Danny is only interested in her for the business of sex.

She answers Danny. "I'm okay. I was looking for Jayne."

"Look, don't worry about her." He takes her over to

where no one can hear or see him; he takes something from his pocket and gives Rosie it.

"Put this in your bag and let me know if you want any more. Now go and make yourself available."

Rosie looks at him, seeing he is very serious. She is about to join Jade who is talking to some of the guests when she sees Jayne coming out of one of the rooms, followed by the fat man and another couple of men. The men are all laughing. Jayne looks awful; her hair is a mess, and she looks as though she has been crying as her mascara has run down her cheeks. She looks to be unsteady on her feet, her dress is pulled over one shoulder and she is trying to pull it up. Danny comes to Rosie again.

"Get her out of here, get her to the bathroom, and see she gets tidied up right now," he says, pushing Rosie towards her.

She takes her to the bathroom and when they get there Jayne starts to cry.

"Come on Jayne, what's happened?"

"They raped me. All of them, one after the other. Danny told me to do as they say, he was really mad at me and he grabbed me round my neck." Rosie tries to console her.

"We have made our bed now we must lie in it. If we don't do as we're told we will be in trouble."

"I don't know if I can do this Rosie. The drug thing is getting worse," Jayne says. She looks pale, and worried.

"I know how you feel. We'll talk about it later."

Rosie picks up her bag, takes some pills out of it and then takes out a few, offering Jayne some. Jayne, still crying, takes two and swallows them.

Rosie sees to Jayne's makeup and does her hair.

"Come on girl, pull yourself together." Soon they go back to join the others.

Natalia and Monika come into the room half-dressed and dancing around the men, who need little encouragement. They are soon dancing with them, encouraging them to take their remaining clothes off. Jade looks to be on a high, and joins them. Danny and Paul are stood together watching Rosie and Jayne; he motions to Rosie to join the others.

Not wanting to get Danny mad she goes to join the

others, taking Jayne with her.

The drugs are taking hold. Rosie is taken to the bedroom by one of the older men and this time she does not resist. Julian is with Natalia now, dancing close to her. She has only her panties on.

It is soon early morning and some of the men are asleep. Some of the girls are laid in the chairs with them, and some on the floor.

Danny and Paul are rousing the girls and telling them to get ready, as they will be leaving soon. Rosie, Jayne and Jade are taken to the vehicle standing by to take them home. Danny gives each one an envelope.

"Here, you've earned it."

He gives Jayne and Jade some drugs, telling Rosie she already has hers. The car drives away with Danny stood in the road watching them leave.

Jayne is slumped in the back seat not really caring or knowing where she is. Jade is in a little world of her own. Rosie is in a place where she doesn't care too much about anything anymore. She helps Jayne up to their room, puts Jayne on to her bed and then goes to her own bed, lays down and soon falls asleep, fully clothed.

It's well into late afternoon before Rosie awakes. She is finding it hard to wake up properly. Her eyes just won't focus; she manages to sit up, gets out of bed and goes to look in on Jayne, who is laid half in and half out of bed but sill fast asleep. She calls out to her.

"Jayne, wake up."

Jayne opens her eyes then starts to sit up, and then falls back down again. She doesn't know where she is for a minute or two then asks, "Rosie how did we get back here? I can't remember."

"We came back in a car. I put you to bed."

"Oh yes, I remember a bit." Jayne gets up and follows Rosie to the kitchen. Rosie makes them a drink and they sit chatting. Rosie reminds Jayne that Danny had given drugs and money last night as they left.

"I put my money in my bag."

Rosie walks across and picks her bag up. Looking inside she

finds the money, and takes it out.

"£200."

She then takes out the drugs. There are a couple of small packets of cocaine, and a container with pills in it. Rosie thinks she had got more money on the earlier occasions she had gone with Danny but, then again, just to have the drugs makes her feel a bit more easy. There's some money's worth there. Jayne, seeing what Rosie had in her bag, goes and finds her bag. She takes the money out and counts it. She then looks for the drugs. She has the same amount as Rosie.

"I'm not going in to uni. I'm off to do some shopping. Are you coming with me?" Rosie waves the money at her, smiling. Jayne recollects Danny getting mad with her and remembers how upset she was. She agrees to go with Rosie; she watches her open a packet and Rosie looks across at Jayne.

"Shall we?"

Jayne nods her head. After they have taken a shower and got themselves ready they head into town.

# 7
# Living The High Life

Danny and Paul are in their flat talking about the night before. Danny tells Paul, "The one we have to be careful of is that Jayne. We have to concentrate on her. I think the other two are in, they seem to accept anything we throw at them so we should get them to London as soon as we can."

Paul agrees. "Do we get Jayne into more of the white stuff? Maybe something harder, some brown maybe. But if we do she will be no good for what we had planned for her."

"No. We will give her a little rough persuasion; we will give them a few days to use up all their money and drugs before we tell them where they are going for a holiday," Danny says laughing.

Both of them are laughing now. Paul adds, "A bloody good working holiday."
They both start laughing even more.

"I am very impressed with the Slovakian girls. They know what they are doing and they'll give us no problems. They really have a good work ethic. I hope the Romanian girls are okay when they arrive in Brighton and Manchester."

Danny tells Paul, "We know they are not good quality but we will get what we can out of them. We're expecting Ramon to bring in some other girls within a week or so and they can be dispersed to where they fit in the best. In the meantime maybe you could try for a new girl or two from the university?"

"I will when we get the others out of the way," Paul says. Danny lays back in the chair smiling.

"Some of these so-called dignitaries, if the public only

knew where their bloody money is going. It's unbelievable just how many of them are at it. Mind you, as long as the money keeps coming in I couldn't care less. No point in taking the moral high ground."

The telephone rings. Danny picks up the phone

"D...a...n...n...y."

"Ramon. How are you? What can I do for you?" Danny asks.

"I wonder how the girls are? Good I hope?" Ramon says.

"Ramon no problems. They are very good, and we're looking forward to a few more like them."

"We try, we try. One of my friends in our business... police take his girls, and him. We be very careful Danny. I let you know if we hear from insider in police we pay."

Ramon sounds concerned, which is most unlike him.

"Okay Ramon, we will be careful. You keep in touch."

"I keep in touch, see you." Ramon puts the phone down. Danny tells Paul what Ramon has said. Paul does not look too concerned and just prepares some drinks.

"As long as they are not connected to Ramon or us who cares? Here, have a drink brother."

Danny takes the drink, thinking the business is going far too well to lose it now. Danny contacts Manchester and Brighton just to put them in the picture and to warn them that they should be very careful with the girls and any new clients.

The girls have had a good spending spree, buying new clothes and occasionally stopping off for a drink of wine in the various bars around the shopping centre. They cannot resist something to help them on their way, and to make them feel rather good. Jayne is able to dismiss her fears, and enjoy herself for a short time at least.

Rosie knows they will have to please the brothers if they are called to go to some party or other. She tells Jayne, "I think you will have to look a bit more enthusiastic if we go to another party or you may have trouble with Danny and Paul. If we don't get the money, and the other things, then we will be in trouble."

"I understand Rosie. I'll do my best," she says, smiling

at last.

"I know you will. Come on, let's head for home."
They pick up their bags of new clothes and head for home.


A couple of days pass and they even manage to show up at the college a couple of times but know they have no interest. They are just going through the motions with the help of the drugs they are given.

Rosie has still not seen her mother for some time and her father has tried to contact her but she has avoided him.

May has seen Rosie and she tried to speak to her. Rosie did not acknowledge her.

They have not heard from Danny or Paul for some time now. Sat watching television, there is a knock at the door. Surprised, Rosie asks, "Who can that be?"

She goes to the door and opens it. To her surprise Danny is stood there. She is embarrassed that he is seeing her in her nightdress, and not looking at her best.

"Can I come in then or shall I stand here all day?" he smiles.

Rosie stammers a bit. "Come in, come in. I'm just surprised to see you here."

He smiles and follows her into the lounge. Jayne sees him and jumps up.

"Well you two look to be relaxing. I wanted to have a word with you both." He sits down and both the girls sit looking at him, waiting in anticipation to hear what he has to say.

"We were wondering if you girls would like to pay a visit to London with me? Only the best hotel and it will be well worth your while. What do you say girls?"

Rosie looks across at Jayne who hasn't said anything and who is just sat staring at Danny. Rosie asks, "Well, what do you think Jayne? I'm willing."

Jayne just nods her head in agreement then asks, "How long are we going for?"

Danny doesn't want to say too much.

"Oh, just a couple of days or so. Can we say you will be able to go then?"

"Yes we will both go won't we Jayne?"

She looks at Jayne as she says it, giving Jane a look enough to say, *'go on, say yes'*.

Jayne answers, "Yes okay."

"That's great. You will have company as Jade will be joining you." Danny relaxes. "Well, am I going to get a cup of coffee then?"

Jayne gets up to go to make the coffee; Danny is sitting on the settee. He looks at Rosie and pats the settee alongside him motioning for her to sit beside him. She walks across and as she sits with him he puts his arm round her. He runs his hands down her back. He can feel her smooth skin under her nightdress. He pulls her closer to him.

"Get rid of her," he says, meaning Jayne, whispering in Rosie's ear.

She is getting excited just being close to him. Despite his treatment she can't help thinking that he is as good looking as ever. She smiles at him. Jayne comes into the room with the coffee and she hands Danny his drink. As she hands Rosie hers, Rosie motions with her eyes trying to tell her to go to bed. Jayne understands what she is trying to tell her.

"Oh I'm so tired. I'm going to bed now excuse me. Night Danny."

Danny just looks at her and tells her, "I will tell you what the plans are later."

Soon Danny is sat alone with Rosie. She asks him how he knew where she lived.

"I know a lot of things about you and the others around here."

He puts his cup down and walks over to the light switch. He flicks it off then walks back to her.

"Where's your room?"

She gets up, unable to hide how much she wants him. She walks to the bedroom with Danny following her and sits on the bed, watching Danny as he approaches her. He runs his hands through her hair then, holding her head back, he kisses her passionately and fully on the lips. She wants him more than ever as his hands feel her body. He stands her up, lifting her nighty over her head, exposing her beautiful breasts. He kisses her breasts, and then her neck. She is breathing heavily with excitement. He sits her back on the bed and then starts to remove his clothes. Rosie is laid back, watching him and waiting for him with anticipation. He lies alongside her. She can't wait to touch him.

"Wait," he whispers.

He gets up and takes something from his coat pocket. He pops some pills into his mouth then puts one in Rosie's mouth. She swallows it, and then lies down alongside her again. She feels his chest, then his inner thighs. He is so aroused and she thinks to herself, *'I've waited for this for so long.'*

He turns her on her stomach, kissing her back then moving slowly down her back, kissing and occasionally using his tongue, making her feel like she is about to experience something she has never experienced before.

His body is now on top of her; her face is sunk into the pillow and she can feel his every move and, as he enters her, she screams out, putting her hands back to pull him closer to her.

"Yes, yes," she cries.

Danny's lovemaking is sometimes tender and loving, and then he can be really rough and demanding. He tells her just what he wants her to do and, without hesitation, she obliges. Danny does to her what no other man has ever done. No other man could make her feel like she does now. He has taken her to places she has never been before. Rosie is laid on her back with Danny laid on top of her and she is perspiring, nearly exhausted with the lovemaking as he moves slowly, teasing her and making her want more. Her fingers are digging into his back, she drags them down his back scratching him, and he feels the pain that makes him want more.

He takes hold of her hair and pulls her head back, kissing and biting her neck until soon they are both ready, their bodies unable to take any more. She has this wonderful feeling, her whole body is now moving in spasms, and with one last thrust Danny lets all the energy inside him go. She can feel him as he reaches his climax. She cries out again with pleasure. Then they both lay there, exhausted. Rosie can feel his dripping body on top of her but she does not want to let him go.

After dozing for some time Danny gets off the bed. She watches him. Seeing him naked excites her. Danny turns and looks at her; he smiles and then carries on to the bathroom.

When he gets back he starts to dress, not saying anything for a while before he tells her, "Rosie, get yourself ready for the weekend. You will both be going to London, and Jade will be joining you. You will be meeting some very influential people. You all have to look your best. Oh and ease up on the pills and whatever else it is you're doing."

"Whatever you say Danny."
Rosie smiles at him.

He walks to the door then but before leaving he turns and adds, "If you can perform like that at the weekend you will be well rewarded. I'll be in touch. Bye."

Rosie just lays there thinking about what has been happening to her. She thinks back to her first meeting with Danny and what has happened since. She has never felt any shame until now. A tear runs down her cheek and she turns and cries into her pillow before falling to sleep.

The next morning both girls are sat drinking their coffee. Jayne knows how much Rosie likes Danny so she does not ask Rosie about what went on last night. Rosie is sat very quietly then she tells Jayne, "When we go to London this weekend we will have to look our best. Danny said we must go easy on the white stuff so we will have to ration it out a little."

"Rosie, we are wasting our time at uni. I've lost all interest. My parents will go mad but I've had enough. We have let things go too far now." She holds her head in her hands.

"Yes, I know what you mean. My mother won't give a damn what I do but my dad is another thing. He will give me some grief and I don't want to face him; I have been avoiding his calls."
As she is speaking she is chopping out a line or two of cocaine. She bends down, and snorts one, and Jayne walks across for the other line.

On Friday evening they receive a call from Danny. He

will send a vehicle to pick them up early on Saturday morning and they are told to pack and be ready. Rosie and Jayne spend all Friday evening packing their clothes away. They are excited but a little nervous.

On Saturday morning the vehicle arrives. The driver takes their cases and, as they get into the car, Jade is sat there smiling.

"Morning... you two don't look too happy. Have you had a bad night? Here take one of these, they will make you feel better."

They take them from Jade, who takes one herself. The chauffeur tells them, "The drinks are in the compartment between the seats. So make yourselves comfortable ladies we have a long way to go."


Danny is already in London, where he has been to see his parents who think he is still in the banking business and doing very well. They are impressed when he arrives in a new Porsche 311 Turbo. He tells them that Paul is unable to come to London because of business but he will telephone them. His father, an ex-banker himself, is very pleased that his sons have taken after him and are working hard.

Danny says his goodbyes to his parents and goes to get things ready for the girls and to see his clients.

Danny arrives at the Savoy Hotel in London. He pulls up outside, he is told to leave his car is to be taken away and parked, and then he is shown into the hotel foyer. The manager comes over.

"Mr Danny Franklin-Smith?"

"Yes, that's me," Danny says

"Follow me sir, this way. Sheikh Fahd is expecting you."

A young woman dressed in a smart uniform is stood outside the lift and waiting for them. Once they are inside the lift the young woman follows them in, standing alongside the control buttons as she closes the doors. The lift stops and the doors open; the young woman stands outside, letting them enter the most wonderful apartment, with marble floors, beautiful furniture, and large oil paintings on the wall. A man in full Arab white dress, with what looks like a manservant alongside him, walks towards Danny.

"Mr Danny Franklin-Smith." He holds his hand out to Danny who enthusiastically shakes his hand and gives a gentle, deferential bow of the head.

"Nice to see you again sir." The Amir motions to Danny to follow him. The hotel manager goes back into the lift and leaves.

They sit down in this very large room with sprawling sofas and the manservant brings them cold drinks and pours them.

"No alcohol Mr Franklin-Smith. I'm sure you will enjoy a nice cold lemon juice," the Amir says, laying back into the cushions behind him.

"That's fine sir." Danny is sat upright waiting for the manservant to leave.

"Tell me Mr Danny, have you got the merchandise we ask for?" he says, mopping his forehead with a white silk handkerchief.

"Yes, three sir, as you requested. I will bring them tonight for you to see if that's okay?" Danny says, feeling nervous and hoping the girls have done as he said and laid off the drugs.

"Tonight is fine. If they are what I wanted then we may take a trip in my private jet for a couple of days. Would that be a problem for you?"

"I think we can arrange that sir." Danny is thinking to himself, *'bloody passports, shit'*.

The Arab man stands up and holds his hand out to Danny again.

"Shall we say 10 o'clock this evening?"

Danny shakes his hand again with a little nod of the head.

"10 o'clock sir."

The manservant leads Danny back to the lift, the doors soon open with the girl in the uniform standing there with a very serious look on her face. When they reach the foyer and the doors open Danny leans towards the girl and says, "Smile, girl." She looks at him and, for the first time, smiles.

"That's my girl," he laughs, thinking, 'I'm partial to a girl in a uniform.'

Danny leaves the hotel to meet the girls.

The girls arrive at the hotel in London where they are staying.

Jade is very impressed.

"Wow, look at this. I hope it is as good inside as it is outside," Jade says smiling.

The chauffeur opens the door for them and as they get out he takes their bags from the boot. A young man from the hotel puts them on a trolley. He takes them inside; the girls follow him and the chauffeur to the reception desk. The chauffeur tells the receptionist, "Mr Daniel Franklin-Smith." She looks at the computer

"Ha! Yes rooms 141, 142 and 143."

She hands the young man with the baggage the keys and tells the girls to follow him.

He shows each one to their rooms. Rosie enters her room; it is very nice and she goes to the window and looks out over London, thinking *'what have we got in store for us?'* She goes into the bathroom and decides to take a bath and relax a bit. Once she has sorted out her clothes she runs the bath. There is everything she needs in the bathroom. She gets into the bath and lays back, enjoying the warmth of the water and the sweet smell of the perfumed salts she has put in. She lays there for some time and is nearly falling asleep when she partly opens her eyes and is surprised to see Danny stood in front of her, watching her and smiling.

"Danny, I never heard you come in."

She says, sitting up with the soapsuds running down her bare breasts. For a moment she is going to cover up then decides not to bother.

"Hello Rosie. The other girls are in their rooms so I'll speak to them later. You need to be ready for about 9.30 tonight and I want you and the others to be at your best. You're going to meet a real Sheikh."

Rosie looks surprised. "A real Sheikh? You're joking."

"No I'm not Rosie. Have you got a passport?"

"Yes, at the flat." Rosie says, getting excited.

"You have to tell me where it is. I'll send someone for it along with Jayne's and Jade's, we may need them."

Rosie looks puzzled, "Why would we need our passports?"

"I'll tell you later. First, where is your passport in your

flat?" He smiles at her.

Rosie explains where her passport is and Danny tells her he going to see the other girls to ask the same question. He leaves the room, telling her he will be back shortly.

Rosie gets out of the bath and puts her robe on. She pours herself a drink from the small bar then goes to her bag and takes one of her uppers out and swallows it before Danny gets back.

Danny is soon in her room after speaking to the girls. Rosie is sat on the settee in her robe. Danny comes and sits alongside of her.

"Rosie, I know I can depend on you." His hand is on her knee and he squeezes her leg and runs his hand up to her thigh.

"I can, can't I?" he says again.

She looks at him. He only has to touch her and she falls to pieces.

"Yes Danny, you can depend on me." She parts her legs but Danny smiles and moves his hand away.

Standing up he tells Rosie, "The others know when to be ready. Until then just relax. I will come for the three of you around 9.30, okay?"

She is disappointed that Danny did not respond to her when he touched her.

"9.30, I'll be ready."

Danny walks to the door.

"See you tonight."

Danny leaves.

Both Jade and Jayne come to Rosie's room. They sit talking for sometime. Rosie asks, "Do you know this person we are going to see is a Sheikh?"

"What's a bloody Sheikh? Is that a King or a Prince or something?" Jade asks.

"Something like that. A head of state," Rosie tells her.

"Is he rich? If he is then I don't mind what kind of state he is in!"

That makes them all laugh even more. They go to their rooms to get ready after sharing out a bit of cocaine. Danny arrives and gets them all in Rosie's room.

"Well you all look very nice, but Jade a little less on the

lipstick. Your passports will be arriving in a couple of hours or so, so if you happen to be asked to fly somewhere there should be no problem, okay?" The girls look at one another and all agree.

"Come on girls, the Amir's Rolls Royce awaits you."

Danny opens the door motioning for the girls to follow him. They arrive in the foyer and a very smart chauffeur is standing waiting for them. Danny has a quick word with him. The chauffeur nods his head, "Yes sir, I understand."

The chauffeur turns to the girls.

"Follow me ladies."

The doorman opens the doors for them and a white Rolls Royce is in front of them. The girls all look at one another, impressed. The chauffeur opens the car door for them and once inside they take in their surroundings. Jade is smiling.

"Very nice. We won't get to ride in anything like this very often."

The Rolls is soon underway. They are all sat very quietly as they drive through London and, when they arrive at the Savoy, the chauffeur opens the door for them and when they are out of the vehicle he leads them inside the hotel. A very smart Arab-looking man comes to them.

"Come with me, ladies," he says.

A few of the male guests are looking at the girls as they go to the lift that goes to the private suites. The same girl in uniform opens the lift doors for them and as they enter the lift the man just stands there not saying anything as they go to the Amir's apartment floor. They arrive at the Amir's apartment and as the lift door opens a woman dressed in a white flowing robe greets the man. He whispers something to her and she looks at the girls.

"Come," she says.

The girls are amazed at the apartment. Everything is amazing; the furnishings, the lush rugs and marble floors. There is very light Arab music playing in the background as they follow the woman, who takes them to this beautiful bathroom with a very large bath which would probably hold six people. The girls have never seen anything like it.

"Take clothes off," the woman says in broken English.

At first they are reluctant to take their clothes off and just stand there. Then again the woman tells them rather abruptly, "Take clothes off."

Jade is the first to start taking her clothes off and the others follow suit. In the meantime the woman is preparing the bath with oils and perfumed bathing soaps. They are all stood naked as the woman motions them to get into the bath. They do as they are told and get into the bath.

Jade whispers, "I had a bath an hour or so ago, do I look dirty?" They all have a good giggle.

The woman just stands watching them as they bathe and then she brings some large white towels for them and three white robes. "Come out now," she tells them.

They get out of the bath, dry themselves and put on their robes. There is a leather couch with a white sheet on, and the woman tells Rosie, "Take off robe on here." She does what the woman tells her.

Rosie is naked as she lies down. The woman has oil on her hands and she starts to rub it all over her. Rosie is amazed how the woman massages her; she is so gentle Rosie feels so relaxed and she can smell the perfume in the oils as the woman's hands massage every part of her body.

When she is finished Jade is next. The woman repeats the same procedure with the other two.

She gives all of them a white silk long gown that buttons at the front, which is practically see through. Then the woman sees to their hair. She will not let them put too much make up on, only what she will allow them. When they are ready they are led into a beautiful room with a four-poster bed in it. She tells them to sit down and wait for her.

They are wondering what will happen next and Jayne looks a little afraid.

"Don't worry Jayne, we'll be okay."

Some time passes and when the woman comes back she tells them to stand up and only speak to the Amir if he speaks to them and refer to him as your highness. Not long after he appears. The girls do not know what to do; they are stood in a line as he approaches them. He is a very smart looking man dressed in long white robes and with dark but greying hair. He smiles at the girls then stops close to Rosie. He looks her up and down, from just inches away, and then he looks at her face.

"Name?"

"Rosie! Your... your highness." He shows his approval by putting his hand to his chin and nodding his head.

He does the same with the other girls, looking them up and down and then he walks back to Rosie. He puts up his hand and touches her hair. He stands looking at them for a while then leaves the room, motioning for the woman to follow him.

The girls are baffled, not knowing what is going on. They are stood there not daring to move; when the woman comes back she tells Rosie to remain and the other two girls to follow her.

Rosie seems to be waiting a long time before the Amir arrives back in the room. He walks past her and lies on the bed, then motions to her to come over to him. She stands close to him and he reaches up and undoes the few buttons on the front of her robe, exposing her breasts.

His touch is gentle as he puts his hand into her robe, still looking at her, then he lays back, undoing his robe and exposing himself. He takes Rosie's hand and puts it on his private parts. Rosie takes hold of him; he is laid back with his eyes closed as she moves with a slow gentle movement. He opens his eyes then takes hold of her, brings her onto the bed and on top of him. He lets her do what she is doing and she has no inhibitions. Soon he is inside of her, she puts both hands on his chest as she lifts up and down slowly. He does occasionally touch her breasts. She is watching him as she feels him, knowing he is about to reach his climax. She moves around on him giving him the utmost pleasure. As he does finally climax, she herself presses down on him, giving herself some pleasure.

He occasionally looks at Rosie and takes in her beauty. He has had many women and not cared if he ever saw them again but this young one has something he likes very much. He already knows he must see her again. He lays for some time with her alongside of him, and then he eventually gets up quietly and leaves the room. The woman comes in and takes Rosie to the bathroom. When she has finished she tells her to get dressed and join the others who are now back in their own clothes. They are shown back to the Rolls Royce and driven back to their hotel. Once inside the vehicle Jade asks, "What went on there then? We were just told to dress and wait. Did you do it with him then?"

Rosie, being a bit embarrassed, does not want to tell them, just smiling instead.

"You didn't did you, Rosie? Tell us what happened, we have to know."

"No, there is nothing to tell."

"I bet," Jade says.

When they get back to their hotel they go to their rooms, having decided to meet for breakfast.

The next morning Rosie gets a call from Danny.

"Well Rosie, you must have impressed the Amir. He wants the three of you to fly to Qatar on his private jet tomorrow. I'll see you later. He has sent you a present so I'll give it to you later, okay?"

"Yes Danny. What about our clothes? What will we need?"

"Rosie you will not have to bother about that. The Amir will send someone to take the three of you on a shopping trip. What do you think of that?"

"We won't be going to Pre-Max then," she says, laughing.

"No. I think something a little better than that. Rosie, I'll see you in an hour or so, so you can tell the girls."

"Bye Danny."

Rosie cannot believe it and heads for the girls rooms to tell them about the trip to Qatar. Jade is very excited.

"When are we going on this shopping trip then? I can't wait. I wonder if we have a limit on what we can spend?"

Rosie smiles, "I asked if we were going to Pre-Max."

They all laugh, then Jayne says, "I bet he could probably buy all the bloody Pre-Max chain of stores."

After an hour or so Danny comes into the room, smiling.

"Well done girls. I'm more than pleased with you. And Rosie, here is something the Amir sent you." He hands her a small box.

Rosie takes the box from Danny, looking at the others as she opens the box and her eyes light up.

She can see a beautiful gold bracelet. The girls cannot get near enough to see it. Jade asks Rosie if she can hold it, Rosie takes it from the box and passes it to Jade.

"Wow! It must have cost a fortune," Jade says, feeling the weight of it in her hands.

"Don't worry girls your turn will come. The Amir is, as I said, a very generous man, that is if you please him," Danny says, looking at Jayne.

Danny takes something from his pocket, "Here, use it wisely girls, you understand what I'm saying don't you?" he says, as he gives Rosie the cocaine.

"Share it out between you."

There is a knock on the door. The man who met them in the foyer of the Savoy is standing there. Danny speaks to him and he turns and leaves.

"Get your glad rags on girls, the Rolls awaits you. That man will be escorting you. He has the Amir's credit card and he'll make sure you get whatever you want."

They cannot get ready fast enough. Danny arranges to see them later. They leave with their guardian and the credit card; first stop is Harrods. The girls look at one another very excited as the Rolls stops and the chauffeur opens the door. People are staring at them as they get out of the Roller. Seeing the people looking at them makes them feel like they are people of real importance. Jade plays it up a bit, walking into the store swinging her hips.

As they follow their guardian into the store they are met by a manager of the store and taken to the ladies' clothing department and then set free to spend.

"Bloody hell, Rosie. I feel like running amok," Jade says, as she and the others are rummaging through racks of very expensive clothes. Any time anyone of them picks something there is an assistant there to help them.

The Amir's man is just sat watching them. Jade is coming out of the changing room, she smiles at him, waving the dress and he just nods his head. She gives it to the assistant. This carries on through the next couple of hours in all departments; coats, dresses, shoes and underwear.

Rosie and Jade are in their element. Although Jayne is

picking up things and trying them on she is not enjoying it as much as the other two. Rosie and Jade stop to talk to her.

"Jayne, what's wrong? How often do we get an opportunity like this? Bloody hell girl enjoy yourself. Buy, buy, buy like there is no tomorrow," Jade tells her.

"I need something," whispers May.

"In the toilet," Rosie says.

Rosie tells the assistant they need the ladies. They are led away by the assistant. When they are inside the ladies' room, and a lady who has just washed her hands has left, they get together. She opens her bag and takes the cocaine out.

"Jade you watch the door." Jade goes and stands by the door while Rosie puts a couple of lines down. Jayne is down sniffing up a line, which has gone in a flash. Rosie follows, and soon Jade is there taking her share.

All three stand there for a while, cleaning themselves up a bit before Rose asks Jayne, "Okay now girl?"

"Yes Rosie I feel a bit better." She tries to smile.

Jade is at the door.

"Come on then, let's empty the bloody store girls," she says laughing.

The girls have lost track of time. They are enjoying themselves that much when the Amir's assistant stands up and motions to the girls and then points at his watch. They take the hint. The assistant calls for a young man to help them with their packages, taking them to the vehicle.

They can hardly get in themselves when all the packages are in, but they manage to do so and then head off back to their hotel, all very happy with what they have managed to buy on the Amir's credit card.

They get all their purchases to their room and once settled in they get together to chat over a few glasses of wine about what will be happening tomorrow.

Jade says, "I bet we will have to pay for what we bought today. When we get to Qatar we better be prepared for anything."

Rosie gives a weak smile, "I hope it will not be that bad. Maybe the Amir will just want the same."

Jade looks at Rosie. "Well what would the same be, Rosie? Tell us, then we'll know what to expect?"

She goes a little red in the face. Jayne has just a vague look on her face, not seeming to take much in.

"It was just hand relief and a bit of sex but it was over in no time," she tells them.

Jade laughs, "I can't see us getting all these presents just for a bloody hand job Rosie, mind you the Amir is good looking, well distinguished and kind of good looking depending on how much we have had to drink and how many tablets we have taken."

They all laugh and then decide to go to their rooms.

Danny telephones Rosie, telling her they have to be ready for 11 o'clock sharp in the morning when they will be taken to the airport. He has told the others but asks her to make sure the others are ready and that she should keep an eye on Jayne.

When they finish talking Rosie takes something to calm her, and then relaxes on the bed wondering why her mother has not been in touch. She has had a few calls and texts from her father but she has not answered him, knowing he will want to know where she is and what she is doing.

# 8
# Little Fat Man

Early the next day Danny has called them and they have to be ready to leave for the airport in two hours. The girls are frantic and start to get ready and to pack. They keep running into each other's rooms asking if they should take this or that but finally they are all ready.

A couple of young men from the hotel come and take their baggage down to the vehicles and then Amir's assistant appears.

"Come, come follow me." They pick up their handbags and frantically follow him. When they get in the foyer Danny arrives.

"Hi girls. I will be joining you on the flight. You all look very nice but we better get going."
The girls follow Danny and the Amir's man to the very large vehicle waiting for them. It has darkened windows and is very luxurious inside with white leather seats and everything they need.
They go to Heathrow Airport but not to the main terminal, the busy part, but to a quiet part where they are taken to a small building and through customs and immigration without being checked, apart from their passports, before being taken out of the building to a private jet standing by.

They are ushered on board and within one hour of arriving at the airport they are in the air. Once they are flying Danny comes across to Rosie, Jade and Jayne.

"When we arrive you will not be staying at a hotel, you will be staying in the Amir's palace so I will see you in a couple of days. Do not take any mobile phones with you. I will take care of them. Just enjoy yourselves, okay?"

They smile at him and then search in their bags for their mobile phones to give him.

Throughout the flight two lovely looking airhostesses who Danny seems to be very interested in are waiting on them. Rosie has been watching him and gets rather jealous.

Jade nudges Rosie, and hands her a pill. Rosie and Jayne take them when Danny is not looking; he is busy chatting up the airhostesses.

As they are about to land Rosie asks Danny, "Where are we landing?"

Danny looks out of the window.

"We are landing at a place called Doha, and then we will be going to a place called Al Wakra. It's on the coast and a very nice place."

The others are listening with interest as Jade asks Rosie, "Do we get to go to the beach?"

Rosie is laughing as she tells her, "Do you think you're going to Scarborough? For God's sake, you'll be asking to go to the bloody amusements next." They all start laughing, including Danny.

The plane lands and taxis to a small building where there is a small group of people all wearing Arab robes. As the jet comes to a stop, Danny ushers the three girls to the door. As the door opens they walk out into the very warm air. A young woman, very nice looking, and dressed in a white robe with her head covered with a white silk scarf which covers half her face, walks up to the girls, and in very good English tells them, "I am Mia. Please come with me."

Danny motions to the girls to go with her, telling them he will see them later.

Two vehicles drive away; one with the girls and one with the entire luggage. The vehicles are air-conditioned which is very nice after experiencing the intense heat. Rosie is looking at Mia, not knowing if she is English or from Qatar. Mia looks at her but does not speak until they have arrived at the most magnificent building. It is surrounded by palm trees and various exotic plants.

Everything seems to be white. The buildings are white and all of the people are dressed in white too.

Rose whispers to Jayne and Jade, "I feel a bit overdressed, don't you?"

Jade giggles.

"Bloody hell, that's a good advert for white emulsion. All they need is the Dulux dog."

They all start giggling again, with Mia staring at them.

The vehicle pulls up, two people outside run to open the doors for them, two others go to the other vehicle to take the luggage to the building. Mia signals for the other girls to go with her. They enter the building and the girls are amazed; everything looks so sterile, clean and crisp; marble floors throughout and flowers everywhere. Once they get to their rooms they are lost for words. They each have a room with a four-poster bed; large scatter cushions are laid around with the largest television anyone has ever seen fixed on the wall. Mia asks if the girls are hungry, then tells them to freshen up, as some food will arrive for them. Their rooms are close so they are able to get to each other quite easily. Rosie is in Jayne's room when Jade joins them.

"My bed is big enough for six people," Jade says.

Rosie looks at her, "Don't say that, you may get six people visiting you," she says laughing.

Jayne is beginning to come out of her shell a little now, probably because she is impressed with what she has seen, and how good they have been treated. She's now ready for something to eat.

Mia takes them to a room near to their bedrooms where there is food laid out on the table.

"Take what you want and I will see you later." She leaves them there with one manservant stood ready to place any food they require on their plates.

"There are drinks but non-alcoholic," Jade whispers to Rosie. "I could do with a nice glass of wine."

"No chance, they are Muslim. They do not touch alcohol," Jayne tells them

"I have heard they do when they are in the seedy clubs of London," Jade says.

They all go quiet as Mia arrives back in the room.

"When you have eaten you can relax in your rooms for the rest of the evening and I will see you tomorrow."

With that she leaves the room again. They get out the cocaine and, as it is quiet, they give themselves a boost while no one is around. Jade comments, "I could do with a glass of anything at the moment."

As Rosie cleans her nose of the white stuff she says, "No chance of that. We better go easy. We haven't got a lot left. I have a few uppers and that's it. Best see what we have between us."

They get their bags and take out various pills that they have. Jade puts them all together and reaches across to Rosie.

"You take care of them Rosie."

She puts them away. She is feeling rather high now and goes to her room, where she lays down; her head is spinning round. She has noticed that the effect of the cocaine seems not to be lasting as long as it did when she first started taking it.

The following morning they freshen up in their bathrooms, which are more luxurious than the Amir's bathroom was in London. They see no one apart from a manservant stood by the food that has been laid out, as before. There are foods they have never seen before, and they are sampling all the unfamiliar fruits, in general thinking being here is not that bad.

Through the day they are not bothered, lounging around in this wonderful place through to the evening. Mia arrives and the girls are sat together. Mia looks at them in their western clothes.

"We must get you ready. You must bathe, and scent your bodies."

While she is speaking two more women arrive.

"You." She points to Jade.

"Go with this woman, and you," she then points to Jayne, " Go with this woman, and you." She points to Rosie, " Come with me."

They all leave the room. Rosie follows Mia to the bathroom and Mia looks her up and down. "Take your clothes off." She does as she asks. Mia is running the bath; she is putting oils and salts into the bath water.

Rosie is a little embarrassed. She walks to get into the bath and, once in, Mia comes to her and starts to bathe her. Her hands are smooth and she massages the oils into Rosie's body. Rosie has her eyes closed as she feels Mia's hands in a way caressing her body, leaving no place untouched. After some time, Mia beckons her to get out of the bath. As she does Mia starts to dry her, then wraps a large white towel around her. She does Rosie's hair, lifting it up in a style she has never had but that makes her look more beautiful. Her hair is finished, and before she gets dressed Mia rubs perfumed oil all over her body.

"Put on this robe and nothing else." She gives a white silk robe similar to the one Rosie wore when she last saw the Amir.

"Yes you look very nice. The Amir will be pleased with you, come," Mia says.

Rosie follows her and they meet up with the other girls who are dressed the same. Jade looks at Rosie and winks. They are taken to another part of the palace and into a very large room. The Amir is laid back on pillows talking to two other men and they are all dressed the same, in Arab clothes. The Amir does not take his eyes off Rosie. He smiles at her. The three girls are standing in front of the men who look at one another, and then at the girls.

A small, fat man with a long dark beard looks at Jayne, and waves her to sit near him. Jayne does reluctantly.

Another man sat near the Amir points to Jade. She is told to sit by him. The Amir gets up and just says to Rosie, "Come."

She follows him to his room. He walks over to his bed that is draped in long, flowing silk curtains. She can smell incense burning. There are candles burning, and light sound of Arab music is playing in the background. The Amir calls her over to him and he undoes the front of her robe, exposing Rosie's lovely round breasts. He touches her like before; she is stood with her eyes closed, his hands touch her in her most intimate places before he makes her to go on to her knees. He takes her hand then places it on him, she knows what he wants and she undoes his robe, exposing his erect penis. She is taken aback; she cannot remember him being like this the last time she was with him. He takes her shoulders, and as she gets nearer to him he gently pushes her head down on him. She does what she knows will please him.

His whole body is taking in all the wonderful sensations he is experiencing and her head moves up and down, slowly taking him more and more.

He moves her on to the bed, exposing all of her body. She can feel his beard as he kisses her body. He then massages her breasts, kisses them while his hands caress her and soon he is on her and penetrates her. She cries out he as he enters her slowly. His body moves up and down, her nails are long and dig into his back. He cannot control himself as he climaxes, she can feel him and he is now still, and quietly he just remains on top of her. Then, to her surprise, he starts to move again. She soon gets herself moving with him. He changes her position sometimes on top of him, and sometimes he on top of her. She is exhausted as he climaxes again.

They lay for sometime before he says to her, "My little one, you go to your room now."

He watches her as she puts on her robe. He enjoys just looking at her. She goes to the door, turns and looks at him and for the first time he smiles at her as she leaves.

The little fat man who cannot get his hands on her fast enough takes Jayne to a room. Groping her, he pulls her on to the bed. Her robe is now open, he bites her nipples, she cries out. She is in pain, pushing his head back from her, and he pulls her legs apart. Jayne tries to resist but he pulls her head back by her hair.

"No, no get off me," she says. This seems to make him even rougher with her. She cries out as he forces himself inside her. She tries again to push him off but as she struggles he hits her.

He has a smell of tobacco and sweat which makes Jayne feel sick. She dare not stop him now. As he abuses her she is crying. He is not concerned and just turns her over. Tears are running down her face as he is grunting. Laid on her back she feels pain but cannot move him, he is so heavy. He lets out a large grunt as he climaxes inside her, and stays there for some time before getting off her. Jayne is still crying and tries to get up and out of the room. He takes her wrist and throws her back on the bed.

"You stay. I tell you when to go." He slaps her head. "Understand?"

Jayne nods her head. She is so frightened of him that she decides to let him do what he wants.


Jade is with the younger man who is very nice. He talks to her, asks her questions and he is so experienced in his lovemaking that he seems to go on and on forever. Jade being Jade, she just does what he wants without any problem. They make love for a long time before Jade goes back to her room.

The following morning Jayne comes to Rosie, crying and looking terrible. She tells Rosie what happened. Rosie looks at her body; she has marks on her back and her legs.

"I need something Rosie, I need it bad."

She needs something herself. She takes it out as Jade arrives in the room smiling, but soon begins to look serious when she sees Jayne.

"What the hell's been happening to you Jayne?"

"That fat pig hurt me," she says as she sniffs a line of cocaine.

"How was your night Jade?"

"Fine. He was very nice and some lover. You must be good, the Amir likes you," Jade says smiling

They both look at Jayne and try to reassure her but she is still upset. She says, "I want to go home. I can't go through with that again. Not with that man, no way."

"What did you do to upset him Jayne? You will make it worse for yourself so just do what he asks, close your eyes and think of nice things."

"Think of nice things while he is abusing me? I can't."

She starts to cry again. Jayne asks Rosie to give her something else to help her. Reluctantly, she gives her a couple of pills that Jayne downs immediately. They bathe again and then go for something to eat. Both Rosie and Jade try to console Jayne and through the morning she calms down somewhat but is pressuring Rosie to give her more drugs.

The day seems to drag on. Occasionally they get together

but spend much of the day sleeping.

Rosie is thinking about her family again, knowing her father will go mad not knowing where and who she is with, and her mother will be wondering where she is; probably just to ask her for some money.

They have eaten in the evening when Mia comes to tell them to bathe again. They go through the same procedure; bathing, oils, perfumes and white robes. Jayne is getting herself into a right state. The woman who is with her comes to Mia and whispers to her. Mia tells Rosie she will be back soon and leaves with the other woman.

Rosie can hear loud noises but is uncertain who it is. The noise seems to fade away and Mia comes back into her room. She does Rosie's hair and then gets her dressed,

"Come now," she says. This time Rosie does not see the others. She is taken to the Amir's rooms, where he is sat smoking his Arab smoking pipe on his own. He pats the cushion alongside of him telling Rosie to sit, so she does so. He smiles again at her, not saying too much, until he says. "My young one, you go home tomorrow. Take this."

He has the most wonderful ring in his hand.

"You try it on."

She puts it on her finger and she looks at the Amir.

"Thank you your highness. Thank you, it is beautiful."

"Just like you, my fair one. I will see you again in the future but before you leave tomorrow. I need you to be with me tonight. Come now." He stands up and walks toward his bedroom, with Rosie following him.

Jade is taken to a room where the same young man she was with last night is waiting. She sees him and smiles and when they are in the room alone he tells her,

"My name is Amir Abdul. I am the Amir's cousin. Your name is Jade, yes?"

"Yes, I am Jade."

"Shall we proceed then Jade?" he says, taking his robe off and standing naked in the middle of the room.

Jade takes her robe off.

"Yes, let's proceed," she says, smiling at him. She sees that he is so aroused already. Soon they are on the bed, exploring each other's bodies through the night. There is very little talking, just complete raw sex.

Morning arrives and Rosie looks for Jayne but cannot find her. She goes to Jade.

"Where is Jayne? I can't find and her bed does not look as though it has been slept on."

Jade looking rather puzzled, "I haven't seen her. I came back and went straight to bed."

They sit talking and when Mia arrives in the room she tells them, "You will leave this afternoon. Pack your things and get yourselves ready."

"Mia, where is our friend Jayne?" asks Rosie.

Mia just looks at Rosie, "You just do as you are told. She is okay and you will see her later."

Jade just gets out a word. "But..."

"You do as you are told. Get ready," Mia says angrily.

When she has left Rosie is feeling a bit concerned. "What has happened to her, where is she?" she asks Jade.

"We cannot do anything. We will probably see her later."

Jade goes to pack her things and leaves Rosie.

By late afternoon some people come to take their baggage and they notice someone has packed Jayne's clothes for her. The vehicles are outside and both Jade and Rosie are taken to one of the vehicles and are shocked; when they get in Jayne is sat inside on her own and she looks like a zombie, her eyes are dark underneath. She just looks at them, not showing any emotions, not greeting them, just looking right through them. Rosie sits alongside her.

"Jayne what's happened? Where have you been?"

Jayne does not respond she just stares at Rosie. Both Rosie and Jade try to get her to speak but she says nothing.

"Look at her arms," Jade tells Rosie.

There are bruises on her arms and what looks like needle marks on the inside of her arm. Rosie shakes her head, takes hold of Jayne's arm and is inspecting it more closely. Jayne just lets her do what she wants.

"We better not say anything Rosie, let's just get out of here," Jade says.

Through the journey to the airport no one speaks and they are a little worried now. Rosie is trying to tidy Jayne's hair, but Jayne still does not speak. Jade takes some pills out, and hands Rosie a couple. She looks at them and wants to say no but she cannot because she needs them that bad.

The vehicle stops and Danny gets in.

"Bloody hot out there. We fly back to London shortly. I hear things went good, apart from her." He points to Jayne.

"She isn't too well," Rosie tells him."

Danny is looking really mad.

"She is going over the top with the hard stuff. I told her to take it easy." Rosie is about to butt in when Danny shouts at her.

"Don't make frigging excuses for her, just look at the bloody mess she is in. I'm really pissed off. She could have fucked up the whole set up here."

The girls sit quietly, not daring to say anything. Jayne did not even flinch when Danny shouted in her face, she just let her head drop to one side. Rosie and Jade try to sit her up straight but she just goes back into the position she was in before.

Rosie has the ring on that he Amir gave her and Danny notices it.

"Well, well, you must have impressed the Amir. Let's look at that, he gave you this," he says holding her finger, and looking at the ring more closely.

"And what did you get Jade? Something nice? I know this one got nothing." He is only inches away from Jayne's face as he says it.

"No I did not get anything either," Jade tells Danny.

He laughs. "Don't worry, I have a surprise for you both later and a little something else, okay?"

Jade and Rosie smile at him.

The vehicle stops at the airport and they are all taken to the Amir's private jet. Jayne has to be carried on to the plane. On board they are given drinks and made comfortable before take off.

Jayne is left on her own occasionally and Danny goes to her; they notice he puts something in her mouth then forces her to drink some water.

Once they are in the air Danny calls Rosie over to sit with him.

"Listen Rosie, I want you to stay with Natalia and Monika who are now in London in a very nice apartment. What do you say? I will be staying in London for a while." He touches her leg and smiles.

"What about Jade and Jayne?" she asks.

"Jade will be with you. As for Jayne she will be moving on because she has nothing to offer. Look, she is high all the time; she's a bloody wreck. By the way has she any family in Leeds or anywhere else?"

Rosie is quiet, Danny shouts at her. "Answer me - has she any bloody family?"

Rosie is now frightened of him. "She was in care before she came to uni. I don't think she is in contact with any of her family. She has no idea if any of her family still exist."

Danny smiles and his mood changes immediately. "You don't worry about Jayne, leave that to me."

She dare not ask him where Jayne will go and she asks Danny reluctantly, "What about uni?"

"Rosie, you will get rich, and all the white stuff you need, but don't overdo it, you understand? I have money for you and Jade, money like you have never seen before. You and Jade have to control your habit; you don't want to finish up like her, do you?" Danny smiles at her then turns to look at Jayne again.

He knows Rosie can't shake off the habit now, and that she could never afford to stay at uni and get what she needs.

"Okay Danny, I'll stay in London with Jade and the other girls."

"That's my girl. You'll have to sort your family out. You can decide what you want to tell them. I'll tell you when you can contact them." He kisses her cheek at the same time as feeling her body.

When they land they are rushed through customs and immigration without any problems. They are met by two Rolls as before.

Jayne is taken along with the luggage to the other Rolls. Danny speaks to the driver before joining the girls, who are in the other Rolls waiting for him.

They soon speed away along the motorway, and then through the very exclusive areas of London, arriving at some very swanky apartments. Danny ushers them out and into the entrance, which is very nice. Jade is looking all around and is very impressed. She nudges Rosie, Rosie looks at her, and she is smiling enough to say *'I like this'*.

They go up in a lift to their floor and along the corridor; Danny opens the apartment door inside and into a very beautiful lounge area. Then the two Slovakian girls come to them; Natalia and Monika call their names.

"Rosie, Jade, here we are in L...o...n...d...o...n. Nice to see you." Both Natalia and Monika are laughing.

"Apartment very nice, L...o...n...d...o...n very nice, plenty money and plenty jigi jig."

All the girls are laughing. Danny shows the girls their rooms and then calls Rosie and Jade together, away from Natalia and Monika.

"Here is your money." He gives them both envelopes, which Rosie thinks feel very bulky, as though there is a lot of money in it, and then he gives them a small bottle of different pills, and some cocaine.

"Just remember what I told you both. I'm going now; the girls will show you around. I'll be in touch. Oh and don't use the landline for any personal calls, do you understand me? You know what I said Rosie?" He sees the girls are a little afraid of him and they just nod their heads.

He leaves calling to the other girls. "See you soon, be good," he says laughing.

Rosie and Jade go to their rooms and Rosie opens the envelope.

"Wow!" She says out loud, running to Jades room. She is stood looking at her money and she looks up at Rosie.

"I'm lost for words. I have never seen so much money."

"We better put it somewhere safe," she tells her. They both put their money where they think it will be safe before joining the Slovakian girls.

Rosie looks at Jade and says, "Danny never gave us our mobile phones, and we cannot use the iPhones here for any calls. What do we do? He told me we can contact our families when he says?"

Jade shakes her head. "I don't know, when Danny comes back you ask him for our mobiles."

"You bloody ask him, I'm not," Rosie says.
Jade shrugs her shoulders. "I knew you would say that. I'm not going to ask him. Sod the mobiles."

"If we ever get to go out shopping or something we can buy one, " Rosie says, wondering if they will be able to.

"Bloody hell Rosie, I bet we will be closely watched. We will have to see how things go. Shall we join the girls?" Rosie follows Jade to the lounge area.

Natalia and Monika are sat drinking and chatting away in their own language when Rosie and Jade join them. Natalia looks at Rosie.

"We have been in L...o...n...d...o...n now a couple of days, where have you been?"
Rosie looks at Jade, thinking she better not tell them where they have been.

"Nowhere special. What have you been up to?"
Natalia puts her hands in the air.

"One very good party here, and lots of men with lots of money we like very much. Paul says we get very nice presents, and, you know, some very good quality cocaine."

Jade takes the bottle of wine, and pours Rosie and herself a drink. They sit talking for hours and listening to Natalia, who has lots of stories to tell.

# 9
# May Flowers

Not hearing from Rosie, her father goes to her flat but nobody answers. He is getting concerned now and is wondering where she has got to. Then he remembers May, the girl Rosie shared her flat with before she went to live with Jayne. He recalls where it was and makes his way to her flat.

May is in her flat when there is a knock at the door. She goes to answer it and as she opens the door a man is standing there.

"Are you May?" he asks.

"Yes I am May. What can I do for you?" she says.

"My name is Robert Lambert. I am Rosie's father and I have been trying to contact her. I have not had an answer from her either by text or her mobile, and there was no answer at her flat. Do you think she has gone somewhere with Jayne, her flat mate?" He is looking rather concerned.

May does not want to say too much about Danny, nor his brother.

"I spoke to her a few days ago but only for a minute. Since she moved in with Jayne I haven't seen too much of her at all. She hasn't been to uni for some time now."

"Have you any idea where she might be?"

"I don't know. As I told you, I have not seen her or Jayne at uni for a couple of days now. If I see them I will let you know. Have you a number I can contact you on?"

Robert Lambert gives May his card, and tells her, "Please telephone me if you see her or get to know where she is, I would appreciate it very much. If you see her will you tell her to please contact me immediately. I have something very important to tell my Rosie. "

May takes the card from him with his number.

"I will Mr Lambert. I am sure she is okay so I wouldn't worry too much."

He thanks her and leaves. May is mystified; she wonders where she could have gone. May feels something is not right and is determined to find out where Rosie is.


May is in the restaurant a day or two later when she sees the girls gathering around a good-looking chap. She is curious, and makes her way across to them. Some of the girls are giggling and chatting to the man. He sees May and smiles at her. May smiles back at him and he makes is way towards her.

"Hi there, my name is Paul. What's your name? Have I seen you before somewhere?"

"My name is May. Sorry, I can't remember meeting you before." Then May remembers Rosie telling her about Danny and his brother.

The girls start to thin out, seeing he is talking to May. They see he is taking a particular interest in her. May plays along with him, wanting to know what he is up to.

"How about meeting up sometime for a drink or two?" he says, flashing his lovely smile at her.

"You say a drink or two? That sounds nice, when?" May is stringing him along now, although she likes what she sees. He is so good looking and she thinks she may find out something about Rosie.

"Here is my mobile number. How about this weekend?" He hands her the piece of paper he wrote his number on, having folded it up.

"I'll be in touch," he says, smiling and leaning close to her.

As he leaves he is waving to some of the girls who seem to like getting his attention. May goes back to her seat and opens the piece of paper he gave her. Along with his number he's added a note.

"Do you like games?"

May thinks *games?* She doesn't understand, then thinks *wait a minute*, she remembers Rosie had told her Danny's brother was called Paul and he looked so very much like him. She just cannot remember everything she told her. She is now more than just interested in him and what he said.

May cannot wait for Paul to call her. She has had her hair done and has bought herself something nice just in case he calls and asks her out. Just when she is about to give up waiting the phone rings. She runs to the phone then stops herself. She just lets it ring a couple of times then slowly she picks the phone up.

"Hello."

Then she hears his voice, "Hi there, how are you May? I thought I would give you a call to see if you're free Saturday night. I would like us to get together, just you and me... what do you say?"

May is smiling to herself, "Yes, I would like that."

"Great. Shall we say around eight? I'll send a car for you, okay?"

May is thinking, why send a car for me?

"Why can't you pick me up?"

"I have a bit of a surprise for you. Just come in the car - I will send for you." Paul thinks yes, I have a surprise for her but will she fall for it?

"Okay, I'll be ready." May really cannot wait; all the time she is wondering what she will wear.

"I hope it is going to be a very intimate evening, May," Paul says in his sexiest voice.

"Who knows Paul? We will have to see." She feels her face flush.

"See you Saturday. Bye for now."

"Bye Paul."

May sits for a while. In one way she is very excited; she likes Paul and thinks he is a good looking guy with lots of sex appeal. She does not usually pull men like Paul. Then again, Rosie comes to mind and May wonders why she has been away and not contacted her father or anyone.

Danny telephones Paul on arriving back in the UK.

"Hi bro, how are things with you? Has Ramon sent any

more girls to replace Natalia and Monika yet? They are doing a good job here in London?"

"Apparently they should be arriving anytime. Three or more from Romania. He assures me they are the best he has had up to now. I am working on another young girl from the university who could be okay, just trying her out. We should soon get things going again here. I take it the girls will be staying in London now, so any problems on that?"

Danny puts Paul in the picture regarding what has happened since he went to Qatar.

"No, I think we have things in hand. I will watch over things just to see how things are. Rosie was the Amir's favourite, he told me to make sure she is always available when he visits London. Jade is okay, she just does what she is expected to do. Unfortunately that Jayne is a dead loss and we have to get rid of her. Ramon is placing her in one of the peep shows in Soho. She is out of her head and doesn't know what she is doing. She caused us problems with one of the clients in Qatar. She had to be subdued if you know what I mean. We have to be careful and cover her tracks because we don't need any problems. I know she had little or no family and she was in care before she went to uni so there will be very little interest in where she has got to."

Paul's never concerned too much about anything. He tells Danny, "Well, Ramon will see to that. One of us will have to go to Brighton soon just to see everything is going okay there."

"You get everything running in Leeds and then you can go to Brighton. I need to be here for a while."

"Okay Dan, keep in touch. Bye for now. I'll give the new girls a try out," Paul laughs and puts the phone down.

Paul has sent the car to pick up May and everything has been organised for her. May is ready as the car arrives; the driver opens the door for her and she gets in, hardly able to move in her tight dress.

May sits, waiting in anticipation. She just does not know what to expect. They arrive at their destination, the driver opens the door and May gets out of the car with much difficulty due to her dress. Her legs and are more exposed, the driver seems to be getting a good look and he smiles. May tries to close her legs so he cannot see. She thinks to herself *'Perv'*. He tells her to head to apartment 103 and just go in. He gives her a key.

She is looking round as she enters the apartment lobby thinking, *'Yes, very nice'*.

She finds apartment 103, opens the door and it is dark inside with only a very low light, with soft music playing. May walks around the apartment looking in rooms then, once back in the lounge, she finds a mini bar and pours herself a drink of wine from a bottle. She still walks around drinking her drink then she hears someone enter. She hurries back into the lounge again and sits on the sofa, waiting for Paul to come in, when someone from behind covers her eyes.
She giggles.

"Paul, what are you doing?" She giggles as she feels someone kissing the back of her neck. She puts her hands up to pull the hands from her eyes.

"Ssshhh."
A blindfold goes on to cover her eyes.

"No, Paul." Then she feels his hand exploring her body. She feels a little light headed knowing she has only had a couple of sips of wine. She wonders how she could feel like she does but she likes what he is doing.

"Paul, come on, stop and take this off me." She reaches to remove the blindfold again his hands stop her. Her breasts are being squeezed and a hand goes in between her legs. His hand touching her, she responds now and is breathing heavily as her clothes are being removed. She feels strange not being able to see Paul but she likes it more and more as he does things to her that she has never, ever experienced. She is now in just her panties as he stands her up. She is giggling as he leads her to the bed.

"What are you doing, Paul?" He lays her down, his lips kissing her all over her body. She arches her back to meet him and her hands get hold of his head, pushing him further into her thighs.

"Oh yes, yes," she says as his tongue does magical things to her. She is now far from being bothered about being blindfolded and soon he is on top of her, thrusting himself inside of her. She screams out, he is biting her neck; she caresses his now naked body, making him more aroused. She is loving every minute. The sex goes on and she has multiple orgasms. Something she has never had with the young lads she had been with.

Soon she is exhausted. He whispers to her to wait here, her body is wet through with perspiration as she lays there. She thinks she can now take off the blindfold while waiting for Paul to come back. She rubs her eyes, the room is in darkness and she feels strange and rather sleepy, and more than contented. While waiting for Paul she falls asleep.

When she awakes after an hour or so she calls his name as she is still laid on her own.

"Paul, where are you?" she giggles.

There is no answer so she gets up and looks around the apartment. No one is there, just a note near her clothes that have been folded on the sofa. She reads the note. *'Sorry, had to go. Hope you enjoyed everything. Here's a present for you - get something nice for our next meeting.'*

She looks and to her surprise she finds a few £20 notes are laid on her clothes and she picks them up. May being May she counts the money then, smiling to herself, puts the money in her bag considering what she will be able to buy. She gets dressed and then leaves the apartment thinking *'Sodding hell, he could have given me a lift home.'* She manages to hail a taxi to get her home.

She had only had a drop of wine, and yet she still feels more than a little drunk. She is thinking about Rosie when she was buying new clothes, and is trying to put things together. No, she thinks, I'm imagining things. She wonders if she will hear from Paul again and when?

The next few days pass like normal. She has managed to spend her money on a few new clothes and shoes. Then out of the blue and to her surprise she gets a call.

"May, did you enjoy your evening? Would you say it was a little different? Do you like the intrigue? I was wondering if you would like, shall we say, a little more of the same?"

May cannot get over him calling her again. She thought it was just a one-off.

"I can honestly say I did enjoy the evening and, yes, I would like to see you again, although I never saw too much of you last time." She doesn't want to question him too much on why he left her to find her own way home and she doesn't want to put him off.

"Okay May, if you would like to go out this coming Saturday I'll send a car for you around eight."

"I'll be ready," she says happily, as she has never pulled a man like Paul who she thinks has class.

"Right, May, see you Saturday. Bye."

"Bye Paul."

She smiles to herself, not believing her luck.

# 10
# Comatose

Over the past few weeks the girls have settled down in their apartment. They are all enjoying the luxury and the easy life they are experiencing. Rosie and Jade get on well with Natalia and Monika; they all are taking drugs; cocaine and, often, amphetamines. They have been in the apartment for a few days now; Danny has been to visit only once since they moved in just to check up on them. Rosie and Jade dare not ask him for their mobile phones knowing he could blow his top if they upset him.

Things have been a little quiet recently in the evenings. They usually watch television and down a couple of bottles of wine before going to bed. Natalia has become very friendly with Rosie; Rosie likes her because she can be so funny at times and nothing seems to bother her. She is talking to her, when Rosie asks, "Natalia how did you get to the UK? We hear a lot about girls being forced to come here."

Natalia laughs, "Forced? No, no we were not forced to do what we doing. Monika not either. We like the nightlife back home and we approached by a man who ask us why just do it for fun? When in the UK you can earn lots money. He introduces us to people who help us come here. So, no, not forced."

"Well you could say the same. We really were not forced, we just got into it, it just happened," Rosie says.
The girls are listening to the conversation. They agree, and Jade picks up her glass.

"To us, girls." They all repeat the mantra and then down their wine.
They are all very tipsy when they decide to go to their rooms.

Rosie takes a shower, getting her nighty on and getting into bed. She is still worried about her mother and father and that they will be very worried and wondering where she is. Being a little drunk she gets a little emotional and tears run down her cheeks.

Natalia appears at her room door. "Can I come in?" she asks.

Rosie nods her head. Natalia is a little drunk too and dances around. She smiles at Rosie as she comes over and sits on the edge of Rosie's bed.

"Why you cry? You not happy?" she asks.

Rosie wipes the tears from her face. "I'm okay. I was thinking of my family."

"I the same. I think of my family too. I send them money. I make them happy."

"You always have good answers for everything Natalia." She smiles at her.

She takes hold of Rosie's hand, "You nice Rosie I like you." She strokes Rosie's hand then brushes her hair from her face.

"You very beautiful woman."

She just looks at Natalia. "You are beautiful too."

Natalia leans forward slowly until she is very close to Rosie's face. She turns her head away from her but she takes hold of Rosie's chin, and moves her face towards hers. She kisses her on the lips. Rosie can smell her perfume and wants to pull away but lets Natalia kiss her.

She kisses Rosie's neck. Again she does not resist but lies back as Natalia moves her hand down the sheets, lifting her nightgown and starting to touch her. Rosie moans then Natalia whispers in her ear.

"You like me stay?" She is looking at Rosie, She does not speak she just nods her head. Natalia stands up and takes off her nightgown. Rosie is watching her and she sees what a beautiful body she has; large breasts and long legs. She is soon under the sheets with her and she takes off Rosie's nightgown, their naked bodies soon entwined. Natalia touches her gently and she takes Rosie's hands, placing them on her own breasts. Rosie squeezes them, making her cry out, then, not needing to be led on, she kisses Natalia's breasts, then moves her hand down between Natalia's legs. Rosie is getting more excited as they both enjoy each other's bodies. She is kissing Rosie's body, her tongue searching and exploring every part of her. Soon Rosie is doing what Natalia does to her and she is more than enjoying the experience, not wanting it to end. Rosie cannot contain herself. She is amazed just how fast they both reach their climax. They both fall asleep holding each another.

In the morning Jade comes into the bedroom. As she enters the room, she calls Rosie's name then both Rosie and Natalia lift their heads up. Jade is just stood there looking at them,

"Oh sorry I…. sorry." She turns to leave the room, smiling to herself.

Rosie looks at Natalia. "We best get up," she says, giving her a bit of a look.

"No problem, and no worry. If we like do it, no problem. She could join us maybe sometime." Natalia jumps out of bed, bursts out laughing and then Rosie starts to laugh with her.

As Natalia leaves the room laughing she turns to Rosie as she stands in the doorway.

"And maybe Monika, too." This makes her laugh even more.

She does feel a little embarrassed when she sees Jade.

"Each to their own," Jade says.

Rosie is about to make an excuse as to why Natalia was in bed with her. Jade just puts her hand up.

"Rosie, you don't have to explain yourself to me."

Rosie goes to make a coffee.

Through the day the girls are restless and desperate to get out and do some shopping. They all have money to spend getting out means less drugs and drink that have been taken, probably due to the boredom.

Just when they were giving up hope Danny pays them a visit. As he enters the room he is smiling.

"Well my beauties, I have some work for you tomorrow night. Some very important clients need your company. I think you can go out and treat yourselves. I will have a car pick you up; you can go to your favourite store. No, not Pre-Max. How about Harrods? What do you say?"

Natalia is clapping her hands in delight and the others are very happy too. Rosie runs over to Danny and kisses him on the cheek; Danny is laughing.

"Rosie, I need a quick word with you." Rosie is concerned, wondering what could be wrong.

Danny takes her to her bedroom. He sits on the bed; she joins him and sees she is concerned.

He looks at her. "I don't want you to go with them tomorrow night. You have to stay here, okay?"

"Why Danny? Why am I having to stay here, is something wrong?"

"Don't worry Rosie. You can go on the shopping trip with the others, it's just the Amir would like to, shall we say, keep you for himself. You will get substantial rewards from him I can assure you," says Danny reassuringly.

Rosie only wants Danny. She feels she is losing any chance of him getting closer to her.

"Okay Danny, if you say so."

Danny puts his arm around her, puts his free hand in his pocket and takes out her mobile phone.

"You can phone your family. You can make any excuse you like. I trust you to be careful in what you say. Okay Rosie my sweet?" He pulls her to him.

"Tomorrow I will see the girls alright, and you can get the drinks ready. I will come to visit you, what do you say?"

Hearing him say this makes her brighten up.

"Yes I would like that. And you will come, won't you?"

"I am looking forward to it." Danny wants to please her. They join the other girls. Danny tells them what is planned and, before he leaves, tells them to enjoy themselves.

Rosie is going to call her mother and father to make some excuse but decides to do it after their shopping trip. She tells the others she will not be going with them tomorrow night as Danny has something else planned for her. They ask what but she will not tell them why. She tells Jade she has her mobile, and suggests Jade and her wait until they come back before ringing anyone. A couple of hours pass, and the car comes for them. They get into the vehicle like children going to the candy store.

They do their shopping and have to have another car to carry the things they have bought. They had spent hours rooting through dresses, shoes, bags and very sexy lingerie, not knowing when to stop.

Pleased to get in their apartment they throw off their shoes and start opening their bags and boxes of clothes.

Later in the evening Rosie calls Jade to her bedroom.

"We can call our parents if we want. Danny said he would trust us and we could tell them what we want. Apart from the truth that is. I'm going to say I met a man and I am not going back to uni. I know I will get some flack from my father but at least he will know I'm okay."

Jade bites her lip as she looks at Rose.

"I don't know whether I should call them at all. I don't know what to say."

"Say the same as me. Tell them you met someone and you'll keep in touch, you can't do anything else." Rosie puts her arm round Jade.

"You'll be okay. I'm going to ring my father now."

Jade leaves Rosie to telephone her dad and is still wondering what she should say.

Rosie sits on the bed. She can see how many calls she has had from her father but only one from her mother, which was just before Rosie left for London. She never answered it but now she wishes she had. She calls her father's number. He answers the phone.

Rosie simply says, "Dad."

Her father shouts, "Rosie, Rosie where the bloody hell are you? I have been worried sick, why didn't you answer my calls? Are you okay?"

"I'm sorry dad. I wanted to telephone you and I knew you would be mad at me. I met someone and we went to Spain for a while. I know you will be very mad in what I am about to say but I am not going back to uni."

"Why are you not going back to uni? It's your future. Who is this person, where did you meet him and where are you now Rosie?"

"Dad, I'm in London. Don't worry about me please, I am going to telephone mum just to let her know I'm okay."

"You cannot call her Rosie. I have some bad news. I have tried and tried to telephone you to tell you." He pauses.

She asks, "Tell me what it is, dad?"

"It's your mother. She was found unconscious. She is in hospital in a coma. They think she may not pull through. It was said she has been taking heroin, injecting it, and it was made worse by the heavy drinking, I knew this would happen. She had been getting worse day by day so I have been told."

She is so upset that she can hardly speak. Her father, although he is very mad with her, understands how she must feel. He asks, "Are you okay my darling? I know it is a shock for you. What are you going to do, are you coming home?"

She waits and thinks, deciding what she will do or even if she is able to do anything.

"Dad, do you think she will be okay? I don't know if I can get home. Please don't be mad at me."

"I hope this guy you are with is worth it. What are you going to do?" Her father is disappointed with her.

"I will telephone you later dad if that is okay." She is crying and feels so bad not being able to see her mother.

"Look my darling I will telephone you. Make sure you answer my calls and we will discuss uni and this chap you are with later. I will let you know if anything happens here with your mother, okay?"

"I'll try to get home. Look dad I have to go but I will answer your calls, I promise you. I have to go now."

"I am obviously disappointed with you Rosie. Leaving without telling me. All I can say is please let me know in the future where you are or if you need anything, anything at all. Again, if anything happens regarding your mother I will let you know right away."

They say their goodbyes; Rosie sits on the edge of the bed crying, asking herself what has happened to her, how did she become so dependent on drugs? She tries to convince herself that what has happened to her mother won't happen to her.

Jade comes in Rosie's room and Rosie tells her what

has happened and what she had told her father. Jade is very sympathetic but is more worried about her own situation and what she will tell her parents. She leaves with the phone to call her parents from her room.

Sometime later Jade comes back into Rosie's room; she is crying. Rosie looks at her.

"What happened with you then?", she asks.

"They went bloody ballistic. They wanted to know where I am, who I have been with, and why I have left. I think they were more concerned I had left uni than who I am with or what I have been doing." Jade is still crying so Rosie consoles her.

"There is not a lot we can do. At least they know we are safe, that is if you could call it that. I am so worried about my mother and I just do not know what to do. I may ask Danny if I can go and visit her. Come on, Jade, pull yourself together. Let's join the girls and check out what they bought."

They both wipe their eyes, tidy themselves up and join the others. There are clothes everywhere. Monika is looking through the underwear she has bought.

"Look at these, they should turn them on. Very good, very sexy," Monika says, running her hands over her hips sexily.

"We put nice underwear on, and they want pull them off." She bursts out laughing, falling back on the sofa, and all the others start laughing. Jade soon forgets what has happened and is enjoying the girls company. Unfortunately Rosie cannot; she is in a quandary not knowing what to do, how she can tell Danny that she needs to go and see her mother.

The next night they are all dressed up and ready to go. They take a little cocaine, making sure to clean their noses before Danny arrives. She is feeling a little left out not going with them, but she is hoping Danny sticks to his word and comes back to see her after he has dropped the girls off.

Danny arrives and comes into the apartment, smiling, as he looks them all up and down.

"Wow! You all look great. I fancy the lot of you." Monika pulls up her short dress revealing black stocking tops.

"You like this Mr Danny?" She gives him a sexy look.

"Yes Monika, who could resist you? Hurry up girls we're

running late."

He turns to Rosie, winks at her then goes he goes to her and whispers, "See you soon."

She smiles at him and is excited now knowing he is coming back to see her. She better make herself look nice for him, more so after him seeing sexy Monika flashing her stocking tops at him.

She is on her own now and it is hard for her to get her mother out of her mind. She knows she will have to ask Danny now and hopes he will let her go home but thinks she must do her best to make him like what she has in store for him, then when he is relaxed she will ask him.

Rosie looks at the amphetamines she has, tries her best not to take any but decides to neck one to keep her going.

Danny enters the apartment. He looks at Rosie who is now in a silk see-through dressing gown.

He walks towards her and kisses her, feeling her body through the silk material; he kisses her neck.

"Get me a drink Rosie."

He lets go of her and is watching as she walks to the bar. She pours two drinks and walks back to him. He takes the drink from her and he kisses her again. They sit on the sofa. She makes sure he can see her stockings as she crosses her legs.

Danny smiles, "How old are you? 18?" he says, stroking her legs.

"Nearly 19," she says, looking at him and showing just how sexy she is and how much she wants him.

He puts his drink down and at the same time he takes her drink from her. He stands her up in front of him. She is now looking down at him as she slowly takes off the dressing gown, revealing her lovely body. She just stands there, as Danny puts his hands out and Rosie walks towards him. He feels her body, she just leans back enjoying what Danny is doing as he stands up, and takes his clothes off. She helps him and sees how aroused he is. He takes her hand and they walk to the bedroom and towards the bed. He is about to lay her on the bed then Rosie says, "No."

She pushes him down on the bed. He lays watching her as she is kissing his body then, using her tongue, going down his body. She takes hold of him and he cries out as she devours him.

Danny is enjoying everything she does. She is kissing him, and then she lays on top him, he turns her over and kisses her back, touching and caressing her. She is in ecstasy and she wants more of him. She sits on him now and she is looking down at him as she moves, taking him. Soon, she can feel him inside of her. She moves, knowing how to bring his sexual feelings to their peak. Rosie calls his name, "Danny, oh please, Danny, yes."

Danny, unable to take anymore, rolls over on top of her. He takes hold of her head with both hands, moves towards her, kisses her on the lips as he pushes more and more. She is moving with him, and she cries out again as she climaxes at the same time as Danny. He falls on top of her, exhausted. They both lay there for a while then Danny sits on the side of the bed not saying too much.

He looks at her, smiles, and asks, "You okay?"

"Yes, of course. Why shouldn't I be after that?"

He stands up and says, "Rosie, I have to go now. I would like to stay but I can't."

She wants to ask him if she can go to see her mother.

"Danny could I ask you something?"

He is putting his clothes on, "Yes sure, what would you want to ask?"

"I phoned my father and told him I was with someone in London, and I would not be going back to uni. He wasn't pleased but then he told me my mother is in hospital in a coma. I need to go and see her. Please Danny, can I? You can trust me."

She does not want to tell him how her mother came to be in a coma. Instead, she waits; Danny turns, and looks straight at her. She is thinking he will blow his top any minute and then he replies in a very calm voice.

"Yes okay, you can go. You keep in touch with me and I want you back here in three days otherwise I will come looking for you, okay?"

"Yes Danny, three days. I will be back, thank you, three days is no problem."

Danny is dressed now and walks to the door. "I will organise everything, where are you going to?"

"I'll have to go to my fathers place in Chesterfield, just

south of Sheffield."

"I'll organise everything for you tomorrow. I'll phone you later but don't let me down."

As he is leaving Rose calls to him, "Thanks Danny."

He turns and smiles.

She cannot believe Danny is letting her go. She cannot wait to call her father but decides to wait until Danny telephones her tomorrow. She goes to bed thinking about Danny; she adores him and thinks, why can't it be like that all the time with him?

She wakes up in the morning to the noise of the girls laughing. Jade comes to her room.

"Hi there sleepy head, what a night we've had. Talk about filthy rich, these people were filthy and filthy rich bastards, all of them. Their wives they were worse than the men. I'm going to bed."

Rosie calls, "Wait Jade, I'm going home today to see mum. Danny is letting me go and is telephoning me this morning when he has organised it."

"Bloody hell Rosie, how did you fix that? Or can I guess?" Jade says, pulling a face.

"I will be in touch with you Jade. I'll keep the phone."

"How long will you be Rosie?" Jade asks.

"Only three days. I promised Danny I will come back. I'll see you before I go if you're still in bed."

Jade goes to her bed. The other two are already in their beds asleep.

It's not long before Danny telephones Rosie, and tells her the car will pick her up within the hour and take her to Chesterfield. She tells Jade and the girls and gets herself ready. Remembering she must telephone her father she gets the phone and calls him.

"Hello."

Rosie immediately tells him, "Hi dad, I'm coming home. Can I come to your place?"

"Yes darling of course you can."

She is pleased she can stay with her father.

"It is okay with Mandy, isn't it dad?"

"Mandy has nothing to do with it anyway. She will not mind you coming. You get home as soon as you can - your mother is still the same."

She tells her father, "Dad I am so sorry I did not telephone you. Anyway, it will be nice to see you."

"Okay. When do you expect to get here Rosie? Are you coming on train?"

"No dad, by car. Someone will drive me. I will let you know for certain but I should be about three hours or so. I have to go now dad so see you soon."

She puts down the phone and gets the things that she will need. She makes certain her money is safe in her bag, the car arrives, and they are on their way.

All the way home in the car she is thinking of her mother, feeling so guilty for not telephoning her. Close to home Rosie calls her father to give him a more precise time of her arrival.

It seems a long time traveling. As they arrive in Chesterfield she tells the driver where to go. When they arrive at her father's place she gets out and takes her case. She knocks on the door and her father answers.

"Come in my darling." He holds her and gives her a kiss then takes her bag from her and carries it in at the same time calling, "Mandy, she's here." Mandy comes to her and gives her a hug.

While Rosie is settling in her room Mandy is chatting to her about her mother and the circumstances; how and where she was found, and how her father had been there and seen to everything even though he had really broke off all relations with his wife.

Rosie tells Mandy, "Mum went downhill when you got with dad. I'm not blaming you, mum was already drinking before she found out about you and dad."

Just as she finishes talking her dad pops his head round the door.

"Come on you two I have fixed a bit of a meal."
They all go to the lounge and sit down to eat. Rosie knows what is coming when her father talks.

"Tell me about this chap you are with and why can't you still carry on at uni and still see him?"

Rosie is wondering what to tell him. "He works in London. I am sorry dad but I don't want to carry on at uni. I know it is difficult for you to accept it but that is how I feel."

Her father raises his voice a little. "How are you going to live then, is the chap rich? Are you going to try to find work? What kind of work could you do? A bloody shop assistant?"

Mandy takes her father's hand and calmly tells him, "Robert, can you discuss this later and let Rosie have her meal? It won't do anyone any good just shouting and arguing about it." He is quiet now and starts eating. She looks across at him, hoping he will let it drop for the rest of the evening. Rosie asks quietly, "When can I go to see mum?"

He has calmed down now and tells her, "We can go after our meal or if you want you can wait until morning."

"I would like to go after we have eaten, if that's okay with you dad?"

They eat their meal with nobody having too much to say. When they finish Mandy clears the table while Rosie and her Dad get ready to go to the hospital. They leave the house. Her father is driving.

"Rosie, you will not like what you see. I want you to be brave okay?"

Rosie feels as though she is about to cry then tries her best not to.

"I'll be okay dad."

When they arrive at the hospital her father leads the way to the room where her mother is. Outside the door Rosie is hesitant to go in at first then enters the room. Her father stands near the door as she goes to her mother's bedside. There are machines at work all around her. Rosie takes her mother's hand and looks at her. She has no colour at all in her face and her eyes are dark. Rosie knew her mother had lost weight recently but she looks so thin now. A tear runs down her cheek.

"Mum I'm here, I'm here."

Everything is quiet as she stands looking at her mother. A nurse comes into the room, checks some of the equipment, and, as she is leaving the room, Rosie asks, "Is there any change at all?" Her father just looks at the nurse waiting for her to say something.

"The doctor will speak to you before you leave." She

leaves the room.

Rosie and her father sit close by her mother. Her father looks at her, and gives her a faint smile.

He says, "Things could have been so different. Remember Rosie she was not always like she has been in these last few years. When you were a baby she was a wonderful mother and wife." He looks at his wife with all the misgivings he has about her, and has a tear in his eye. They sit for some time before the nurse comes back into room.

"Mr Lambert, could you please come with me? The consultant wants a word."

"What about my daughter? Can she come?" Mr Lambert looks to the nurse.

"Yes, of course."

They follow the nurse to a room close by.

"Please wait here," she says.

They sit down and it's not long before the consultant comes in.

"Mr Lambert."

He shakes his hand then explains the situation to Rosie and her father.

"I have to tell you that we have come to a conclusion. I'm very sorry to say this but we do not think Mrs Lambert will ever recover or come out of the coma and if she did we could never say what she would be like. Yes, we can leave her, and hope she does, but in the end it will be up to you to say if we can or cannot remove all the equipment that is keeping her alive. I think we should let her go."

Rosie is crying and holding on to her father. He looks at the consultant.

"Is there any way, any chance she could pull through if we leave her?"

The surgeon runs his hand through his hair. He looks at Mrs Lambert then at Rosie.

"We can never be certain in cases like this that she will not come out of the coma but if she did she would have lots of other problems too, damage to her internal organs. In our experience it is unlikely she will come out of the coma. Look, I will leave you both for a while to think about it. You can go back to your wife's room and I'll come and see you again in half an hour."

He leaves the room, and then Rosie and her father go back to Rosie's mother's room. Rosie is still clinging to her father and crying.

"Rosie darling sit down." She sits near her mother again and takes her hand. He walks across to his wife, stands close to her looking at her and Rosie is watching him. He talks to his wife as though she can hear him.

"I don't want you to suffer. Shall we let you go?"

He looks at Rosie. He is crying when he says to her, as he holds his wife's other hand, "I think we should let her go Rosie."

She walks round the bed to him and holds him again.

He asks, "What do you think darling, do we?"

She nods her head then she puts her arms around him. Her father holds her tight, kissing her head. The consultant comes in with the nurse. He just stands quietly then asks, "Have you come to a decision Mr Lambert?"

He tells him, still holding on to Rosie, "We will take your advice. Yes, we agree." There is a long pause before he says, "We will let her go."

The nurse gives Mr Lambert some papers to sign. The consultant tells him they cannot do anything until he has signed the papers. Mr Lambert signs all the papers and gives them to the nurse.

The consultant whispers to the two nurses now in the room. They walk close to Mrs Lambert's bed and stand waiting for the consultant to tell them to carry on with the procedure. Rosie goes to her mother's side and her father is close by. The consultant gives the nurse the nod, she turns off the ventilator and the other nurse starts removing the other equipment. Soon all the things that were connected to Mrs Lambert have been removed.

Rosie is looking at her mother and thinking to herself that she looks peaceful now, just laid there. There has been no movement from her mother at all and she looks as though she is now in a peaceful sleep.

The consultant walks to her and feels for a pulse then looks at Mr Lambert and says, "She's gone."

The surgeon and nurses leave the room, leaving both Rosie and her father to spend a few last moments with her. Rosie just tries to think of the good times she spent with her mother. She remembers coming out of school as a child, seeing her mother stood there smiling and waiting for her, how she would run to her mother, and how she would pick Rosie up and kiss her. They say their final goodbyes.

They leave after some time, both not saying too much while they are on their way home. Rosie is thinking that she must try to stop taking the drugs. She does not want to finish up like her mother. Unfortunately, she knows it will be difficult and how does she ever hope to get out of the situation she is in? She knows both Danny and Paul will soon be looking for her if she does not go back.

When they arrive home her father looks at Mandy, shaking his head. Mandy guesses something sad has happened, and just by looking at Rosie she knows what that is. She goes to Rosie and holds her, trying to console her.

A little later Rosie makes her way to her room. She lies on the bed, again thinking of the good times as a child she had with her mother. After a long time she falls asleep.

The next day Mr Lambert has to organise his wife's funeral arrangements. Rosie just wanders around the house. For all she had told herself the night before she succumbed and took some cocaine while in her room, saying again to herself that this is the last. Yet another voice is telling her, *'No, it's not'*.

Later in the day she goes to her room and telephones Danny.

"Hi Rosie, you coming back already?"

Danny is waiting for some time for her to answer.

"Danny, my mother has passed away... I have to stay for the funeral." She is waiting for a bad response.

Then Danny answers quite calmly, knowing that she is upset.

"Okay Rosie I understand. How long before the funeral do you think?"

"I don't know yet, my dad is organising it. I'll let you know when he tells me."

Danny is sensing something is wrong in her voice.

"You are coming back aren't you Rosie? Are you okay for the stuff?" He thinks he better keep her going on them.

"Yes Danny, I'm okay for now."

"If you get short I'll organise things with Paul. Sorry about your mother. As I said, keep in touch."

"Okay I have to go now Danny. I will phone you soon." She wants to get off the phone.

"Keep in touch do you hear?"

"Yes, bye Danny."

She turns her phone off.

# 11
# A Warning

Danny sits for a while thinking that she better come back. He is about to telephone Paul to tell him to keep an eye on her when he gets a call from his brother.

"Dan, the new girls have arrived. Three Romanians as Ramon said and they are very nice. One speaks a little English but the others can just get by. They are settled in now and know what is expected of them. 1 will be putting them to work very soon. Nick in Brighton tells me his new girls are doing fine and that it seems that our operation is going nicely. If and when I have time I'll go to see Nick and check the books. How are things with you? "

"Good bro, but Rosie will be delayed because her mother has died. I must admit I am worried. You may have to pay her a visit in Chesterfield if she is there too long. We need her back here just in case the Amir turns up as he will expect her to be available. I'll keep you informed if I need you."

"I'm still working on a new girl from the university. She is not what you would call a beauty and as nice as Rosie or Jade, not so slim a body, but you know some guys, especially the Arabs, like a bit of flesh sometimes. I will give a her a couple of more testers and see how she goes."

"Okay Paul, I'll leave things in your hands. As I said, I will give you a call if Rosie gives us any problems. See you."

Danny is happy with all the new girls coming, and he knows he needs people he can trust in the other operations. It will be more difficult for Paul and himself to keep an eye on everything all the time so they may have to get someone they can trust.

Rosie needs to get out. It has been some times now since she had been out on her own anywhere. She tells her father she is going out for a walk around the town. Mandy agrees to drop her off in the town. While they are in the car Mandy tries to find out about the man, and where she has been.

Rosie tells her, "Mandy, I really do not want to talk about that at the moment."

Mandy apologises. With there not being a lot of difference in their ages Mandy seems to understand why Rosie would want to keep it to herself. She drops her off in the town and for the first time in a while Rosie feels free. No one is watching over her, no one telling her what to do, it is like it was for her before she got involved with Danny. Although she would like her life to be as it was she knows it is now impossible because she needs the money and more than anything she needs the cocaine and amphetamines. Twice since she had said to herself she would not take any more drugs but she has had to admit defeat. They pull her out of the deep depression she falls into without them. It's become a problem.

She has enjoyed walking around the town for a short time as it has taken her mind off her mother. It is still hard for her to think she has gone. After shopping she decides she must go to her flat in Leeds. She still has a few things there and so does Jayne. She does not know where Jayne is or if she is safe; she does not know what to do about giving notice to the landlord and maybe she will wait until she has spoken to Danny. She takes a taxi to the flat. It is a distance but she needs to go.

She gets to the flat and once inside she collects the clothes. There are bits and pieces everywhere and it looks a bit untidy. Both the girl's things are left all over. She can see the drawers where their passports were left open as though someone had come in, got them and left in a hurry. She goes through a few things, taking what she thinks she needs and leaves the other things. She telephones for a taxi to take her home to her father's and while she is waiting she thinks of May. She knows she should not have been so abrupt with her the last time they met. She was a good friend, and maybe she will call her later just to let her know she has been away. The taxi arrives and she leaves for her father's house.

He is waiting for her. "Rosie, where have you been? We have arranged the funeral for Friday. The funeral directors tell me everything will be ready for then. Do you want to go and see mum?"

She knows she does not want to see her. She saw her at the hospital and it is different now.

"I don't want to go and see her dad. It is so hard for me, I hope you understand."

Her father goes to her and holds her.

"I understand. Of course I understand."


The first chance she gets she telephones Danny. He answers the phone.

"Hi Danny. I will be able to come back to London on Sunday. The funeral is on Friday, is that okay?"

Danny is pleased. He thought he would have some trouble getting her back.

"Rosie, that's no problem. Look, Paul will arrange a car for you if you give me your address again." Rosie gives him the address and then he tells her, "If you need anything at all, money or the other things, you call Paul, okay?"

"Yes thanks Danny. Danny I have been to the flat and collected some of my things. I see Jayne's things are still there. If we are not going back there maybe we should inform the landlord?"

Danny is quiet for a while. "Do you know the name of the landlord, his address and all that? Tell me and I will tell Paul to go to the flat and see to the clothes and that other things are removed before informing the landlord and paying anything owed."

She gives him all the information he needs before ending their call.


Rosie is a little hesitant about telephoning May but thinks *'I just have to telephone her'*. She rings her number hoping she is in. May's pleasant voice comes on the phone. "Hello, who is that please?"

"It's me. I thought I would give you a ring."

May is so pleased to hear from her.

"Bloody hell Rosie, where have you been? Your dad has been looking for you. I was worried sick wondering where you were. I'm so pleased you telephoned me, Rosie, are you okay?"

"Yes I'm fine...mum...has passed away... I'm staying at my father's house at the moment, the funeral is on Friday afternoon."

"Oh Rosie I'm so, so sorry." May wants to ask her what caused her mother's death but decides not to ask. "Can we get together for a chat?"

"Yes I would love to. We can meet tomorrow afternoon if you like?" Rosie is looking forward to seeing her friend again.

"Where shall we meet? Do you want to come to my flat and we can have a good old natter?"

"Yes, it's a long way but I'll come. I'll see you tomorrow at noon."

They end their conversation both happy that they have spoken to each other.


It is Thursday and Rosie takes a taxi to May's flat. She cannot wait to see her; she knocks on the door and then opens it.

"May? It's me, Rosie."

May comes running out of the bedroom.

"Come in Rosie, come in." She runs straight to her, hugging her and, after holding on to her for some time, she moves Rosie away from her, looking her up and down.

"Wow! Rosie, you look a million dollars. I can't believe how you have changed in such a short time. You look as though you have just won the bloody lottery."

Again May looks her up and down then turns her round.

"You could pull any man the way you look. I feel a bit of a slag compared to you."

"You're lovely May, don't put yourself down."

They both sit down then May asks, "Come on, where have you

been? Obviously you haven't been walking the streets?"

They both laugh. Rosie does not want to tell her the full story.

"You remember Danny? I have been with him in London."

"You lucky shit Rosie, with that good looking guy and with all that money as well. You have definitely fallen on your feet. Well, I have something to tell you." May wriggles her bottom in her seat.

"You are not going to believe this I have been on a date with, wait for it....Paul, Danny's brother. And I'm going out with him again on Saturday night. What a date I had with him, wow."

She does not know what to say. May sees she does not look too pleased at what she has told her.

"I thought you would be pleased for me pulling a good looking guy like Paul?"

"May, I can't say too much but please listen to me. Stay away from him." She takes May's hand and pleads with her.

"Why? Bloody hell Rosie, you're with his brother and look at you. Why, why should I not see him? You have to tell me."

Rosie knows she cannot tell her the truth. She shakes her head.

"May, trust me. If you go on seeing him you will regret it."

May sits for a while quietly then tells her, "I need to know why Rosie, otherwise I will just have to see him again. Look at me Rosie I am not like you. It's my chance to be with someone with a bit of class and, might I add, a lot of money."

She is afraid she says too much. "Well May just don't say I didn't warn you."

May, not wanting to fall out with her, tells her, "If it makes you happy I'll be careful of whatever it is I'm suppose to be careful of." She laughs now, trying to get off the subject.

"Rosie, where is Jayne? Did she go with you? Have you seen her?"

She feels she is getting in too deep with May's questions.

"Yes, she came to London and later left. She said she was, like me, not going back to uni. She said she was going to see some friend, some bloke she knew."

"So you are not going back to uni then? I bet your father was pleased?" May says.

"You could say he wasn't very happy but at the end of the day it's my decision. With mum gone now I'm definitely going to go back to London."

May takes hold of Rosie's hand and looks straight at her.

"Are you sure you're doing the right thing Rosie? Are you happy?"

"Yes, I'm happy. Come on now; tell me all the news from uni? How is quick Kjell doing - getting slower I hope?" They both start laughing.

They spend a couple of hours together, May being her happy self trying to cheer Rosie up and taking her mind off her mother. They enjoy their time together; it's a bit like old times. They part, telling one another they will keep in touch.


The funeral takes place the next day. There are only a few close relatives at the funeral and after the service at the crematorium the few people who are there go to a nearby pub for a few drinks and something to eat. Rosie and her father go around the people thanking them for coming to the funeral. They both want to get away as soon as they can. Mandy did not attend the funeral; her father said it would not be right and Mandy agreed. Soon they are able to leave for home. At home Rosie is sat quietly and her father comes and puts his arm around her. He can see she is still upset.

"Rosie, please stay. Please, go back to the university. This chap can't mean that much to you."

She is wiping her eyes. She looks up at him.

"Dad I have definitely made up my mind."

Her father, knowing now he cannot change her mind, tells her, "You must keep in touch. Let me know if you are okay or if you need anything. You will won't you?"

"Thanks dad I'll call you regularly, I promise." She kisses him on his cheek.

During the evening Rosie telephones May but gets no answer. She thinks about what May had said about seeing Paul and, if she is seeing him, she guesses what could be happening to her. She prays she is not going to be as gullible as she has been.

May is dressed ready and waiting for the car to arrive. The car comes for her and she gets in, wondering where she is going. To her surprise the car pulls up at a very large house. The driver opens the car door for her. She gets out and the driver points to the front door.

"Just ring the bell madam. You are expected."
May is laughing to herself because the driver called her madam. She rings the bell and a young man opens the door, smiling at her.

"Please come in." He never asked her name or who she was, which seems strange.
He takes May's coat. She can hear music and laughter coming from one of the rooms close by.

"Come, follow me." She does as he asks and as she enters the room there are a few men and a couple of youngish girls. The men are all well dressed. May looks around then she sees Paul coming to her, holding out his hand. May feels a bit embarrassed as he calls out to everybody.

"This is May everyone." They all smile at her as Paul gives her a drink.

"Champagne. You do like it I hope?"
May smiles at him. "Love it. I drink it all the time," she giggles.

"Don't be afraid. Just mix, enjoy yourself, we have all night in front of us," Paul tells her.
She watches Paul go over to one of the men and they both look at May. Paul's sees she is watching him so he lifts his glass up to her and gives her a smile. May is feeling a little more comfortable as the man who was talking to Paul walks across to her. He has a bottle of Champagne in his hand and he tops her glass up.

"Come on, drink up," he says.
May takes a couple more sips from her glass.

"My name is Roger. You're the lovely May, correct?"

"That's right, May." She looks at him thinking he isn't bad.
Others are dancing as Roger asks May. "Shall we?" He takes hold of her while she still has her drink in her hand. He swings her around, May is laughing.

"I'll spill my drink."

"Who cares? Drink up my beauty, enjoy." He holds her even closer and then he is kissing her neck. She looks across at Paul who is just smiling. He winks at her.

As the evening progresses May has consumed a lot of champagne. Roger is stuck to her like glue and May has hardly seen Paul. The other girls had said hello to her but were more interested in the men. Roger had taken her round the men who were all very nice to her. She feels so relaxed now. In fact more relaxed than she has ever felt before, she feels so light headed.

Roger is getting a little more intimate with her and he is kissing her neck and his hands are wandering but May doesn't stop him. One of the girls is dancing on her own rather sexily, and the men are all watching her. Roger pulls her onto the sofa. The girl is going around the men slowly letting them take off an item of clothing. May is mesmerised by what is happening, but feels unable to focus her eyes now. Her whole body seems to be tingling and Roger's hands are now everywhere but May just giggles. She likes it.

The young girl is now naked as two of the men carry her out of the room. Others are starting to undress; Roger takes May to another room. May can do nothing; she just lets him do what he wants. He lays her down on the bed and removes her clothes. She can see others in the room. Roger is now undressed himself and he lays on top of her. She can feel him penetrate her, she moves with him at the same time and she is watching a couple of the men who have come into the room. They are close by and looking at them and they are sometimes touching her. She just moans with pleasure at every touch. Roger is soon finished and she sees and feels another man lay on her. She is so aroused she does not care and lets him do things to her and she doesn't try to resist. She is made to do things to him and again does not resist. She has no sense of time; she feels her body is now being abused but never has she felt like she does now.

During the early hours May wakes up. She has no clothes on and Roger is asleep alongside her. She feels a little sickly and tries to get out of the bed but her legs are unsteady as she heads for the bathroom. When she comes out of the bathroom she is still unsteady and after putting on her underwear she climbs back on the bed, covers herself with the sheet then lays down again. Roger snores and moves, turning over and then putting his arm around May. She doesn't push him off and she is soon asleep again.

A loud voice is calling her name. May jumps up and, opening her eyes, sees Paul looking down at her.

He says, "You definitely had a good night girl. It's twelve o'clock. I have just woke up myself."

He has a glass of water in his hand. May watches him take some sort of pill from a small box. He looks at her.

"Here, take a couple of these. They will make you feel better." May takes the pills and the water and she starts to get up, pulling the sheet to cover her. Roger just moans and turns over again.

"Come on May, get yourself tidied up and I'll take you home."

May feels a little embarrassed. She smiles at him and makes her way to the bathroom.

Paul goes to the other room. There are a few empty bottles laid around and a few underclothes scattered across the floor. May comes into the room dressed.

"Good, you're ready. Let's go then."

May just follows him and gets into his car with him; he looks at May who now feels more relaxed and confident.

"I remember some of what happened last night. Did I make a fool of myself Paul?" she says rather sheepishly.

"No, don't worry about it. Who knows, we might go to another party like that very soon. That is if you want to?" He laughs.

They arrive at May's flat. She says bye to Paul and he puts his hand on her leg, stopping her from getting out of the car.

"Wait," he says.

May sits back. Paul takes some money from his wallet and he hands it to her. May takes the money from him asking, "What's this for?"

"Don't you want it?" he asks, looking quite serious.

May has never had so much money and really wants to keep it.

"Of course, if you insist," she says, smiling at the same time as putting the money in her bag.

"Do you fancy doing it again then sometime? It's okay if you don't want to." He knows she will say yes because he sees she likes the money.

"Will you be with me?" May asks.

He kisses her on her cheek smiling. "Yes, I'll be with you. I'll ring you then, okay?"

May gets out of the car clutching her bag.

"Phone me Paul. You will, won't you?"

"Yes, soon. Bye for now." He drives off with May watching him.

Again she feels a bit unsteady on her feet and cannot wait to get to her flat. She just goes to her bed and lays down. She is soon asleep.


The day after the funeral Rosie telephones Paul to find out what time the car will be coming for her. His phone is ringing for what seems like a long time, then he answers, "Yeah, who's there?"

"Paul, it's me Rosie. What time will the car be coming tomorrow?" Again she waits for him to speak.

"It will be there for you around ten o'clock in the morning. Had a late night last night and just woke up. What's the bloody time?"

"Three o'clock."

"Sodding hell, three o'clock. Look, you be ready in the morning okay? My head is banging, bye." Rosie hears him coughing and cursing before the line goes dead. She is thinking to herself that he must have a bad headache.

Rosie is still taking a little cocaine when she can, taking great care to ensure that neither Mandy or her father catches her.

She telephones May a couple of times but gets no answer so she gives up.

The car arrives to pick her up and her father tells her again that she must keep in touch; she convinces him she will take care and will let him know if she needs him. He stands in the street waving as she is driven away. No sooner are they clear of the street than she opens her bag and takes some pills out of her bag and swallows them. She lies back with her eyes closed thinking about what is in store for her when she arrives back in London.

They arrive at the apartment. She is looking forward to seeing the girls and as she enters the apartment Jade comes running to her, followed by the other two, each giving her a hug and telling her how much they have missed her. Jade helps her unpack and tells her what they have been doing for the last few days.

"Rosie, it's been hectic since you left. I'm exhausted. The couple of places we have been to were absolutely fantastic, never seen anything like them. How some of these people live, and wow are they into the partying and the sex thing. You would think it was just the men but the women, who look like butter would not melt in their mouths, are sometimes worse. I hope everything went well at the funeral. We were thinking of you."

Rosie sees just how relaxed Jade is now at what they are doing and then asks her, "Have you seen Danny?"

"Have we seen Danny? He has been at the parties with us, although he does disappear now and again with some of the female clients, if you can call them that. I think he may be dropping in to see you. You know you are one of his favourites," she says, laughing.

Rosie does not like to hear about Danny going with other women but she is not that stupid to think he will ever ride off into the sunset with her.

The other girls come into her room. Natalia sits next to her.

"You okay now? I miss my little Rosie." She kisses her on the cheek.

"We have very good time, plenty money, very generous people we soon be very rich," Natalia laughs.

"You know why she miss you Rosie." Monika, who is always very quiet, is laughing,

Natalia playfully slaps Monika on her head; this makes them all start laughing.

It is very quiet over the next couple of days. They have their own little parties with wine and the occasional drug taking. Danny has not been in touch with them. Rosie seems to be a little more affected by the drugs and drink than ever before. She has been going over the top a bit. Natalia had approached her, trying to get into her bed but she would not let her. She hasn't been taking too much care of herself and is not looking her best.

Then Danny telephones the girls. He tells Jade they have to be ready but tells her to tell Rosie she will not be going and he will come round with the driver.

As soon as she knows this she makes an attempt to tidy herself up before he comes in the evening. She is looking rather pale and has the shakes, which she cannot seem to stop. Danny arrives and enters the apartment.

"Where is my Rosie?" he asks the girls. As he says that she comes out of her bedroom dressed very nicely. But the smile on Danny's face changes. He tells the girls to go to the car and tell the driver to take them to their destination and to come back right away for him. He says he will see them later.

When they have left and he is alone with her he walks across to her looking very mad. He takes her shoulder and drags her across to a mirror.

"Look, take a good look at yourself. I have fucking warned you about being heavy on the bloody drugs. You either ease up or you will be in a lot of trouble. When the driver gets back you're coming with me."

"I'm sorry Danny. It's been difficult." She starts to cry.

"Difficult? I let you go to your mother's bloody funeral and this is what happens? I'm bloody mad, very mad."

Danny is walking up and down. Occasionally he stops and looks at her.

"The Amir is coming any day now. Do you think he wants some bastard druggy?"

He goes on ranting until the driver knocks on the door.

Danny shouts at Rosie to get her coat on; as soon as she is ready he drags her to the car and shoves her into the back seat before getting in himself. He tells the driver to take them to somewhere in Soho. Rosie is frightened as she as no idea where they are going.

Danny does not say anything and when the car stops she can see what looks like a number of strip clubs and a lot of men going and coming from them. He drags her out of the car then takes her into this dingy building along a dark alleyway. He opens the door and there is a man sat on a seat looking at a girl through a small window. The girl is sat naked on a stool doing things to herself. The man turns. He is sitting with his trousers undone and he tries to cover himself up when he sees them. Danny grabs hold of him and throws him out of the cubical then he says to her.

"Take a look around. Do you want to finish up like her? Take a good look?"

Then to her horror she sees it is Jayne. "Oh no, not Jayne."

She starts to cry, and stands looking at her. Jayne does not recognise her, she just carries on 'performing'. There are numerous booths with small windows in them, which the men are peering through watching Jayne.

Danny grabs Rosie again, pulls her out of the booth and then takes her back to the car, to her relief. She was thinking he was going to leave her; he pushes her in the car and tells the driver to take them back to the apartment.

They are now back in the apartment and Danny pushes her onto the sofa and puts his face only inches away from her face.

"I only warn you once. You get your act together now or you will finish there with your friend, okay? Do you hear me, okay?"

She is really shaking now, more to do with fear than the drugs she has consumed.

"I'm sorry, really sorry, Danny. I will ease up on the drugs I promise."

Danny looks to be calming down now. "Get me a drink then come sit with me."

She is relaxing more now. This is what she has always wanted. She closes her eyes as he kisses her on the lips. As he touches her she can feel warmth in her whole body. She wants to touch him, she is on her knees and she is about to give herself to him as he suddenly pushes her away and stands up. He looks down at her, walks to the door and pauses a moment.

He looks at her again, turns and tells her. "You remember, no more chances." Then he leaves the apartment. She is still on her knees and she puts her face on the sofa. She is now crying uncontrollably.

After some time she stands up and walks to the mirror. She stands looking at herself, her mascara has run down her face, her eyes are dark underneath, her face is pale and she is so depressed. She goes to her room, she takes the pills from her bag and the cocaine she has, she lays everything on the bed, she pours herself some wine, filling the glass to the rim then drinks it all. She is looking at the drugs, she is thinking of her mother; she says to herself how much she is like her.

She wants to take all the tablets thinking this is the only way out of the mess she has got herself in. She picks them up, trying to force herself to take them, and lifts them up to her mouth then suddenly realises she cannot do it. She throws them across the room before falling back on the bed and crying herself to sleep.

The girls come back in the early hours. Jade comes to Rosie's room and sees her laid on top of the bed. She sees the tablets all over the floor and is really worried

"Rosie, Rosie, please wake up. Wake up." She just opens her eyes slowly looking at Jade.

"What, what's up?"

Jade is relieved that Rosie seems to be okay.

"What's happening? Why is all this lot all over the floor?"

She points to the pills scattered around.

Rosie does not want to tell Jade about seeing Jayne. "I had too much wine after Danny went."

Jade looks interested in what happened with Danny.

"How long did he stay? Come on, tell me?"

"Not long. Don't look like that. No, we never did anything because he was mad at me, very mad. I have been taking too much…" She sits on the side of the bed holding her head in her hands, crying.

Jade shakes her head.

"Yes I know what you are trying to say. I did not want to say anything to you but you have been taking more than usual. Rosie you have to be careful, we all have to be careful or we could be in real trouble."

Rosie says to herself, *'If she only knew what can happen.'*

"Come on, get yourself in bed and we'll talk about this later."

Jade helps her undress and get into bed.

"Get a good night's sleep Rosie."

Jade goes to her own room.

# 12
# A Gift From The Amir

Everyone is moving by lunchtime and Natalia, as usual, is the liveliest.

"Anyone eat breakfast? Good English bangers."

"God I feel sick, not for me." Jade puts her hand to her mouth,
Natalia is laughing when Rosie comes into the room. She looks at her and then at Jade and Monika.

"Rosie what happened? You no look good, you have problem, we help you, you know that don't you?"
She feels so bad she can barely look at them she is so embarrassed.

"I will start from now to get myself straightened up. I am determined."

"First you take plenty coffee, then you shower and freshen up. Maybe we go shop later, what you say?" Natalia smiles at Rosie.

"Yes, I'll do that." The girls make a fuss over her. They all do what girls do; chat, bathe, do their hair and make up before taking a walk to do a little shopping, which Danny allows them to do now.


Danny does not show himself for quite some time. When he does decide to give them a visit he enters the apartment and looks around, looking for Rosie. She comes out of her room; he sees her, and then smiles.

"Well, well, I cannot believe it. You look great - have you had a wonder drug or something? Come here?" He motions for Rose to go to him.

Rosie walks over to him and he takes hold of her and turns her round.

"Very nice." The other girls are laughing, they are happy and he is now okay with her.

After he has playfully slapped Rosie's bottom he turns to the girls.

"Right my lovelies, I have a few very, very important clients who need some female company tomorrow night. You all have to be your best so are you ready for it?" He looks at them all again, smiling.

Natalia is the first to speak, "Very important and very rich I hope? Yes we ready, right girls?"

They all nod their heads.

"You, Rosie, have to see a certain very rich fellow. Come, we will talk about it."

He walks to her bedroom, with her following him.

"Rosie, the Amir will be arriving tomorrow. He wants you to be at his apartment tomorrow night. I know you have seen the error of your ways, and there will be no repeat of what happened. I don't want to see you like that again. The Amir's chauffeur will pick you up around eight thirty. Look your very best because he tells me he is looking forward to seeing you again."

"I'll be ready Danny." She just gives him a slight smile.

They go to join the others. Danny looks like a changed man to the Danny that Rosie had seen a couple of days ago. He is joking and playing and flirting with all of them.

He pulls Rosie on to his knee and gives her a big kiss.

"You are going to be very rich if you play your cards right. The Amir can, as you know, be a very generous person, so make hay while the sun shines darling. The same goes for you bunch of beauties. You give them a good time and they will pay generously for it. Right, up you get my sweetie, I'm off."

She stands up. He gives them one last pep talk before leaving.

Jade looks at Rosie. "You are a lucky son of a bitch Rosie. The Amir requests you join him, you must be good Rosie girl."

Jade grabs hold of her and dances around laughing then

the others join in.

Things quieten down and Rosie is in her room. After having a few words with her father she decides to call May. May answers.

"Hi Rosie. I have telephoned you a couple of times but could not get you."

Rosie tells her she had phoned May after the funeral but she got no answer either. She asks May what happened with Paul on the so-called date. She does not want to tell Rosie what really happened at the party so she makes something up, telling Rosie she went to dinner with Paul.

"It was a nice quiet night really." May feels rather guilty telling her lies.

Rosie does not believe her, as she knows what probably happened.

"So you did not go to a party or anything?"

"No it was just the two of us."

"Are you seeing him again, then?" she asks, trying to get something out of her.

"It's been a few days. No, I haven't seen him but I'm sure he will call," May says with a bit of uncertainty in her voice.

Rosie knows now she is not telling her what really happened.

"Look May, I know how Danny and Paul operate. Tell me the truth, what happened?"

May feels very awkward now.

"What's the point of lying? Yes, there was a party and yes, there was a bit of sex, and yes, he gave me some money. There, I have told you everything."

"Sex with Paul?" she asks.

"No....with someone else. I had too much to drink and it happened. I can't remember that much to be honest. Anyway, he hasn't been in touch since so you don't have to worry Rosie."

"I do worry May because I know their game." Jade comes into the room so Rosie decides to end the call. "Okay, look I'll telephone you later. Bye for now."

May wonders why she stopped the conversation, and sits wondering what is going on with Rosie? She is in London with this rich, good-looking guy and she is warning her not to get too involved with Paul and his brother. She cannot understand.

Rosie is ready and waiting for the Amir's chauffeur to pick her up. She looks so beautiful and she sits looking at herself in the mirror and for the first time, she says to herself, *'Prostitute. I'm a prostitute.'*

She does not want to cry so she holds back the tears, thinking to herself that she has to be strong and promises herself she will sort her life out soon.

The chauffeur is waiting for her and she goes to the Rolls. The chauffeur opens the door for her and she sits in the back seat, quietly.

When they arrive at the Amir's private rooms at the hotel she is greeted by the same woman - Mia - who beckons Rosie to follow her. She knows what will happen as they go through the same ritual; the bathing, oiling and dressing before going to the Amir.

Mia takes her to a large mirror and she looks in the mirror with Rosie, smiling.

"You very beautiful and the Amir will be very pleased with you." She sees herself dressed in this long silken robe. Mia takes her to his quarters and she enters his room. He is laid back, dressed like always in his white robe. He beckons Rosie to go to him and he is smiling as she stands in front of him. He looks her up and down then takes her hand; she sits next to him.

"You look sad my little beauty. Are you not happy?" The Amir brushes her hair from her face.

"I am happy, sir, I am happy," she says, forcing a smile.

The Amir points to a large box. "This is for you," he says with a big grin on his face, pushing the box towards her and motioning for her to open it.

She takes the box and opens it; inside are several undergarments in pure silk with a white rose and a smaller box laying on the top of them. She opens the smaller box, and inside is a beautiful bracelet with diamonds. She does not know what to say so she looks at the Amir.

"They are beautiful. Oh thank you, thank you."

The Amir takes the bracelet and puts it on her wrist. She leans across and kisses him on the cheek, and then she wonders *'should I have done that?'*.

He smiles at her then stands up, looks at her and walks to the bedroom, with Rosie following him. She knows what he expects now and she is very relaxed about it. Everything is so sterile, and so immaculate.

She goes to him as he lies on the bed and she undoes his robe. He has his eyes closed as she does what he wants.

A couple of hours have passed. He is not in such a hurry to go like before; he lays with her on the bed, occasionally touching her face or feeling her hair before telling her, "You can go now. Mia will show you your room. You can stay here tonight."

Rosie gets off the bed still naked and he watches her as she puts on her robe. She smiles at him and leaves the room. Mia is there as if she had been waiting for her and she leads her to her bedroom. Mia says, "If you need anything just press the bell beside the bed. The shower room is there, do you need anything?"

"No, thank you."

Mia leaves, closing the door. Rosie walks around the beautiful apartment before taking a shower and going to bed. She sleeps late into the morning again until Mia appears with a tray of coffee and with various fruits on it. She puts it on Rosie's lap as she sits up.

"Thank you Mia."

Mia looks at her, hearing Rosie call by her name; she nods her head and smiles and then leaves her.

She eats and showers wondering if the Amir will call her. She watches television and just relaxes. People seem to be coming and going, making beds and cleaning around. Mia is there asking her all the time if she needs anything. Through the day she is attended to by various servants and into the evening when she expects to see the Amir, Mia comes. "You can dress as you will be leaving shortly and the Amir will see you when he comes back to UK. Please hurry, you must go. I have your bag and these things that the Amir told me to make sure you take."

She is soon dressed and is taken by car back to her apartment. She wonders what is happening as she was expecting to spend another night with the Amir.

Jade is in the apartment when she gets back.

"Here she is. What's all that you've got? Come on let's have a look?" Jade says, trying to take the box from her playfully. Rosie is trying to hold on to it and they are both laughing. Finally, Jade gets the box off her and opens it.

"Wow! Look at these," She shouts to Natalia and Monika. She takes the underwear from the box.

"These are pure silk and what's this, a white rose? You lucky sod, what's that on your wrist?" She looks closely at the bracelet.

"That must be worth a fortune." Jade cannot stop looking at it.

Natalia is laughing at Rosie. "You must give a good blow job. You show us and maybe we get nice expensive presents. We do good last night but not as good as you."

Danny comes the next day and he is in a very good mood.

"Rosie my darling, come here." She goes to him and Danny hands her an envelope.

"This is from the Amir. He has had to go back to Qatar for some very important business, and you are very lucky that he wants you to have your own apartment." Danny is waiting for a good reaction from her but Rosie does not look too happy.

"I would rather be here with the girls Danny. I'll be lonely on my own."

Danny's face changes. "You will have your own apartment and that's it. It is in a really expensive area of London. Think yourself lucky my girl, as you would only live in a place like you're going to if you were a millionaire. You will move in a day or two and that's final."

Rosie does not say anything, as she is afraid he will get mad again with her.

When Danny has left, the girls tell Rosie about their night out. Jade is laughing.

"I had this guy who was not the best of lookers but when he told me he was a property millionaire he got better looking. I don't know where he got his strength. He was at it all night."

Again they are all crying with laughter. Monika shares her story.

"You see my man he older than my poppa with long white hair and big beard and he look like... I think you call him Father Christmas. Natalia's man, or was it two men Natalia, young and good looking."

"I have good night with both... when one tired the other take over very nice, and we all got plenty money. People get up to go work. We have easy job as we lay down," Natalia says.

That really creases them up. Rosie has tears of laughter rolling down her cheeks.


May has almost given up on Paul when she finally gets a call from him.

"Hi! May how are things?"

May is surprised to hear from him but happy he has called.

"Okay, thank you. I thought you had forgotten me."

"How could I forget you May? Listen, tomorrow night are you free?"

"I'm always free Paul." May is thinking she should not have said that but she liked the money she got before.

"Right, usual time, eight o'clock is that okay?" Paul tells her.

"Fine, I'll be ready." May is a now a little excited, wondering who will be there.

Paul smiles to himself thinking, *'This one will be easy'.*

The next night May is ready. She has a tight red dress on which she has to keep pulling down, and with her being rather plump it shows a few odd shapes and makes her bottom stick out like a camel's hump. She looks in the mirror, and tries to breathe in to get rid of the spare tyre she has around her waist, which is made worse by the tightness of her dress. She is now tugging at her dress and she looks over her shoulder. She knows that is the best she can make her figure look and gives up trying anymore. Soon the car arrives with the same chauffeur she had before - the one who ogles her legs.

He opens the door for her and as she gets in and he is staring at her legs. She tries her best to keep them shut but finds it difficult. Her legs part as she tries to move along the seat. The chauffeur smiles at her and before closing the door he looks straight at her and licks his lips. May just pulls a face at him.

The house is quite large with a lit drive leading to the house. May gets out of the car again, trying to stop the chauffeur looking up her legs but again she gives him a treat. As she walks past him she whispers.

"Dirty old man."

"Have a nice night, miss," he says sarcastically

May turns and gives him another dirty look before going to the door.

Paul answers the door.

"Ha! Come in May," he says at the same time eying her up and down.

There are a lot of people; more than the first party she went to. Paul gets her a drink and while she is looking around Paul puts something in her drink and stirs it round before giving it to her.

Paul tells her to get acquainted with the other girls that are there. She notices that some were at the other party. May takes a sip of her drink.

"Come on girl, drink it up because there is plenty more. Enjoy yourself."

She drinks half of the glass. "Was that gin and tonic?"

"Yes, a large one. Right May, get mixing and I'll see you shortly. I'm just going to speak to a friend." He walks across to a couple of men and starts chatting to them.

May is feeling good, quite relaxed and starts talking to a foreign girl. She is the one who stripped off before.

"I'm May. I was at the same party as you before, do you remember me?" May is slurring her words.

"Yes, I see you before," she says giggling.

The music is quite loud now and the party is livening up somewhat when Paul comes across with another drink for May. She takes it from him and again drinks half of it. Paul puts his hand on her bottom and gives it a squeeze. May just smiles at him. She really fancies him.

Paul whispers something to her and she nods her head then he takes her by the hand and leads her to another room. Once inside he closes the door then pulls her to him. May can't wait; her hands are all over him.

He pulls the zip down at the back of her dress and after a bit of a struggle he manages to get it down to her waist. He gets his hand inside her dress and is squeezing her bare bottom.
She is undoing his zip on his trousers and then she puts her hand inside his trousers. She can feel he is aroused. He pushes her gently to her knees. May is really sexed up and does not need any guidance and she takes him without hesitation. He pulls her head towards him. She is so carried away now with what she is doing that she does not realise another couple of men have come into the room. They are stood watching them and Paul is stood with his eyes closed until he can't stand it anymore. He calls out, "Yes."

May just carries on until she feels him gently pulling away from her but before she can move a hand grabs her head and pulls her closer. She realises it is someone else but without hesitation does the same to him, then after a short time he pushes her back on the floor, kneels beside her and starts to help her undress. May sees a blurred face looking at her, voices that sound in the distance. She feels out of control and she is seeing flashes of light across her eyes but she has a strange sense of freedom and has no inhibitions. She is now naked, as the man has sex with her like before with Roger. He and someone else manoeuvre May into various positions with May more than obliging.

When they have finished they leave May laid on the floor, she lays there still naked for some time and just when she is about to get up Paul enters the room with a couple of men. They stand watching as he gives her a drink and forces a couple of tablets down her. She is laid down on the floor again as the men do what they want with her. May does not fight them off as they take it in turns, sometimes two having sex with her at the same time.

What seems like hours pass before May is left alone. She is so unsteady on her feet as she stands up and her mouth is so dry that she needs a drink. She finds her clothes laid around and manages to put them on, staggering as she does. She sees a tray on the table with drinks on it. She pours herself a drink, unable to stand without swaying and she sits in a chair trying to pull herself round. She knows some of what had gone on but it all seemed to be a kind of dream. She could hear voices, men laughing, but could not make out their faces, which were so blurred. She falls asleep in the chair and the first thing she hears next is Paul.

"Come on, get up, let's have you home. You really like it don't you?" He pulls her to her feet.
He gets her in the car and takes her home. May is uncomfortable; she knows part of what had happened and she tells Paul, "I'm not usually like that."

"Like, what, you mean the sex?" he says, laughing
May tries to say something but her words are still slurred.

"I won't do that again. I should not have come. Rosie tried to warn me," she says, trying to straighten her clothes.
Paul looks at her. "What did you say about Rosie?"

She knows now she should not have told him anything about Rosie.

"No I didn't mean."
Before she can say anything else Paul shouts at her, "You didn't mean what? Your friend Rosie is in serious trouble."
The car pulls up outside May's flat.

" Get your arse out of here. I'll see you later."
May gets out of the car. Paul waves an envelope at her saying, "You can forget this my girl."

May is sorry she said anything now. At least she would have got the money. She wonders if she should tell Rosie that Paul knows she had tried warning her. She tells herself, *'I will telephone her later today when I feel a bit better. Yes, I'll do that.'* She staggers to her flat.


Later that morning Paul telephones Danny and he answers the phone.

"Hi bro, how's things?"
Paul knows that Danny will blow his top.

"Your little angel Rosie has warned the girl May I told you about. She had told her she should keep clear of us and the set up." Paul waits for Danny's response.

"Bastard, bastard, shit. After all that she has got. I'll kill her." Danny is now fuming. "Who's this May then? I guess the one from the university, is that how she knows her?"

Paul is thinking about what she said. "Yeah, they must know one another and obviously they have been in touch."

"Well we'll put a stop to that. She has her own pad now paid for by the Amir, the ungrateful cow."

Danny is thinking about how he is going to deal with her.

"Look Paul, you sort things out at your end and be careful. I'll see to things here. This does not have to get out of hand."

"This May is easy meat Danny. I should not have any problems because she is hooked." They finish their conversation.


Danny cannot get to her apartment fast enough. He bursts open the door and all the girls look at him as he marches past them looking for Rosie. He makes for her bedroom and pushes open the door. She is sat on the bed reading. He slams the door shut and walks across to her. Rosie can see how mad he is.

"You tell that friend of yours, what's her name, May? To be careful of my brother and me."

Danny lifts his hand up as though he is about to strike Rosie. She immediately cowers on the bed, closing her eyes expecting him to land a punch on her. Suddenly he stops shouting. Everything is quiet and she opens her eyes slowly, not daring to look at him. He is just stood looking down at her and his anger seems to have gone. He sits alongside of her.

"I just do not understand you. You have not been forced to do what you're doing, you have been well paid for what you have done, so why? Why, when you have this opportunity to be able to get anything you want from the Amir, do you want to balls it all up? Tell me?"

"I'm sorry Danny. I know I shouldn't have said anything. She was a friend who I roomed with."

Danny knows the Amir will be arriving at any time so he tries to be a little calmer.

"The apartment is ready for you, and you will be moving later today. You put things right with your friend May, and Paul will be seeing her later. I think the Amir will arrive tomorrow night and he will expect you to be available if he wants to see you. Now, do not give us any more problems. This is, and I say again, this is your last chance, okay?"

"Yes Danny, I understand. I'll pack my things."

"Good. Someone will pick you up later. If you have any problems let me know immediately. I think you better call your friend now."


She gets her phone and telephones May. After several rings no one answers, "No one is answering Danny. I won't leave a message. Shall I call later?"

"Okay, call her later. I will phone you if there is any change in our plans." Danny gets up and leaves, not speaking to anyone as he passes them.

"Shit he not happy Rosie, you in trouble again." Natalia looks at the others.

They ask her what the problem was with Danny. She will not tell them.

Rosie does tell them that she is moving later in the day and the other girls are disappointed, as they don't want her to leave. Jade is not happy either.

She says, "Rosie, you must call us and give us your address. We may be able to get to see you and go out sometime together."

"I will if Danny lets me. I don't want any more trouble." Jade helps her to pack her things, and when they are alone she tells her what happened, and why Danny was mad.

"Rosie, we all know what we are doing. It's not for us to cause trouble and get on the wrong side of Danny and his brother. Just tell your friend you should not have said what you said. If she wants to get involved it's up to her and leave it at that."

"I will if I can get hold of her," Rosie tells them.

They finish packing her things, and Jade is laughing.

"Rosie, you have more bloody clothes and shoes than Victoria Beckham."

"I hope they are as good as hers." They both are laughing. She is all packed and waiting to be picked up when the car arrives. The girls say their goodbyes, asking her again to get in touch as soon as she can to let them know where she is.

She is sat in the car and she has not been able to contact May. She is thinking maybe May is avoiding her, knowing Paul will have told Danny what she said.

She is sat looking out of the car window as it drives through one of the most expensive parts of London. When the car stops the driver tells her to go into the building while he follows with her bags. She walks into the foyer and looks around it. It is fantastic and she feels a bit out of place as the driver takes her to the apartment.

The driver rings the bell and a Eurasian looking woman dressed in a maid's outfit opens the door. She smiles at Rosie,

"Come, please, come in Miss. My name is Susie."

Rosie follows her as the driver puts the bags down and leaves.

The maid shows her around the apartment. Everything is so immaculate and she just cannot take it all in. Susie goes to bring in her cases, leaving her stood in shock. She walks into the bathroom and shakes her head in disbelief, thinking if the girls could see this, well, wow they think theirs is great but look at this. She follows Susie in to a walk-in wardrobe where there is enough space for all the clothes in Harrods to fit. The maid starts to unpack her clothes. Rosie tells her she will do it but the maid insists.

Rosie walks over to the large window that looks out over London. She cannot believe she is stood in her own luxury apartment. Her mind goes back in time to when she was a young girl in Chesterfield and how she and her friends would fantasise about their futures like all little girls do. How could she have ever known something like this would have happened to her? She smiles to herself. Apartments like this, a maid and then, like many times before, she realises the price she has paid.

She feels so guilty about giving herself to strangers, and the drugs. She is remembering when she was young and her first kiss when she was only 13 years old and she was with a boy named Jimmy. He was around the same age as her, and when they were alone in a friend's garden and thinking no one could see them he quickly gave her a kiss on the lips, and then tried to touch her non-existent breasts; she remembers pushing him away, then running away from him thinking she had done something really bad. Now, well, all her inhibitions have gone and there are no limits to what is expected of her.

She asks herself why is it that, if you want a good life, love, money and everything else, does it have to have all the bad things that go with it? She stands daydreaming for some time before coming back to reality. She turns and watches Susie.

"Susie," she asks, "do you stay here in the flat?"

"No, no Miss. I only come each day and I take care of apartment and if you need anything you ask Susie."

"Thank you Susie." She smiles at Susie.

"No thank me Miss, my job." Having finished unpacking her clothes, she asks Rosie what she would like to drink or eat.

She now appreciates just what she has and she knows she could only dream of a lifestyle like this. Soon she is settled in and has made herself familiar with the layout. The TV room is like going to a cinema with a screen that covers the wall and large seats for half a dozen people.

She gets a call from Danny. "Hi! Danny."

"Well, what do you think? Now do you believe me when I said the world could be your oyster? Enjoy it while you can and let's have no more trouble. Have you spoken to your friend yet?"

"No, I have tried but I get no answer," she says nervously.

"Okay, keep trying. If the Amir wants to see you he will let me know. It could be tomorrow or the next day. Just relax and we'll talk later."

"Okay, Danny. And Danny, I do appreciate what you have done for me."

"Pleased you can see that now, okay bye for now. Rosie, just before I go we will get together sometime when things are quiet."

"I would like that Danny. Bye."

"Bye." He knows there is something about Rosie he has a soft spot for but also knows that business must come first.

She puts the phone down and smiles to herself. She cannot wait for Danny to visit her; sex with him is something more than special. She has done as Danny said and cut down on the drugs, although it has been difficult at least now she is only using on a few occasions. But it is hard.

May has been feeling very irritable. She needs something to calm her and she has dabbled with amphetamines and a little coke before but never has she felt like she needs them like she does now. She has seen on her phone that Rosie has been calling her but she has been reluctant to answer her. She knows she could probably have caused Rosie a lot problems.

The telephone rings. May sees who is calling and answers. It is Paul, who wants to reassure her that things will be okay if she cooperates.

"May, look, you have nothing to fear from my brother or me. It has to be your decision at the end of the day. I have something this weekend if you want to join me."

May is thinking about the money that she never got last time she was with him.

"I will if you want me to, Paul I... I was wondering that you did say it would be worth my while but I never got anything before and I am a little short at the moment."

May wants some money to buy some drugs.

"Look May, I have something for you when I see you. So I can count on you then?"

May is relieved. Her parents have not got very much and she knows she cannot get anything from them.

"Yes. What time and where should I go?"

"I'll send a car for you like last time, between seven and nine o'clock. Be ready, look nice, okay?" If she can, he thinks.

"I'll be ready Paul."

They finish talking and Paul knows she's hooked and keen to join his girls in Leeds. He telephones Danny.

"Danny, I have sorted our little problem here. She is all for it and I want to try to get her to join the girls here in Leeds, what do you think?"

"Yes that's good Paul. Lay off the university for a while now though. We have girls coming in from Eastern Europe, nice lookers, so there's no need to struggle to get them from there now."

"Okay Danny, it looks like things are going well," Paul says.

"No need for you to visit Nick in Brighton either. We are having a meeting with Ramon. I need you, Nick and Luke from Manchester to come to London. You can see mum and dad while you are here, as they are wondering why you have not been to see them. You know what dad is like."

"You give Nick and Luke a call. When is the meeting Dan?"

"Some time next week. I'll let you know and, yes, I will call the others."


Rosie is enjoying living in the apartment. She has called the girls who are dying to see the place. She decides to wait while the Amir has gone back but she has promised the girls they can pay her a visit.

Danny calls her to tell her the Amir is now in the UK and will expect her to visit him tomorrow evening. He said he would send his chauffeur for her. Danny says, "Rosie, look your best. I know you will."

"Yes, okay Danny."

When they have finished talking she is feeling a little nervous, although she knows the Amir has always been good to her. She thinks he can probably have any woman he wants with the wealth he has, and she thinks *'why me?'*. And how long will it last before he is tired of her?

She wakes up in the mornings unable to believe she is living in this place. Susie is always happy and does everything for her. She is preparing her things for the evening, trying different clothes and underwear on. Susie is giving her opinion.

She has decided on her clothing and in the evening she dresses, taking great care to not over dress. She looks in the mirror and sees that Susie is watching her.

"You look beautiful miss. Really beautiful."

"Thank you Susie. I don't know when I will be back so can you take care of things while I am away?"

"Yes I take care. No problem Miss Rosie." She smiles at her.

It's not long before the Amir's chauffeur arrives and escorts Rosie to the Rolls. She sits in the back enjoying the attention she is getting. Again she is escorted to the Amir's suite where she is met, as always, by Mia who greets her with a smile. She seems to have mellowed somewhat since she first met Rosie. Mia takes her through to the rooms, where she knows Mia is going to go through the same ritual as she has been through the times before; the only difference is she is more relaxed and enjoys the experience.

She is all ready to meet the Amir and is led through to his quarters. The door opens and the Amir is laid back on a large sofa, reading. He looks up at Rosie; a big grin comes on his face as he motions to her to sit by him. He takes her hand and kisses it.

"My white Rose. Do you like your apartment?"

"Yes, it is really beautiful," she says shyly.

He looks down at his book and says, "Do you like Shakespeare? Have you read Romeo and Juliet? I find it tragic but compelling. His poems Venus and Adonis and the Rape of Lucrece are very erotic. He wrote these poems in 1593. You can read them. I would like that. Take the book with you when you leave."

"I have read some of Shakespeare," Rosie tells him. "I find it very intense reading."

He smiles at her again. He puts the book down and takes her by the hand and leads her to his bedroom.

She knows what he expects and does all she can to pleasure him through the night. She does not leave him until nearly daylight, when she is taken to her own room where she falls asleep more or less instantly.

Through the next day she is pampered and looked after. She does see the Amir until late in the afternoon, when he calls at her room - something he had never done before. He sits and talks to her, asking her questions about various things. Thankfully Rosie is able to answer without being too embarrassed as she feels she is not afraid to speak to him now. Before leaving he tells her he will see her later in the evening.

After eating she prepares herself to visit him again. Mia puts her hair up, telling her she looks so much better with it up. When she is ready Mia stands in front of her.

"Beautiful, beautiful."

She smiles as she goes to his rooms.

He is tender with her, taking in her beauty as he enjoys her every touch. The night passes and he is reluctant to let her go to her own room.

"I must leave today unfortunately. I cannot take you with me but I may be back in a week or so, depending on my commitments. You must see me before you leave, my little one." Rosie looks at him and he looks sad.

"I will. I will." Then she leaves for her room.


Later in the morning she is all dressed and packed, ready to leave when the Amir comes into her room with his manservant. He stands in front of her and smiles then snaps his fingers, holding out his hand. The manservant gives him a folder he then gives to Rosie.

"You take this. All the information you need is in this folder along with my chauffeur's number. If you need anything, anything at all, you call my man Mustafa and he will see to it. If you need a vehicle to go anywhere you call the number and my man will be available. Whenever you need him."

Rosie does not know what to say. "Thank you, thank you."

The Amir takes her hand and kisses it.

"Take care my little one. You can buy whatever you need." He kisses her hand again before turning and leaving, with the manservant running behind him.

When she is on her own she looks into the folder. There is a lot of money along with a credit card and a pin number for the card. She has a big smile on her face as she says out loud, *"Buy anything."*

She sits down, looking at what else is the folder, and unable to believe how fortunate she is. The chauffeur comes for her bags, she says goodbye to Mia before leaving. Mia just smiles as she leaves.


Once back in her apartment she has to pinch herself to believe this is all hers. She is smiling and enjoys the rest of the day lounging about with Susie who, as usual, sees to her every need.

She decides to telephone May. This time she answers.

"Hello."

"It's me, Rosie. I have tried to phone you numerous times. Have you been avoiding me?"

"Avoiding you Rosie? Why would I do that?" She knows that Rosie knows about her telling Paul about the warning.

"Look May, it's not my business what you do and if you want to see Paul then you see Paul. Anyway, let's forget it. What have you been up to? Been to any parties?"

"Well to be honest I am meeting Paul tonight." Thinking she maybe should not tell her.

"You enjoy yourself May. I have a new apartment now, something rather special. I will tell you more next time we speak. You take care and let me know how things go.

"A special apartment? You are doing well for yourself. Okay, I'll telephone you in a day or two. Bye for now as I must finish getting ready."

"Bye May."

May thinks things can't be that bad for Rosie. A bloody new apartment. Smiling to herself she says to herself that she wants some of that.


May is ready. She is rather irritable as she is waiting for the car to arrive, hoping that when she gets to where she is going Paul has something to calm her. The car arrives for her and when she gets to the car she sees it's the same driver as before. He is stood smiling, holding the car door open for her. She slides by him, getting into the back as he closes the door slowly looking at her.

*'Dirty old shit,'* she says to herself as she tries to adjust her dress.

They soon arrive at a large apartment building. May gets out of the car, and looking up she sees it's not for people like her to live unless you win the lottery. The driver leads the way, with May struggling in her high heels to keep up with him. Inside the reception the driver shows her to the lift.

"Please madam, this way."

May gets into the lift and the driver is stood alongside her, still with the same silly grin on his face while at the same time he is looking her up and down. They get to the floor where they want to be and go along to the apartment, where the party is. He points to the door.

"Just go in miss, they are expecting you."
May opens the door cautiously and as she does she can hear laughing. She can now see a number of women and men in the room. A few look at her as she enters and it is not long before Paul is alongside her. "May, how are you"?

"Fine Paul." May smiles at him.

"May, come with me." He takes her hand and leads her into another room there are two women laughing and taking drugs. They smile at May.

Paul walks across to a small table. He takes a packet from his pocket and as he looks at May he puts a line or two of the white powder on the small table, motioning to May to take some. May slowly puts her head down close to the table and puts her finger to one side of her nose and sniffs up, and lifting her head up she closes her eyes then goes in for the second line, which she snorts up her other nostril. Paul is impressed that she does not need telling what to do and it's clear that she could not get it fast enough.

"Come on, let's get you a drink May my darling. The party is about to begin." He grabs hold of her bottom and squeezes it.

May just smiles at him as she goes back into the other room with Paul. The cocaine is taking hold. She now feels light headed, her heart's racing and she's giggly as Paul gives her a drink.

"Here, get this down you."
May drinks it all in one go and Paul tops up her drink immediately. He puts his arm around May and guards her to a couple of men talking to another woman. Paul pushes May playfully towards one of the younger men and the other couple are laughing as the young man grabs hold of her.

"Well I'll have to keep you to myself then." May just giggles holding on to the young man.

"Mmm, I have no objection to that."

152

Paul leaves her with him and the others. Music is playing and a couple are dancing, rubbing their bodies up close together and occasionally kissing. The young man whispers in May's ear as he starts to dance with her.

"I'm Damian, what's your name sexy?"

"May," she says, snuggling up to him.

Later on some of the couples are dancing together and some of the women start removing their clothes. May joins them with no inhibitions. It soon turns into a near full orgy. May is just going along with whatever happens. The drugs and drink have made her mind wander and she occasionally sees different faces on top of her. Sometimes she cries out as both men and women touch and feel her naked body. She is laid on the floor among other naked bodies and later, as she comes around, she sees Damian lying across her with another woman. She has no strength to get up and she lays there for sometime. Other people are getting up now as Damian attempts to have sex with May without success. May manages to push him off and makes her way to the bathroom, collecting her clothes, or at least what she can find strewn amongst other people's clothes.

There is no sight of Paul and she cannot remember seeing him since he was with Damian.

She is in the bathroom with another woman who looks rather pale and as she opens her bag she looks across at May. "I feel like shit," she says as she pops a tablet in her mouth.

"Here take one, it will make you feel better."

May takes it from her. "Thanks." May takes the tablet with a drink.

The woman takes one last look at herself in the mirror before leaving the bathroom and as she leaves she says to May, "God, what a night. Bye, see you."

May tidies herself up and then goes back into the room as Paul enters.

"Ha, here you are. Shall we go?"

May smiles as best she can. "Yes I'm ready."

Damian walks across to her, wearing no shirt and buttoning his trousers.

"Would you like to meet again May? Give me your

number?"

Paul says to Damian, "May's number is not for you now Damian. If you want to see May again call me - you know the rules."

"Okay Paul, my friend." He carries on getting dressed.


Once outside Paul helps May into the car and once in the car he gives her an envelope with money in it.

"That's for the last time we were out and for tonight I think you will be happy with that. |Oh, and you may like this."

May sees it's cocaine and some amphetamines; she takes them from him.

"Thanks Paul."

As they are driving along Paul asks, "Listen would you like to join a couple of my girls here in Leeds? You would have no worries about money. If you think you would like to you would have to say goodbye to uni. But you will be well taken care of and live in a very nice apartment. What do you say?"

While he has been talking May has looked into the envelope. She cannot believe how much money he has given her. Paul laughs seeing her face.

"You like? There is a lot more than that out there waiting for you. You would meet a lot of important and very wealthy people. If you need a little time to think it through that's okay."

She sits quietly for a while then she just says to Paul, "Yes."

Paul looks at her, "That didn't take you long. You do mean yes to joining us, right?"

"Yes, whenever you like." May thinks her parents won't care as long as she sends them money now and again.

"I'll see to a few things. You pack your things and I'll call you and let you know when I'll pick you up."

They arrive at the flats and Paul tells May she will not regret it as she leaves. May is clinging on to her envelope with the money and the drugs and she cannot get to her flat fast enough.

Once inside she checks the money saying out loud, *"Shit, shit."* She has never had so much money in her life. Although she is still affected by the drugs she takes one of the tablets Paul gave her before falling on the bed, holding on to her money.

Rosie is enjoying everything. She loves the apartment and a few days have passed. Danny calls to see her. Rosie looks more beautiful than ever. Danny enters the apartment and she runs to him to take his coat. Danny stops her in her tracks. He holds her slightly away from him; he looks her up and down then turns her around. When she is facing him she gives him a beautiful smile.

"Give me your coat. I'm so pleased to see you."
Danny gives her his coat. "My darling Rosie, you just get more beautiful every time I see you."

"Can I get you a drink? " she says, giving him her very sexy look just to encourage him.
Danny sits on the sofa, "Never mind the drink. Come sit down next to me."
She walks over to him and sits next to him.

"I was thinking of staying with you for a while. If you want me to, that is." Danny takes her hand.

"Danny, you know I love spending time with you, you must know that." Rosie lowers her head shyly.
As she speaks Susie comes in and sees Danny.

"Can I get you anything before I go Miss Rosie?"

"Miss Rosie is okay Susie, you can go now," Danny laughs.
She leaves Danny who lays back on the sofa laughing.

"You are being spoiled Miss Rosie. Could Miss Rosie come a little closer as I would like to hold her?"

"Miss Rosie would like that very much," she says seductively.
Danny takes hold of her and kisses her passionately, feeling her beautiful body. He whispers to her, "You are so, so beautiful."

She stands up and holds her hand out to him. Danny gives her his hand and she leads him to the bedroom. As he sits on the bed she starts to undress herself slowly and sexily. Danny cannot take his eyes off her. He wants so much to touch and caress her body. She stands in front of him and, naked, he pulls her to him once more. He kisses every part of her body, her skin is like silk to his touch and he feels an overwhelming urge to explore her body. She feels so relaxed and she can let her real feelings come out when she is with him. She adores him and it's not just the sex with Danny. No one could ever make her feel like she does with him, and when he touches her she is in ecstasy. She has taken very few drugs in the last day or so and she is pleased because she has a clear mind and is able to enjoy Danny's every intimate touch. Time stands still as they make love like never before; their bodies are there for each to enjoy - and they do.

It is the next morning before either attempt to get up. The night has been short naps and sex throughout and when Rosie manages to get away from him he makes a grab for her as she gets off the bed. She playfully slaps his hand.

"You want a drink don't you, you sexy man?"

"Yes I am a little thirsty. But I'll have you for my breakfast."

He laughs as she wiggles her bottom at him and then gives him a big smile as she leaves the room.

Rosie is made up. She has left all the sex with other people behind her and, for now at least, it's just Danny and her, which is all she has ever wanted. Before Danny leaves she asks if it is okay for the girls to come to see her, and go on a bit of a shopping trip with her. Danny tells her it's okay but not to make it a regular thing as the Amir could turn up any time.

She cannot wait to call Jade.

"Hello."

"It's me Rosie. How are things there?"

Jade is excited hearing Rosie. "Rosie it's great to hear from you. Everything is okay here; the girls as always are enjoying themselves. How are you doing?"

"Great. Listen Jade, would you and the girls like to visit me in my new apartment?"

"Yes of course we would. Is it okay with Danny? Don't want to drop you in the shit girl."

"Yes it's okay with Danny. He knows. If you come tomorrow I'll send my driver to pick you up."

"Listen to her! My driver. How you have come on Rosie - don't make us jealous. No really Rosie, I can't wait to see you." Jade is giggling on the end of the phone.

"Shall we say two o'clock tomorrow then? I'll be

waiting."

"Bye for now Rosie. I'll tell the girls."

"Bye Jade."

Jade tells the girls about Rosie's apartment and that they are going to visit her.

"Are there any men going to be there?" Natalia asks.

"Aren't you getting enough Natalia? No, it's just us girls."

Natalia just shrugs her shoulders.

"I only ask. Be nice to see my Rosie."

Rosie is so happy and the next morning she calls the Amir's chauffeur and gives him the girls' address, and tells him to pick them up at two o'clock and bring them to her apartment. Rosie tells Susie to get some nice food and drink ready for the girls.

"Susie, make it special because these are my best friends." She wants to make a good impression on her friends.

"No worry Miss Rosie. I make something very nice."

Rosie cannot wait to see them and she wants to look her very best and makes sure she is dressed in her finest clothes.

Everything is ready as the girls arrive at Rosie's apartment. The doorbell rings and Rosie opens the door. The girls run to her, hugging her and then Natalia kisses Rosie telling her how beautiful she is and then she walks round the apartment with her arms up in the air.

"Rosie, Rosie! You are so lucky, what a place."

The others follow her, looking in every room. Jade is unable to believe just how beautiful it all is.

"Rosie, oh Rosie."

"Come on, come and see my TV room."

Natalia stands in the doorway.

"It like a proper cinema but with better seats nice, very nice."

Once they have seen everything they sit down and have a good chat, asking Rosie many questions. They have a few drinks and Natalia hands a couple of unknown pills round. Rosie asks, "What are they?"

"Who cares if they make you feel good?" Natalia says.

At first Rosie is reluctant to take any until she has had a few glasses of wine.

They enjoy the afternoon together and Rosie has told Jade while they're on their own about Danny visiting her. Jade can see when Rosie talks about him how happy she is.

Monika tells her about the parties they have been to and the men they have met.

"Only Natalia can wear them out. English men very sexy but never satisfied," she says.

They all laugh, enjoying their time together. Before they go they make arrangements to go on a shopping trip.

"We go Harrods and spend, spend, spend."

They have a great time together shopping until they drop and as usual Natalia has them in stitches telling them about her many sexual exploits.

When they have left Rosie is relaxing, thinking how good it was to be with them again.

## 13

# The Demetrio Problem

Danny, Paul, Nick and Luke are meeting at Danny's apartment and are discussing certain things about their growing operation; the money they are taking and the cost of their operation.

"We will need to speak with Ramon about girls coming in and the money we are going to have to pay for them," Danny says.

Nick is eager to make an impression on Danny and his brother, and makes a suggestion.

"Maybe we can expand to other places around the UK? That is if we can get some reliable people to run the other operations with us."

Danny agrees, "We are already considering that Nick. I must congratulate you; you are doing a good job so keep it up. Luke we need you to do the same and we will give you some more girls so let's see what you can do. We best leave for Ramon's place now. Nick you come follow us, with Luke in your car. Paul and I will go in my car."

They leave the apartment. Danny and Paul are leading the way.

"Oh Danny, remember Rosie's friend May," says Paul, "she has now joined the girls in Leeds and she can't get enough, she is game for anything. But I don't think she will last that long and she will be ready for dumping in a couple of months or so."

"It does amaze me just how easy some of these girls can get into it. Mind you, Rosie is another thing. She definitely has that something that most don't have; the Amir thinks there is no one like her. Pity we don't get many like her."

"Yes, she is a good looker. And I think you like a piece of her now and again, am I right?" Paul slaps his brother on the back, laughing, before adding, "Then again, who wouldn't? Dan, I would not say no myself."

Danny looks at Paul rather seriously. "You have no chance, so don't even think about it brother."

Paul is laughing now, teasing Danny.

"Don't worry Danny just joking. Remember Damian who we worked with? He is partial to a bit of rough stuff and he really took a liking to that May. I think he needs to go to Specsavers." They are both laughing now.

They arrive at Ramon's house. Victor opens the door and greets them; they go through to the lounge where, as usual, Ramon is sat with a very nice looking girl on his knee.

"Danny, Paul come. Good to see you. Introduce me to your friends?" He pushes the girl off his knee and walks across to them to shake hands. Danny introduces him to Luke and Nick, telling him they are running the other operations.

"Drinks for my friends Anna my beauty. Come, sit down," Ramon says.

The girl asks them what they want to drink and as she walks across the room all of them are looking at her swinging her near naked backside as she walks. Ramon laughs out loud and shouts.

"I see you like her arse." Again he laughs, sitting and leaning back in his chair.

"Victor go and get the other girls. Danny, we have been very busy lots of business. Things have been good for you, yes?" Ramon says.

"Yes, things are good. I told you on the phone Ramon that we want to expand and we will of course need more girls. Do you see any problem?"

Danny is hoping for a good response.

"Danny no, no problem. How many you need? 20? 30?" Ramon says, smacking his knee and laughing.

Danny gets serious as the others look on.

"We need to know, how much for the girls? You know we are giving the suppliers more business, so maybe we could get a better price for taking more girls? What do you think?"

As Danny says this four very nice looking girls come into room in very revealing clothes. Ramon indicates to the girls to sit with the men, at the same time as he replies to Danny.

"Maybe we can do a deal, yes, why not? I put it to them. Look, we talk business a little later. Enjoy yourselves - we have plenty time to talk."

The party livens up and the girls give them a bit of a show, which they all enjoy.

Later in the evening Ramon calls to Danny to go with him into another room where they can discuss business more privately and Ramon can make some calls to his friends who are providing the girls from Eastern Europe.

While on the phone with someone called Demetrio, Ramon seems to get very upset about something and is shouting down the phone. Danny does not understand, as they are not speaking English. This goes on for some time before Ramon slams down the phone.

"I call another friend," he says. Ramon phones another number. He seems to be muttering to himself, and not looking too happy. Danny has not seen Ramon like he is now; he's normally laid back and never gets upset. In between speaking to other people he looks across at Danny.

"That guy I shout at with no brain because he is an idiot. He wants share of business or more money for girls than before. I tell him fuck off."

He carries on telephoning another couple of people and, after a lot of negotiations, the business is done, and Danny is happy about the outcome. They go to join the others. As they enter the room Paul looks across to Danny who gives him the thumbs up. Paul, smiling, carries on enjoying himself with the girl he is with, leaving the others all enjoying themselves with the girls. None of them get much sleep.

Ramon calls to Victor and another one of his heavies to go with him to another room. Ramon talks to Victor in their language.

"Demetrio cause us problem. He has people here in London, he wants to set up here with his own operation and not give our girls to the Brits. We need our own people to be very careful. When we argue he tells me if we want war he will give us war. I not tell Danny and others. They may be too frightened to take any more girls from our other friends in Eastern Europe."

They go back to join the others. Ramon walks into the room smiling, as though everything is okay.

The next morning Nick, Paul, Danny and Luke come out of various rooms, looking rather tired after a hectic night and drinking a little too much. Soon they are ready to leave and Ramon comes from one of the rooms with Anna hanging on to him in fewer clothes than she had on the previous night. Ramon tells Danny not to worry and that the new girls will be coming soon. He says goodbye to them before heading back to the bedroom with Anna.

Once back at Danny's apartment Danny puts them all in the picture regarding what he plans to do and what he wants them to do before they all head off for their destinations.

Once Nick and Luke have gone Danny tells Paul about Ramon shouting and arguing with someone on the phone and what he had said it was about. Danny thinks there was more to it but what he didn't know.

"Maybe you were just imagining it was more than it was," says Paul.

Danny shakes his head.

"No, Paul. Something was going on. We need to be careful when we get these other girls. You drive steady when you are driving back to Leeds and before you go make sure you call and see mum and dad."

"Yes, okay Danny. Keep in touch, see you."

Paul leaves; Danny knows Ramon and is concerned about something but doesn't know what. More importantly, perhaps, who is this Demetrio?

A week or so has passed. Rosie has seen Danny just once more since the last time he spent the night with her. She was hoping to see more of him but he had only stayed for an hour or so. She has been on a couple of shopping trips with the girls and has thoroughly enjoyed the freedom and also not having to worry about money. She could buy anything she wanted and the girls are very envious of her. She wonders when the Amir will be coming back to the UK. She asks herself time and time again how long will this life she is leading last?

Jade and the girls keep her informed on the very interesting parties they have been to and the people they have met; some television stars, politicians and occasionally well known people in the public eye. Rosie occasionally wishes she were with Jade and the girls more, especially when she feels a little lonely.

She is in her apartment when she gets a call from May.

"Rosie, got a lot to tell you," she says sounding excited.

"May you sound very happy with yourself. What as been happening since we last spoke?"

"Rosie I have left uni. I'm living in an apartment with some of Paul's other girls."

Rosie is not surprised to hear what May is telling her. She knew exactly what Paul was doing. Danny had done the same to her and Rosie does not want to criticise her but tells her, "As long as it is what you want May."

"Yes, I'm okay with the set up. I could not earn the money I am getting now Rosie - it would have taken me years being at uni then having to find some kind of work. I see Paul a lot but only when there is some party being lined up. But what parties they are. Well, I guess you know the score, don't you Rosie?" she says, laughing.

She knows there are no secrets between them now and feels she is free to talk about herself.

"Yes May, I do. I told you I have a new apartment and how it came about through Danny? I met the Amir of Qatar and he pays for everything."

"You're joking? A bloody Amir? Oh Rosie, you were always a lucky shit. So, do you just see him now and again and he pays everything for you?"

"Yes, but I see Danny now and again as well as the other girls I stayed with before."

"So Danny is sleeping with you? Girl, you have the best of both worlds. I hope I meet some frigging Amir. Look Rosie, keep in touch. I have to go now. I need a booster if you know what I mean. Bye for now."

"Bye May, take care."

May feels better that she has told Rosie everything and that they can be friends again.


Danny calls Rosie to let her know that the Amir is visiting and he will probably call on her.

"Rosie, you know what he expects. Make sure everything is right for him. He never told me how long he will be staying but be prepared."

"Yes Danny, I'll take care of everything, don't worry."

"I never worry about you now Rosie. I'll see you again when he leaves. Okay, bye for now."

"Okay Danny, bye."

She tells Susie what to do and to make sure she has plenty of food in. She gets herself ready just in case he arrives at any time. She thinks it is unusual for him to visit her because he usually sends for her to go to his apartment. She takes a couple of her pills; she is managing the drugs a lot better as she knows Danny would not be pleased and she is wary of how he would react if he thinks she's hitting them hard again.

Late the next evening she is sat alone relaxing when the bell rings. She goes to the door where the Amir's man is standing.

"The Amir will be here in a minute or two."

The Amir's man dashes back to the lift. Rosie waits fussing round and for others to make sure everything is in place before he enters. The Amir's man opens the door and the Amir enters, dressed in a very smart suit with his dark long hair, greying at the sides, and looking very distinguished. She had only seen him in his white robes but now sees and notices that he is a very good looking elderly man. He walks towards her, smiling and takes Rosie's hand and kisses it.

He asks, "My white Rose, I have missed you. Are you're settled in your apartment? You do have everything you need, yes?"

She finds herself blushing, then only half looking at him, as she answers.

"I have everything, and much more than I need, thank you."

He walks over and sits down on the large sofa. She is a little uneasy being in her own environment but he tries to put her at ease. He beckons to her.

"Come, sit down."

She sits next to him and they are now alone, as the Amir's man has left the room. He looks her up and down, then smiling he tells her, "You are so young and so beautiful. I don't have a lot of time to spend with you, little one."

"Would you like something to drink or eat?" she asks. She is halfway standing up to go and get him something when he takes hold of her hand again.

"No, I am fine. Please sit."

She looks into his dark eyes and sees this gentle caring man. He just smiles at her; he does not say anything for some time before asking, "Where is the bedroom?"

Rosie knows what he wants. She stands up and walks towards the bedroom with him following her. When they get into the room he stands in front of her, watching as she starts to undress slowly he stands motionless until she is completely naked. She walks towards him and attempts to take his clothes off and he tells her to lay on the bed. She watches him as he undresses, folding his clothes neatly and laying them on a chair. Rosie smiles to herself, thinking how she had just dropped her clothes on the floor.

He is now undressed and lays on the bed. Rosie kisses his chest and the Amir guides her head down his body. Soon she has him and his body arches as she takes him slowly. His hand is on her head, pushing as she uses her tongue, taking him then releasing him over and over again. Then she comes up to him and straddles him, taking him inside of her. His eyes are now closed as she performs her most intimate manoeuvres on him until he can stand no more. He cries out, grabbing hold of her bottom and pushing himself further inside her.

They lay still and Rosie dozes off. He gets up and goes to the bathroom. When he comes back into the bedroom he looks at her laying naked on the bed. He smiles, looking at her while he dresses. When dressed, and before leaving, he leans over her, kisses her on the forehead. She opens her eyes, she sees him looking at her, and she smiles at him only half opening her eyes.

"Are you leaving already?"

"Yes. I must go now. Maybe I will see you again before I leave the UK. Sleep now, and dream of nice things. Bye, my white Rose."

She watches him as he leaves, before pulling the covers over herself and falling asleep.


She wakes and goes to the lounge. Susie has not arrived yet and she is about to go to her bedroom when she sees a package on the table with a note. She picks it up and reads the note.

*'For my white rose. I hope you like it,'* it reads.

She opens the package and there is the most beautiful necklace and bracelet. She holds it up to the light, where she can see the diamonds sparkling. She walks over to the large mirror, puts the necklace on and cannot believe how marvellous it is. She puts the bracelet on, holding it away from her and moving her wrist. A big grin comes over her face as she looks at herself in the mirror.

"Rosie, you lucky girl."

She puts the presents away before going to bathe.


Some girls have been delivered from Eastern Europe. Ramon has sent some to Leeds, Manchester and Brighton. Paul, Nick and Luke have called Danny to tell him about the girls.

They all seem very happy and Danny is pleased and is looking forward to increasing his earnings. Paul has really got things going now in Leeds and he tells Danny that business could not be better.

Danny gets a call from the Amir.

"Mr Danny, unfortunately I have to leave the UK. I have small problem so please make sure Miss Rosie is okay. I will probably not be back for some time."

"Yes sir, I will make sure she is okay. Hope the problem is not too serious," Danny says, half smiling.

"Too serious? We can sometimes put things right without too much of a problem and sometimes we can't. We will have to wait and see. Goodbye, I will be in touch."

"Goodbye sir."

Danny is thinking of Rosie and now he knows he can visit her without having to worry about the Amir turning up. This makes him feel good and he decides he will call her when he has sorted a few things out regarding the new girls.

Danny is sat watching the television when, on the evening news, he sees there has been a shooting in London, with two people killed and another seriously injured. The police say it was Eastern European gangs. Danny sits up waiting for more information. The area mentioned is not too far from Ramon's place.

Danny is really concerned and does not know whether he should call Ramon. Then he thinks that this is very important and he must call Paul.

"Hi Paul. Have you seen the news? There has been a shooting here in London quite close to Ramon's place. It is said Eastern Europeans are involved and there's a couple dead. I can't call Ramon until I'm sure he is not involved. We better watch out just in case, call Luke and Nick and tell them we don't think it is Ramon involved in the shootings and that we are just being cautious. Tell them to let us know if they have any problems."

Paul is now worried because the last thing they want is any trouble and more so with Eastern European gangsters.

"Dan, do you really think Ramon is involved? It could be anyone. The bloody Eastern Europeans are all over London."

"Yes I know, but remember Ramon arguing with that guy Demetrio? I may be jumping to conclusions and I hope I'm wrong otherwise we're in the shit. Look Paul, do what you have to do and I'll try to get some info. If I find out anything I'll let you know right away."

"Okay Danny, I will tell the others but until we hear from you we will be very careful."

"Be in touch, bye." Danny puts down the phone and is looking rather worried.

Danny is constantly watching the television, waiting to see if there is any further news on the people killed and injured. The police have made an appeal on the television for anyone who can give any information and anyone to come forward who could have been in the area at the time of the shootings.

Danny is afraid; he knows it will be the end if it is Ramon. Their business will be finished and he does not want to lose everything that they have built up. Danny is finding it unbearable waiting and when his phone rings he can't answer it fast enough.

"Hello." He waits for the person to answer. "Danny, it me Ramon."

"Ramon what's been going on? You seen this thing about Eastern Europeans on the news?"

"The bastards try to muscle in on our operation. They try get to me when we were coming back my place. There was a lot of shooting but we okay. It is their people who have problems, we okay. We at another place just in case they have another go. Don't worry Danny; everything is being taken care of. And one thing, Demetrio will not bother us again."
Danny cannot believe how unconcerned he seems.

"Ramon, you've killed a couple of people and you tell me not to worry. I am fucking worried. What do you suggest we do? Surely we cannot just carry on? What if the bastards come looking for us?"

"Danny they know we not a push over. That is if any of Demetrio's friends are still around. I think we okay, our people come together and help each other at time like this. We lay low for now I think soon it quiet down and no one see us run away frightened when shooting started. In a week or so I go away for a while to Romania and we make sure we have no more problem. I speak to a lot of people. So Danny, I call you if there is any problem and until then just carry on, okay?"

"I'm not going to find that easy Ramon. I hope you can guarantee our safety otherwise we will have to stop our operation." Danny is still feeling anxious,

"Yes, yes Danny I make sure you have no trouble. okay."

"I will tell the others. Keep us informed on what's happening."

"Danny, it best you no tell others too much if you know what I mean my friend."

"I understand. I will not call you, you call me Ramon."
"I will speak to you later, goodbye."
"See you Ramon."

# 14
# Aftermath

Danny sits back in his chair unable to believe what has happened. He never for one moment thought he would be involved with people who used guns. Not only that but to have killed people. Well, he just cannot believe what has happened.

He calls Paul and tells him what Ramon has said but tells Paul not to tell the others too much.

The police are on the television saying they understand that the people who were killed had only just entered the country from Romania. The police had asked for anyone with information about them to contact them immediately, adding that they were seeking information from the Romanian authorities.

After a few days pass nothing more is seen or mentioned neither on the television news nor in the newspapers. Danny is hoping things have cooled down now although Ramon has not contacted him again. Still worried, Danny has not been too far away from his flat for quite some time.

Rosie, not hearing from Danny for a long time, was thinking he was not interested in her now. She had been shopping with the girls but had only had a couple of visits from them. At times she gets lonely and she has found it hard to resist the drugs. She had taken a little more cocaine than usual but she is now afraid Danny will know so she knows she has to stop using for a while, just in case he reappears.

Her father had called her and asked her to visit him but she would always come up with some excuse. He still asks about the person she is supposed to be with. Life is boring and she is spending a lot of time on her own. More and more she asks herself whether living in luxury is enough, when she doesn't see anyone and she hasn't any real friends?

All she does is shop for clothes or go to the hairdressers. Since she met Danny she has always wanted Danny to ask her to finish all this, and have a happy life with him, just the two of them. How wonderful that would be. But in reality she knows it just won't happen. It is as though she is being swallowed up into a big dark hole and there is no way of getting out of it.

She has been out shopping, and to the hairdressers for some pampering. She makes her way back to her apartment feeling a bit depressed. She enters the apartment, takes off her coat, and calling to Susie but not hearing her answer she goes to the lounge, and there, stood smiling, is Danny. She is so happy as he walks towards her, puts his arm around her and pulls her to him, kissing her.

"Hello Rosie, you look nice."

She is blushing as she replies, "Thank you. I thought you didn't want to see me."

He pulls her closer.

"Does it look like I didn't want to see you?"

He kisses her again. Susie pops her head around the corner of the door smiling.

"Can I get you anything Miss Rosie?"

"Maybe later Susie. Unless Mr Danny needs anything."

"No. I have been very busy and that's why I haven't called you. Is everything okay?" Danny goes to sit down.

"Yes, I'm okay. You look tired you must have been busy. Are you staying the night?"

Rosie is standing close to him.

"Yes, I think I will." Danny takes hold of her and pulls her on to his knee.

Rosie giggles as he feels her body; wanting to tease him a little she jumps back on her feet.

"You will have to wait. We have all night and I don't want to rush things. Let me get you a drink, you just relax."

Through the evening she does her utmost to please him. He has been rather quiet, not talking a lot and sometimes just sat with his drink in the chair with a worried look on his face. She just sits close to him, not imposing herself on him, and occasionally he looks at her stroking her hair and gives her a faint smile. The evening passes, Rosie and Danny go to the bedroom and their lovemaking is not as passionate as it has been in the past. Danny is laid on top of her, then for no reason he stops and just lays beside her.

"Danny, what's wrong? Is it me?"

"No, no, I have a lot of things on my mind. It's not you Rosie."

He puts his arms around her and kisses her forehead.

"I'm sorry Rosie."

"Danny, you don't have to say you're sorry. I understand. I'm quite happy just being with you."

He kisses her again and they just lay there and soon they are both asleep in each other's arms. The night passes.


When she wakes Danny has gone. He is not beside her, and when she calls his name there is no answer. She goes into the apartment, looks around and realises he is nowhere to be seen. She is a little upset, thinking that maybe he doesn't want her. She remembers how they had made love before and a tear runs down her cheek, as she walks across to a drawer in the bedroom.

She takes out some cocaine; she looks at it then puts some on the side and snorts it. She puts her head back and closes her eyes and stands for a while and then she goes back to her bed, lays down and stares at the ceiling. Eventually, she drifts off to sleep.

Susie wakes her with a drink of coffee.

"Miss Rosie it is eleven o'clock. It is late for you."

"Yes Susie, I'll get up." She has a bit of a headache but manages to take a shower and get dressed, wanting to telephone Danny but thinking better of it. She decides to wait for him to telephone her.

Danny leaves Rosie's apartment and heads back to his own flat not knowing what to do. Not knowing is making things worse and he just cannot relax. Paul and the others have kept things quiet, waiting to hear from Danny over the next couple of weeks. They are now beginning to lose money. Paul telephones Danny complaining about the situation.

Danny gets very angry, telling him, "Look Paul, do you want to finish up in a bastard box? These bastards play it hard. We are better off losing money than being fucking shot dead."

Paul realises what his brother is saying. "Where's Ramon and when will he be in touch?"

Danny shouts down the phone. "I don't fucking know. He could be dead because he hasn't called me. Look, let's give it another week or so then if we haven't heard anything we will have to decide what to do. I don't think I will stay in London if we don't hear from Ramon. It could be very dangerous."

"I understand Danny. You're right, we will do as you say."


A couple of weeks pass before Rosie gets a call from Danny. He explains that he has had to deal with some very important business and says he is sorry for just leaving her without explaining.

He promises to visit her again soon but not at the moment. She does not say too much. She is just pleased to hear from him but feels maybe there could be someone else. Jade has called her a few times. She tells her they have not seen too much of Danny in the last couple of weeks and things have been very quiet, with not a lot of parties.

They organise a get together at Rosie's apartment. Natalia and Monika are complaining. Natalia says, "No parties, no money, this no good."

"There is nothing you can do about it. Danny will sort it out," Rosie tells them.

"Maybe we do some private business? What you say Jade?" Natalia shrugs her shoulders,

"I think we will be in big, big trouble if we do. I think we should just wait until Danny gets things going again."

Natalia looks at Rosie. "You got something to make us feel good, yes?"

She smiles, then goes to her drawer and gives the girls what they want. Soon they are drinking wine and having a laugh. Natalia tells them of some of the men she has been with. Then she looks

Rosie in the eye.

"I like women best. Men just lie on top and bang, bang, bang, then fall off and take cigarette. I want someone like you have Rosie. A nice apartment, plenty money and only bang, bang now and again."

They all burst out laughing. They all enjoy themselves and this has made a change from the boring couple of weeks they have endured.


Danny is feeling less anxious now, as there has been no more news on the shootings. He thinks Ramon is just keeping a low profile for now and hopes to hear from him soon.

Then, out of the blue, he gets a call from Ramon.

"Danny, I'm back in London. I give you my new address and I sort everything now. We should have no problem. My contacts tell me our friends not bother us anymore. We send some girls to Soho, and soon if you want more girls we can deliver." Ramon laughs and adds, "I tell you Ramon take care of problem. How you doing?"

"I'm pleased you telephoned me, I admit I was worried. I will tell Paul and the others to get things up and running properly again. We'll give it a few weeks then look at getting more girls, okay Ramon?"

"Sure, sure Danny, when you ready. I'll call you later."
Ramon gives Danny his new address and they finish their conversation. Danny is now looking forward to bigger and better things; more girls, more money.


Robert Lambert has not told Mandy his girlfriend or Rosie that his business has been getting into difficulties for some time. This is one of the reasons he has not been in contact as much as he should have with Rosie.

Robert has been very worried. He knows that if he cannot raise any funds for his business it will be finished. He has been refused financial help from his bank and has asked numerous business friends if they can help. Unfortunately, he has only received a negative response from them. He contacts one of his old business friends who he thinks may help him. He lives close to Leeds, and Robert leaves for a meeting with him knowing that he has exhausted all other channels.

On his way there he thinks of what has happened over the last couple of years. This all seems to have happened following the breakdown of his marriage. He has been used to being on his own since both his parents died; he did receive a small inheritance from his parents but that soon went after putting it straight into his business.

He sits for some time outside his contact's office. Going over and over what he will tell him to try to persuade him to invest in his company, he takes a deep breath then makes his way into the office.

After one hour he leaves the office with nothing. He is so depressed. He was told there was not much left to invest in, and that it was not worth giving money knowing that it would not be too long before more money would be needed.

Robert never thought he would be in this position. He is not really concentrating on his driving, his mind is in turmoil and suddenly a large lorry pulls out in front of him. He tries to brake, but the car does not stop and finishes underneath the lorry, with the lorry dragging the car up the road before coming to a stop.

Vehicles stop and people get out to help, the emergency services are called. Unfortunately no one can help him because of the position of the vehicle. When the emergency vehicles arrive they take a long time before they finally get to him and are able to free him. When they see he is in a very bad way the medics try to take care of him until he is taken away by helicopter to Leeds Infirmary.

Mandy is at home when a policeman arrives and tells her what has happened. Mandy is in shock. All she wants to do is get to him. She knows she must contact Rosie. After trying a couple of times and getting no answer she leaves for the infirmary. She is told it does not look good and that they are doing all they can. She cannot see him for quite sometime and when she does see him she is in shock. She has to contact Rosie. She tries and tries and then finally Rosie answers her phone.

## 15

# Daddy's Girl

It has been very quiet for Rosie. Her father has been calling her occasionally, asking how she is and if everything is okay. But she has not heard from him for a week or so, which is unusual. Then out of the blue she gets a call from Mandy.

"Rosie... I have been trying to contact you for a long time. Something has happened."

Mandy starts to cry. She can hardly talk. Rosie can tell by the way she is speaking something is wrong.

"Mandy what's wrong? Where is dad?"

Mandy takes a deep breath before answering.

"He has been in a car accident. He is at the Leeds Infirmary and has some serious injuries. He is in intensive care. You must come Rosie." Mandy is crying and now unable to speak.

Rosie is also crying. "I'll come Mandy. I'll come as soon as I can. I will telephone you when I leave. Please let me know if anything happens."

Mandy composes herself a little. "Yes, I'll let you know. Please hurry Rosie."

"I have to go now Mandy. I have to call someone."

Rosie puts the phone down. She thinks to herself, *'first it was my mother and now my father. Oh my god I hope he is all right'*. She calls Danny and when he answers she is so upset.

"Danny," Rosie is crying.

"What's wrong Rosie? Why are you crying?"

"It's my father Danny. I have to go to him; he is in intensive care after being in a serious car accident. He is in Leeds

Infirmary."

Danny thinks, shit, what can happen? He tries to calm her down.

"Okay Rosie. Look, calm down; get the Amir's driver to drive you to Leeds. Go when you can, and keep in touch with Paul."

"Thank you Danny, I will."

"And Rosie, I hope he is okay. You get going."

"Bye Danny."

She organises the driver to pick her up and in the meantime she calls Jade and tells her what has happened and that she is leaving shortly to go to her father.

Soon she is on her way. Mandy asks her when she will be in Leeds and tells her that she will meet her at the infirmary. She tells Rosie her father was on business in Leeds when the accident occurred. Rosie cannot help thinking *'what else can go wrong?'*. She is praying that her father will be okay.

After a journey that seems to take hours she arrives at the infirmary, where Mandy is waiting. Mandy runs to Rosie and puts her arms around her crying.

"Oh Rosie."

Rosie starts to cry herself as Mandy takes her hand and takes her to her father. Rosie is shocked when she sees him. He is laid with his eyes closed. Rosie cries uncontrollably. She takes his hand she whispers in his ear.

"Daddy I'm here, I'm here." She is unable to hold back the tears.

Mandy just stands shaking and looking at him, with her hands to her mouth and biting on her fingers in an effort to control herself. Rosie just sits alongside him, looking at his swollen face with tubes running up his nose, and other things attached to his chest.

It is a long time before the nurse can persuade Rosie to move from his side and out of the room so the doctor can talk to her.

"Miss Lambert, the doctor will be here shortly. He will talk to you."

"Will my father pull through this? Please tell me he will."

The nurse takes her hand. "The doctor will tell you. I know it is difficult but please be patient."

"Miss Lambert," the doctor says as he walks up to them.

"Yes, that's me," says Rosie.

"We are doing everything we can for your father but he has multiple injuries. I can tell you that the head injuries could mean he will never be the same again."

Rosie grabs hold of Mandy. "Oh no, no."

"It does not look too good at the moment. Your father is in a very bad way. We will know more in a few days when we bring him out of the induced coma. I'm so sorry Miss Lambert but that's all I can tell you at the moment."

Everyone is quiet and the doctor turns to leave. Mandy and Rosie just stand, holding each other and crying.

They spend the next few hours at his bedside. The nurse tells them to go home and take a rest, as they cannot do anything there. Mandy manages to persuade Rosie to go home with her to her father's house.


After some hours at her father's, Rosie is now calm enough to ask Mandy exactly what happened. Mandy tells her, "A lorry pulled out of a road and your dad could not avoid it. He ran underneath it. The firemen took a long time getting him out and he had to be flown to the infirmary by helicopter."

Again, Mandy starts to cry.

"Oh Rosie, what are we going to do?"

She is crying herself. "What can we do? We can just pray for dad. And hope, that's all we can we've got."

Rosie is unable to sleep through the night thinking about her father.

The next morning she is sat with Mandy and asks her about her father's business.

"Mandy, who is looking after my father's business?"

"As far as I know your dad's secretary, Jean, has been seeing to things. Don't you worry I will check it out later for you."

Rosie is thinking about her father, then her mother and can't believe how this has happened to both of them.

What is she going to do? She knows Danny will be

checking on her, but she feels she cannot leave her father as he is at the moment, even if Danny asks her to. What if the Amir comes to London and Danny tells her to go back? She decides she will just refuse to go until she sees just what happens regarding her father. They visit the hospital each day. Things are just the same, though. They are waiting for him to be brought out of the induced coma and hoping it will be good news.

They leave to visit her father at the hospital. Once on the ward the nurse sees them and comes to them.

"Miss Lambert, the consultant thinks your father may be brought out of the induced coma later today. Now, whether he will respond immediately we just don't know. We may have to be very patient."

She feels a little relieved and cannot wait; she is desperately hoping her father will be his normal self. Mandy and Rosie sit with him all day, talking to him as he lays in a coma and only occasionally going out of his room.

The nurse comes to them again and asks for them to leave the room as the consultant is on his way. They leave the room and are full of anxiety as they wait to hear how things have gone.

As they sit waiting they do not say much. Occasionally Rosie looks across at Mandy, who is sat biting her nails. It seems like hours before the consultant enters the room; they both stand up waiting for him to speak. Rosie senses it is not good news.
The consultant pauses for a while. Then he says, "Well, he is now breathing without any help. He is awake and his eyes are open, but he is not responding to anything at all. Things may get better or worse. We will wait and see. To be perfectly honest with you he may remain in the state he is in now.
They both are crying again and holding one another.

"Please can we see him now?"

"Yes, the nurse will take you in. I'll see you tomorrow."
The consultant leaves as they both go back to her father's room. He is laid with his eyes open but he seems to be looking into space.
Rosie leans over him and, from a very close distance, she looks into his eyes.

"Dad I'm here. Can you hear me?"

There is no response at all; she repeats the question over and over again but there is still no response. She sits down holding his hand. Mandy does the same and gets the same response. Mandy looks at Rosie not knowing what to do.

They stay for a few more hours. The nurse suggests that they go home for a rest, as they cannot do anything. They leave, holding on to one another for comfort.

When they get home Rosie says that they should discuss what they should do if the worst happens. They will speak with her dad's secretary tomorrow.

The next day Rosie calls her father's office, and the secretary Jean answers.

"Jean, it's Rosie."

Jean pauses for a while then asks, "What's happening Rosie? How is he? The hospital would not tell me anything with me not being family."

She explains to her just what has happened and that they do not think there is likely to be much of a change in his condition.

Jean says, "I don't know what to do. Your dad's business is in trouble. We are having trouble paying invoices which seem to come in all the time, and the bank will not release any cash."

Rosie is surprised as she always thought he had a good business.

"How long has this been going on?"

"A long time. It has gradually got worse over the last year," she tells Rosie in a quiet voice.

"Just how much do you need?"

Jean coughs, and then says, "At least £25,000."

Rosie is stunned. She cannot believe it. "£25,000? My god, could we possibly sell the business? Is it worth anything or do we walk away from it?"

"No, there is not much to sell. I suppose we could just close down or even go insolvent. With your father being in the condition he is you would have to get advice from a solicitor about how it can be done."

She asks, "Close down? I will be in touch with you

tomorrow."

Jean says she will do what she can and wait for her call.

She explains to Mandy what Jean has told her, and asks, "Did you know the company was in trouble?"

"No, your dad never told me anything."

"Is the house paid for?"

Mandy says, "I do know money is owed on it but just how much I don't know."

Rosie has to pull herself together.

She knows she can raise money on her jewellery and she can raise other cash but she thinks she best hold on to that, as she may need it to pay for her father's future care.


The next day she sends Mandy to the hospital while she makes some enquiries with her father's solicitor.

Rosie tells Mandy, "You go to the hospital and call me if there is any change with dad. I will come later. I'll take a taxi and see you there."

Mandy agrees and leaves in her car for the hospital.

She speaks to her father's solicitor, who tells her he had told her father his business was in trouble and tells Rosie that the house is mortgaged to the hilt. It is explained that the best thing would be to sell the house and close the business down as soon as possible. She is shocked at what he has told her, and asks if he can take things in hand as she does not know how to proceed, given that her father is in no fit state to see to his affairs. He says he will and will keep in touch.

She is on her way to the hospital. Her head is in turmoil with the worry about her father, his business, and Danny. She is afraid that she may get trouble from Danny. As she arrives at the hospital she is about to leave the taxi when her phone rings. As she guessed it is Danny calling and she answers the phone.

"Hello Danny."

"Rosie, what's happening? When are you coming back? I have heard the Amir may be coming in a few days?"

She plucks up the courage and tells him about her father. There is a dead silence, and then he says,

"Look Rosie, I need you back here as soon as possible.

You don't want to f**k everything up, do you? You best get something sorted out regarding your father. I will expect you back here in two days, do you hear?"

Danny is very angry with her even though he knows about her situation.

She is upset and says, "Okay Danny, I'll be back."

"Good," he says, and the phone goes off.

She goes into the hospital and joins Mandy. As she arrives Mandy is holding her father's hand.

Mandy sees Rosie and explains, "Rosie, I was just going to phone you. They told me he will not be able to communicate and he could finish his life in this state. Oh Rosie, what can we do?"

She is crying as she goes to her father and holds him.

"I'll take care of him. I'll find somewhere he can be cared for. I have some money. Mandy, the house has to go, and his business is nothing. I will arrange for him to go to a care home. Only the best, of that I am certain. I have to go back to London soon - probably tomorrow or the next day - and you will have to move out of the house. Have you somewhere to go and live?"

"Yes, I can go back to my mother's, that's not a problem," she says.

"Mandy, you can make sure dad is settled in the home when I go back to London. You will do that for me won't you?"

"Rosie, you don't have to ask me that. I love your father so of course I will."

Rosie is very upset just looking at her father and it makes her cry. He seems to just be looking into space; he is not able to speak or recognise anyone. In the late evening, before they leave, she talks with the consultant. He tells her they will monitor him, for a week or two, then, if they agree, he can go to a home where he can be cared for.

They leave for home. She knows Danny will be phoning her at any time, and she remembers May and thinks that while she is in Leeds she will telephone her.

She rings her mobile number.

"Yes, hello."

"It's me, Rosie. How are you? I thought I would let you know I'm in Leeds at the moment. May?"

"Rosie, nice to hear from you. Why are you in Leeds? And will you have time for us to get together?"

"I'll tell you why I'm here, May. My dad has been in a terrible accident. I will tell you more about it when we meet."

"Oh, I'm so sorry Rosie. Can I do anything for you?"

"No, not at the moment. Can you get away okay, say tomorrow afternoon, without any problem? Don't get yourself into trouble because of me. I know only too well how difficult it is."

"You mean Paul? He can be a shit but don't worry, I'll sort out a place where we can meet"

She tells her to meet her at one of their old haunts at two o'clock the next day.

"Okay Rosie. Rosie, I have to go. Two o'clock then," whispers May, before the line goes dead.

She is so pleased she has been able to contact May. Once, before all this with Danny and Paul started, she was a good friend.

Her father's solicitor tells her he is seeing to everything and he has sorted the sale of the house. He reminds them not to worry about any of this, and that he will keep in contact with her to let her know what is happening.

She goes to her father the next morning. She sits with him holding his hand. He seems to be looking at her. She smiles.

"Dad, I'm here for you. I know you can hear me. I'll take care of you."

She puts her head in her hands and cries. Mandy comes into the room. They sit and talk for a while before Rosie has to go off to meet May.

May is sat waiting for Rosie. As she sees her she cries out.

"Rosie, over here. Look at you. No wonder you pull all the good men."

May has a big smile on her face.

They hug each other then sit down. Rosie tells May

everything that has happened to her, including the Amir, and what has happened to her since she left Leeds. She also tells her what happened to Jayne. May is shocked and is now afraid, thinking that it could happen to her if Paul dumps her. He has threatened her a couple of times because of her drug taking.

"That sodding Paul. I thought the sun shone out of his arse. But I know I have to watch out. The other girls are shit scared of him."

"Is it just the same? The sex parties, and different men all the time?" Rosie asks.

May gives a kind of smirk. "Parties? Are you kidding? Anything goes; you name it we do it. I don't care anymore, I just think of the money. You know the old saying Rosie, lay back and think of England. Well I think it's something like that. My parents have never had it so good and they don't give a shit. I think me, and them; better make hay while the sun shines. I will bail out if I get a sniff of anything happening. You know, like happened to Jayne."

Although Rosie is unhappy about everything she has to laugh at May. She never changes.

"May, you be very careful. Some of the people who Paul and Danny are involved with are very dangerous. They can get very nasty."

"Oh! Don't worry, I will Rosie. When I do go no one will find me if I decide to take off."

"Will you... if you get the chance can you help me out in moving my dad when the time comes? I may not be able to get to Leeds. I think I may have found a place for him. All I have to do is tell them when dad is going."

"Just let me know Rosie. I'll help if I can."

"My dad's partner Mandy said she would help also. But I need someone else just in case."

"Don't worry. Keep in touch, I'll do what I can."

Rosie tells May she must not tell Paul she has spoken to her. Then they go their separate ways.

Rosie has been busy looking for a nice place for her father to go to. She can pay money if the fees are needed upfront. The solicitor will take charge of the sale of the house and business. This takes a lot off her mind. She feels she has seen to everything. All she is worried about now is her father. Will he ever get better than he is now?

She spends a few hours with her father. Mandy knows what is happening and Rosie tells her to contact her if there are any problems. After they return to her father's house she collects any personal things that she can. She has been through and sorted a lot of the paperwork that she has found. She has paid the outstanding bills that needed to be paid. She thinks to herself *'thank god for the Amir's credit card'*. She is hoping he does not say anything about the money she is spending when they next meet.

She is on her way back to London and wondering what will happen next. She has amazed herself because her drug use has been so low since she left London. But sat in the car returning to the capital city she feels that she needs something. She takes something from her bag, swallows it and lies back, waiting for the high to kick in.

She arrives at her apartment. As usual Susie is happy to see her.

"Oh Miss Rosie. How your father?"

"Not too good Susie. Any messages for me?"

"Only Mr Danny. He came round, he never say much, he look around and, after maybe 30 minutes, he leave."

She wonders what he was looking for. Why did he come round to the apartment when he knew she was not there? She thinks, *'my jewellery'*.

Rosie goes to where she has stashed the jewellery, knowing it would be very difficult for Danny to find it. She's right, it is still there.

She gets unpacked and is almost sorted out when her phone goes.

"Hello."

"Ha! Rosie, you're back. I'm pleased, I will come and see you tonight okay?"

"Yes Danny, it's okay."

"How are things with your father? Not so good I gather?"

"No, not good." Rosie starts to cry.

"These things happen in life Rosie. You have to be

strong."

There is a silence before he talks again.

"Rosie, are you there?"

She pulls herself together. "Yes."

"Okay. I'll see you tonight."

The conversation is finished. She goes to freshen up. She guesses what he is coming for.

Although she does not want any sex she knows that once he touches her she will give herself to him.

## 16
# Taking Care Of Business

Danny had been to Rosie's apartment checking things out. He was worried that he would come across a huge stash of drugs. He is still suspicious of her excessive drug taking. He had talked to Paul who had been checking on things in Leeds. Paul had given him information on Rosie's father, and had been able to tell him about her whereabouts while she was there. Paul knew of the meeting with May and Rosie but did not read anything into it, aside from that they had been friends at uni.

Danny tells Paul that they must get things running like they were before the troubles with the Romanians.

"If not more girls than before. How are the new girls? Are they all doing what is expected of them?" asks Danny.

"I was going to tell you. One girl, one of the newcomers, was going to do a runner but the other girls told me. She has been taken care of. I gave her a good talking to, if you know what I mean, and a few more drugs to help her be a bit more loyal. Oh and that friend of Rosie, you know the one that was at uni with her, well although she will do anything, and I mean anything, she's piling on the weight. Of course some of the punters love fat girls but unfortunately she is not taking care of herself, and is getting too bloody rounded. She is partial to a few more drugs than the others. I will give her a little more time then we may have to send her to Soho."

"That's okay with me. Don't let our standards drop, whatever you do."

"Don't worry bro, I won't," Paul says rather confidently.

"By the way, I will call Ramon for more girls in the next

couple of weeks. He tells me everything will be okay with those Romanian bastards. I'll call you in a day or two unless anything comes up before. See you Paul."

Rosie is waiting for Danny to arrive. She has always been very smart, and her beauty remains exceptional. Danny comes into the apartment, and sees no one. She is in the bedroom when he calls out, "Rosie?"

She hears his voice and hurriedly goes to greet him. As she enters the lounge he is stood looking at her, unable to take his eyes off her.

"Rosie, you get more beautiful every time I see you."
She smiles at him. "You tell me that every time you see me. You're embarrassing me Danny."

He holds his hands out to her, she walks towards him and he takes hold of her, pulling her close to him. Her body is limp with just that touch. She wants him more than ever. She thinks *'how could I not want him? I love him'*.
He kisses her then runs his hands over her bottom, squeezing it. He moves her just slightly away from him. He looks into her eyes then kisses her. She holds him tight now. She can feel he is aroused. This makes her want him more. They stand there kissing for a few minutes then she takes him by the hand, and leads him to the bedroom.

No words are spoken; they do not have to speak. Clothes are scattered on the floor as they hurriedly undress. Danny now slowly, but with confidence, takes her to those places she has only ever experienced with him. Their passion is much more than bodies touching. It is coming from within, with exceptional bursts of pleasure throughout the night, and into the early morning. Never tiring of one another and waiting for the next wave of desire. Then they are ready to start all over again. They eventually fall asleep. The next thing they hear is Susie opening the bedroom door.

"Miss Rosie?"
She can't apologise enough when she sees Danny in bed with her. She quickly closes the door.
Rosie leans across and kisses Danny. He smiles at her and she leaps out of bed naked, grabs hold of her dressing gown, looks

back at Danny and asks, "You want a drink darling? Coffee, tea? What would you like?"

"Coffee Rosie. But seeing you like that I would like a bit more of what I had last night."

"You best have a rest just in case you decide to stay tonight," she says, laughing.

They get themselves freshened up and she explains to Danny what has happened to her father and how difficult it has been, but that she has sorted things out the best she could. Danny listens but does not really show too much interest.

He is more interested in her being ready for the Amir, who will be arriving at the weekend.

"He will probably contact you and let you know where and when he will see you."

She feels disappointed with Danny and wonders how he can want her and then let her go, not only with the Amir but also all the others.

After making several phone calls he tells her that he cannot stay tonight. In fact, he has to leave more or less right away as he has some very important business. He kisses her on her forehead, picks a slice of toast off the table and leaves. Again, she feels so let down. If only it was just he and she, how wonderful it would be. From the very first day she saw him she just wanted him and there had never been anyone else that she has thought the same about.

Later that day she calls the girls. Jade answers the phone.

"Hi Rosie, how are things going with your father?"

She tells her the full story about what happened, and what she has to do for her father. Jade is very sympathetic.

"You poor darling. What you have been through in the past few months, first your mother and then your father. Well, I just don't know how you have coped."

"How are Natalia and Monika? Are they around?" she asks.

"Yes, just a minute I'll call them."

"Rosie my darling, how you are?" Natalia says she is her usual bubbly self.

She does not want to go through the entire story about her father again. She tells Natalia, "Oh not too bad. How are you lot? What have you been doing? I bet you've been up to no good again with them dirty old men?"

"You joke, all men dirty. Always want to be in where they all came out of." She starts to giggle.
Rosie is laughing now.

"Oh Natalia, where do you get your sayings from? You do make me laugh."

"My sayings? What you mean? I learn good English from clients, bend down, take this, and move faster, I learn very fast, yes. Men usually come and then go if you know what I mean. Anyway, who cares Rosie? We get the money, they get satisfied and every one is happy."

All the girls want to get together but Rosie tells them they will have to wait until the Amir has gone back. Jade asks Rosie to let them know when she can see them and then the conversation ends.


Danny informs Rosie that the Amir will be in the UK the next day and that she should be ready for him, either at her apartment or be available if he should send for her. She knows she must look her very best for him. She is afraid that something may be said about the money she spent on the care home for her father.

Mandy is supposed to inform her on a regular basis what is happening, in order to put her mind at rest. Unfortunately, Rosie has been unable to contact her. She thinks she must be busy with something. The hospital has told her that her father is still in the hospital. Everyone there is seeing that he is comfortable, and will only let him be moved when they are satisfied that he his ready for the upheaval. They say it could be in a few days. Rosie is satisfied at this news but a bit concerned, as she has not spoken to Mandy. She knows the care home thinks he is able to go and that they will give him the best care available.

Late the next afternoon she gets a call from the Amir's secretary telling her the vehicle will come for her around seven o'clock that evening. She is ready and just before the car is about to arrive she gathers her bags. She stops to look in the mirror, smooth's her dress over her bottom, fluffs her hair up, and looks closely at her face thinking, *'do I see a wrinkle or two around my eyes? Could it be the drugs?'* She leans even closer; inspects the lines on her face, that shouldn't be there at her age.

She takes a pill or two just to make her feel more relaxed. The doorbell rings. Susie answers the door. The chauffeur comes into the room, he takes her small bags, and she then follows him down to the Rolls after telling Susie to take care of everything.

They are soon in the Amir's suite. As she enters there is a strong smell of incense. It is not an unpleasant smell but is quite strong. She is greeted by Mia, who treats her so much differently now in comparison to when they first met.
Mia gives her a big smile.

"Please follow me Miss Rosie."
She is taken to the usual place. Mia has already prepared her bath, and the towels and her robe are all laid out. Mia asks her this time, "Can I assist you?" She is calm and pleasant.

"Of course I would appreciate your help, Mia." Rosie smiles back at her.
Mia helps her to undress. She is now naked and gets into the very large Jacuzzi. While she is bathing herself she is thinking about all the work she has to put in to look her best and how stupid it is, because every day you have to start again.

When she is finished bathing Mia holds the towel up for her. As Rosie gets out of the Jacuzzi, Mia wraps the towel around Rosie, and then starts to dry her before motioning for her to follow her to the bench. It is covered in white towels. Mia helps her to lie down and makes her comfortable.

Rosie is completely naked now as Mia rubs different oils into her skin. She is so relaxed and she enjoys Mia massaging, and rubbing the oils on her body. Mia's hands are so gentle as she rubs the oil all over. Mia's hands move up and down her body, sometimes just stopping in one place. She then makes a circular movement with just her fingers. Rosie finds this so very erotic. When Mia is finished she helps her dress in the white silk robe. She does her hair for her, and then spays her with a most wonderful smelling perfume.

"There Miss Rosie, come this way and I will tell the Amir you are ready to see him now."

Rosie follows her again. She is left in a room on her own, waiting for Mia to come back. Then soon she comes back to her, telling her to go with her again. She knows where they are going. Soon she is entering the Amir's bedroom, and Mia leaves her there telling her to make herself comfortable. After a minute or two the Amir comes in. He looks at Rosie and smiles.

"Come here, my dear," he says, holding both hands out to her.

She walks across to him. She stands in front of him and he takes her hand and kisses it gently.

While still holding her hand he kisses her forehead then asks, "How have you been my dear? Have you had everything you needed, no problems I hope?"

"Everything has been fine sir," Rosie says, feeling embarrassed and not finding it easy to make conversation.

The Amir lets go of her hand. He walks across to the very large cushions scattered on the floor. He sits down then lays back on them. He beckons her to come to him.

She sits close. He is very quiet, and then he tells her, "My little white Rose, I have missed you so very much. I am always happy to come to England knowing that I will see you."

She looks at him closely. His dark eyes, his greying beard, his long dark hair and his tanned skin. She finds him a very attractive, mature man. She is feeling a little more relaxed now; she does manage to have a conversation with him. He asks about her family but she gets very upset while telling him. She is thinking of her father and what has happened. He looks very concerned.

"Why are you crying my dear?"

She explains what happened to her father. She has tried to not cry but she cannot help herself. He sees how upset she is. He knows everything about her dad and the accident. He tries to console her.

"Don't cry. Where is he now?" he says, while wiping her tears with the handkerchief he has in his hand.

She has told him everything but is thinking now that she should not have told him about her father. If Danny found out he would kill her. She never thought the Amir would respond like he has.

"You will not have to worry my little one. Your father will be well taken care of."

She can see he is sincere and wonders what he will do. She feels a load has been lifted off her mind. She thinks she must please him. She has so much respect for him. They talk of many things. He asks more about her family. She tells him only what she dare tell him. She does not want him to know how she first got to be involved with Danny.

She is wondering when he will be wanting her to have sex. He does not seem to be in any hurry. A woman servant dressed in robes comes in with various foods and fruit drinks. He is eating and drinking while talking to her. Rosie just picks at a little bit of the food. It must have been an hour or two since she first joined him. He leaves the room for a short period before coming back to her. He smiles at her as he walks over to the bed. He just sits at the end of the bed. She is sat watching him, waiting for him to say something.

"Come," he says.

She goes to him and stands in front of him. He starts to undo the buttons on her robe, exposing her beautiful body. His warm hands stroke and caress her breasts. He kisses her nipples and then slowly moves his hand down between her legs. His eyes are half closed as he feels her; she closes her eyes and all she can think about at this moment is Danny and what they did the last night they spent together. She is imagining it is him who is caressing her.

The Amir takes her hand. He places it on his now erect penis. She moves her hand slowly, letting him enjoy what she is doing to him. He slowly takes her hand, stopping her, and then he lays on the bed. He is looking up at her as he pats the bed alongside him. She moves to lay with him. His robe is open. He is naked as he pulls her to him then, in a whisper.

He says, "Pleasure me my little one."

Through the night he just lays with her, not demanding any more sex. She just keeps taking small naps, thinking he may want more. Next thing she knows it is daylight and he is about to leave. He tells her she can stay with him for the next two nights and that if she needs anything at all she should tell one of the servants.

The next two nights are more or less the same. They spend a lot of time talking and afterwards he just wants the same company and no actual sex. She thinks he is so easily pleased. All the time she is there, anything she needs is there too, and always someone there to see she gets it.

The Amir talks to her on the last night that they spend together.

"You should not want for anything. I have taken care of everything. No more worries about your father. I have a small present for you."

He hands Rosie a small box.

"Take it, and open it," he says, watching her closely.

She takes it from him and opens it; inside there is the most beautiful ring with a very large diamond, which is glittering in the light. She takes it from the box and places it on her finger.

"You like?" he smiles, seeing her response.

"Oh yes, it's beautiful. Oh thank you," she says, as she looks at the ring.

She leans towards him. She is about to kiss him, then she checks herself thinking he may not like it. Then she decides to throw caution to the wind and kisses him on his cheek. The Amir gives her a big smile, showing his very white teeth. He runs his hand through her hair.

"You bring so much joy to me little one. I like to see you happy, not sad."

She so much wants to please him for his generosity but he asks for so very little from her. In the morning, the Amir tells her to give his assistant all the information he needs on her father, where she wants him to be and all of the necessary details. He comes to see her before she leaves.

"I leave today. You take care and I will see you in a month or so. Maybe you can visit me in Qatar. Anyway, we will see." He takes her hand and kisses it before leaving.

She is ready to leave for her own apartment when the Amir's assistant comes to see her. He asks her where she would like her father to be, whether in a Leeds or London hospital or home. He asks what his health problems are. She explains everything to him, telling him if he could be brought to London she would be able to visit him without any problems.

Once he has all the information he tells her he will contact the hospital where he is at the moment, and tell them a private ambulance will go for him and he will brought to a private hospital in London, or a nursing home. She is so happy knowing that her father will be close to her.

When she is back in her flat she phones Mandy again. And again she is unable to contact her. She wanted to tell Mandy where her father is going but she gets no answer. She wonders what is happening. She calls the hospital and asks to speak with the nurse looking after her father.

"I am sorry I have had to telephone you, but could you tell me how my father is? Mr Lambert?"

The nurse tells Rosie, "Not much of a change but he can leave the hospital as long as he is going to a good nursing home. Somewhere we discussed when you were last here."

"Someone will be contacting you shortly to arrange for my father to be brought to London to a very nice home or private hospital where he will get all the care he needs. Could I ask if my father's partner Mandy has been to see my father since I was last there?'

"No, Miss Lambert. I'm sorry to say that nobody has been to see him for a couple of days now."

She is concerned. Surely she hasn't abandoned her father, not now of all times.

"Well, thank you for your help. Could I give you my number and if possible can you call me if there are any problems?'

"That's no problem. Give me your number," says the nurse.

She gives her number and when she puts the phone down she sits for a while thinking about Mandy and if she has gone and left him. Or maybe she has not been able to go to see him for some reason or other. But there again why has she not answered her phone? She decides to give Mandy another call. She tries again and again without any success. She is so disappointed that she calls May.

"Oh May. I think my dad's partner has just left him. I have not heard from her. Dad is going to be moved to London. We don't know when exactly but I know that wherever he goes the place will have everything he needs."

"Rosie, that Mandy must be a real shit to leave your dad now. But it's great news about your dad going to London, and being near to you. How did you manage that? You must be loaded?"

She gives a little laugh then says, "The Amir is seeing to it. He is paying for everything."

"Sodding hell, Rosie. Has he got a brother who likes big women?" she says, laughing.

"May, you would not believe what a marvellous man he is," she tells May, sounding very serious.

"I don't know about a marvellous man. You must be shagging his head off for him to look after you the way he is."

"No, he is really nice, and a caring man. He has gone back to Qatar, so I'm on my own for a while, that is if Danny doesn't visit me. Could you go and see dad May, just to see he is okay?"

"Yes I'll go today. I'll call you if I find out anything about that lousy shit that has left your father."

"Thanks May, I really appreciate it.'

She relaxes at her apartment. She has not heard from Danny for a couple of days. The girls are going to visit her when they can and she is looking forward to seeing them. May has phoned her, telling her there has been no change. Her father is as well as can be expected and will be moved within the next 24 hours. And there has still been no sign of Mandy.

She is waiting to find out from the Amir's man where her father is going so she can visit him. It is not long after that she gets a call from the Amir's man. He tells her, "Your father will be moved very shortly to a private Nuffield hospital, in Queens Street close to Oxford Circus, and he will have a private suite. They will call you when he is settled in. You can visit him whenever you want. If you need anything Miss Rosie you can call this number. Whatever it is will be seen to immediately."

196

He gives her the number to call.

"Thank you for your help. I really appreciate it," she says, feeling more relaxed and knowing that her father is being taken care of.

"I am here to help you. Goodbye for now," he says.

She is so happy. He has given her the number to call if she needs anything. She can soon visit her father now. She knows he could not be in a better place, and he will have all the necessary care he requires and people to look after him. She telephones Jade and tells her about her father and what the Amir has done for her. Jade tells Rosie how lucky she is to be in the position she is in.

# 17
# The Cost Of Living

Ramon has asked Danny to go to see him. Danny goes to visit Ramon thinking it is about more girls because things have been getting back to normal. He notices the place Ramon has moved into is nothing like his last place. It is not in a good area of London.

As he arrives, the usual people are about but they seem a lot more tentative than usual. Victor greets him before taking him to Ramon; Ramon is sat talking to some man as Danny enters the room.

"Hello Danny, come sit down." Ramon stands up and shakes his hand then introduces the man.

"Danny, this is Mikael my friend." Danny shakes his hand, wondering who he is. "Mikael speaks very little English. He is Romanian. He has a few people in London who help some of our people with protection when and if needed."

Ramon says something to the man in his own language; he just sits there until Ramon turns to speak to him,

"My friend, I know I tell you our problems have been taken care of but since we last speak we hear certain people are still, shall we say wanting cut from our operation, we may need Mikael to provide extra muscle if we need it. And, of course, this will cost money...so... the girls... the girls will cost you more money, plus the protection."

He stops talking, waiting for Danny's reaction.

"I thought everything was sorted now but obviously it isn't. Just how much are we talking about?"

There is a silence. Ramon looks at the other man and then back to Danny, he strokes his chin with his hand.

"Well... five thousand extra."

"Five thousand extra for what? A year, a month a week, what?" Danny says, not happy at all.

"Five thousand a month. Protection and delivery of girls when required."

"Every month? You're kidding." Danny gives a sarcastic laugh.

With that Ramon jumps up. He bangs the table with his hand.

"You get girls fucking cheap, you want these bastards shoot you? You make plenty money. Five thousand or your business stop. You tell me what you want? More nice girls? Or some of the shit from here in UK? Tell me, tell me."

Mikael is looking at Danny with a scowl on his face. Danny has nowhere to go; he is boxed in a corner. He has to say yes otherwise he will have to watch his every move and probably be put out of business in a bloody week. He has never seen Ramon as angry as he is just now. He wants to settle things down for now and get out of here as soon as he can.

"Okay, okay five thousand a month with a guarantee we can see our protection and we can turn down any girls that are not good enough."

Ramon's attitude changes immediately.

"Dan...ny. We don't want to fall out, do we?"

Danny feels he is being told, not asked, "We start the payments next month Ramon."

"No, no, no. Payments start now." Ramon stares at Danny.

"I don't have five thousand in my pocket for god's sake." Ramon taps his fingers on the table for a few seconds before looking at Danny.

"Okay, okay tomorrow."

Danny cannot get out of the place fast enough. He says to Ramon, "Tomorrow then, late tomorrow."

"We are waiting Danny. You won't let me down, no," Ramon says, tapping the arm of his chair.

"No, I'll get the money. I best be going now." Danny gets up not feeling too happy at all.

"Oh come Danny. You stay for drink. We have nice girls?' Ramon, smiling, calls, "Alexi, come."
A very nice girl comes into the room half dressed. She walks up to Ramon and puts her hand on his shoulder as she smiles at Danny.

"No, Ramon I have to go."

"How about Alexi giving us show before you go? What you say?" he says, squeezing Alexi's bottom.

"I really have to go Ramon." He stands up, shakes hands with both of them and leaves. Once outside he takes a deep breath. A couple of heavies are stood smoking outside. Danny thinks, *'God we're in the shit,'* before driving away.


Danny arrives home and immediately calls Paul; Paul picks up his phone.

"Hello."

"We're in the shit. Fucking Ramon wants more money. Some for the payment for protection from the same fucking Romanians we are suppose to not be bothering with again. Now hear this, he wants five grand extra a month for the girls, and the protection."
There is a deathly silence before Paul answers.

"Five grand? That will take a chunk of our profits. When does he want it?"

"Tomorrow and not a day later. We won't be able to continue like this. I can see that prick Ramon upping the price again very soon again. He will not be happy until he bleeds us dry."
Paul pauses a moment before answering.

"Looks like we can't trust him. Maybe we could look for another source?" Paul says, showing his frustration.

"Another source? Not possible," says Danny. "Ramon would never let us do that without some repercussions. Look, we pay for now and try to sort something out. I'll call him and let him think we'll go along with what he wants. In the meantime get them girls working and try and get more business to up our take, okay?"

"Will do Danny. Talk later, see you."

After speaking to the others in Manchester and Brighton he tries to relax but all Danny can think about is how he can get himself out of this mess with Ramon. He feels Ramon is taking him for a ride and fears things may get worse. He thinks of Rosie and decides to go to see her.

Rosie gets news that her father is in the hospital in Queens Street. She tells Susie where she is going and if there are any calls or messages to take the names and tell her when she gets back.

She takes a cab to the hospital. When she arrives she is very impressed. Everything is so immaculate and the staff are very professional. As she entered the building she was asked her name and was immediately taken to her father's room.

Rosie stands for a while, looking at her father who is sat in a wheelchair near to the window, just looking out with a vague look on his face. She walks across to him. His eyes do not move as she takes his hand.

"Daddy, daddy." There is not a lot of response. She sits close to him, pushing his hair back and kissing him on his forehead.

The nurse comes in asking if she needs anything and makes sure her father is comfortable.

Rosie knows there is nothing they can do. She thinks it goes to prove that no matter how much money you have sometimes it can make no difference at all. She spends a couple of hours with him before leaving for her flat.

Danny arrives at Rosie's apartment. Susie greets him as he enters.

"Mr Danny. Miss Rosie not here. She gone to see her father."

Danny just motions to her and goes into the lounge, takes a drink and sits down.

"Can I get you anything, sir?" Susie asks.

"No, no I'm okay. I will wait to see Miss Rosie, thanks Susie."

She leaves him sat with his drink.

After a few drinks he is nearly falling asleep as Rosie returns. Susie can't get to her fast enough to tell her of the visitor.

"Miss Rosie, Mr Danny here. He wait for you."

She thanks her, takes her coat off and walks into the lounge. Danny is slumped back in the large armchair with a half empty bottle of whiskey alongside him. She walks across to him, bending down and kissing him. There is just a slight movement from him. She sits for a few moments on the arm of the chair, just looking at him. Her stomach churns with desire. He always does this to her. Always did it, from the very first moment she saw him.

She goes to the bedroom then goes to the bathroom to shower. She chooses her underwear, wanting to look her best for him. She puts on her dressing gown before going back to him.

Susie brings in two coffees. Rosie places one on the table beside him before going over to the sofa. She curls up, just drinking her coffee and looking at him. He stirs, and then half opens his eyes, looking across at Rosie.

"Hello Danny. I did not want to disturb you."

"Rosie," Danny says, as he sits himself up. "I must have dozed off," he says, rubbing his eyes.

"You seem to have had a bit to drink Danny. That's not like you," she says looking concerned.

"A few problems Rosie. Anyway, it's not your problem. How are you? Was the Amir here very long? He contacted me before he left."

She always feels embarrassed when he mentions the Amir.

"He was here a while and I stayed at his apartment. I have been to see my father. He's in the Nuffield Hospital in Queens Street, close to Piccadilly Circus," she says, not telling him who is paying for it.

"That must be costing you a pretty penny or two," Danny says.

"Danny, the Amir is paying for my father's care. I didn't ask he just found out about my father and offered."

Danny sits with a bit of a look on his face. She fears he is getting mad because the Amir is paying.

"Are you mad at me Danny?" she says, looking at Danny.

"Mad? Why should I be mad? It's his money. Whatever you can get out of him you have earned it."

He pours another drink for himself.

"Look Rosie, every time the Amir comes to London and sees you I get a large amount of money, so why should I think any less of you for getting as much as you can out of him?"

He takes a sip of his drink.

"He gives me money, yes, and presents but I have never asked the Amir for anything. He is a very generous man," she says getting upset.

Danny looks mad now. "Don't kid yourself Rosie. He gets to fuck you; he pays you for your services, and me I get paid for organising and introducing you to him. We are both just as bad."

He pours himself another drink. She is upset, thinking *'why is he so cruel?'*. She gets up and runs to her bedroom, crying. She throws herself on the bed. She is laid there for a long time. She wonders if Danny has gone but will not get up to see if he has left. She hears a noise. The bedroom door opens. Danny is stood in the doorway.

"Rosie, I'm sorry. I should not have said what I said. Things are not going well for me at the moment. I have had a lot to worry about."

She just stares at him. He slowly walks across to her. He sits on the bed, takes her hand and kisses it.

"Forgive me Rosie, I'm sorry." He leans over her, holding her face in his hand and kisses her full on the lips.

She cannot stop herself from responding to him. She puts her arms around him, holding him close. She asks, "Why does it have to be like this? I love you so much that I don't want to be with anyone else but you, you must know that, that's how it as always been."

"I wish it could be but this is how it is and it will be hard to change anything. Yes, of course I have feelings for you."

Danny lies beside her. She pulls him close.

"I need you Danny. I want you so much."

He sits up and takes his clothes off. Soon he lies beside her again. He takes hold of her and kisses her body all over. She digs her nails into his back and then she pushes his head down.

"Yes, yes Danny," she cries out, her legs clamp around his head as his tongue makes her body want more.

She needs to take him in her hands, and caresses him gently using all the techniques she has learned. She gets on top of him. He takes the cheeks of her bottom then moves her from side to side, making her cry out again with pleasure. Through the night they only sleep for short periods. As always, they cannot get enough of one another.

In the early hours Rosie, half asleep, feels for Danny. Not being able to touch him, she opens her eyes. He is sat on the side of the bed with his head in his hands.

"Danny, are you okay? What's wrong?"

"It's nothing for you to worry about or know."

He stands up and is getting dressed. She is watching him; she is a little worried because she has not seen him like this before. He turns and looks at Rosie and gives a smile.

"I'll call you. If you need anything let me know." He is about to leave the room when he turns and walks back to her. He kisses her then leaves, not saying anything else. She has seen both sides of Danny; the good and bad. She is confused as she never knows which person he'll be next.

Danny has paid Ramon the money and he has tried to assess just how much it will cost him in profits. He wishes he had more girls like Rosie and the simple but very profitable business that is just dealing with one very rich client.

The whole operation depends on Ramon cooperating with him and providing the girls and protection as there are now so many Eastern European gangs not only operating in London but everywhere.

Danny does not want to get involved with the very seedy aspects of the business and would prefer to avoid Soho and other London locations. All that part of the business is run by gangs who have no qualms about how badly these girls from all over the world are abused, and then discarded like pieces of old meat when they are past their best.

These gangs are now looking at the business models of the likes of Danny; the most profitable side of the business that provides for the very rich who only want the very best girls. This is why people like Ramon, once they see how an operation is being run, want to run it themselves.

Danny is fully aware of this and he knows their time running this operation is limited.

The girls he has are very good and doing a good job, though. He has taken a liking to one of the Russian girls, who seems to be a lot more sophisticated than all the others. She apparently comes from a very good family in Russia but, through mixing with the wrong people, has finished up here in England. Since the very day she arrived she has made a play for Danny which the other girls have obviously seen, and Danny seems to have responded to her and taking a liking to her. When Christina has not been working they have left together, often for Danny's place, and on many occasions she had not got back until the next morning, or days later.


After a few days not hearing or seeing Danny, Rosie is wondering what could be wrong with him, and what has happened? She manages to take a few amphetamines; she is still trying to cut back on the drugs.

After a day or so not hearing from anyone she contacts Jade to see if she knows anything.

"Jade, it's Rosie. How are things with you?" she asks.

"Rosie, we have been worked off our frigging feet. I'm knackered; the girls are all the same. Oh, by the way we have another couple of girls here with us. They are Russians. It's getting like the United Nations here."

"How's Danny? How has he been with you all? Are you seeing much of him?"

"Occasionally Natalia is around somewhere. She has been after one of the Russian girls if you know what I mean. But the Russian girl is playing hard to get." Jade is laughing.
She knows just what Natalia can get up to.

"She never changes does she? Oh by the way my dad is here, close by in the Nuffield Hospital. I can go and visit him when I like."

"That's great Rosie. Has there been any change?"

"No, just the same but he is well taken care of. I have not seen Danny or heard from him for a couple of days now. I would have thought he would have at least telephoned me."

"Things have been a bit hectic at times. I have seen him but only occasionally over the last few days. We are told where to go and what to do, and we do not see him all the time," Jade tells her.

"Jade, how about doing a bit of shopping and having a gossip if you can make it?"
Jade wants to tell her that Danny is showing a lot of interest in one of the Russian girls called Christina but thinks it's best not to tell her. She knows how much she idolises Danny.

Jade tells her, "I would like that but no, not at the moment. We are going to some big party tonight and there will be some big wigs there. Bloody politicians. I hope they can't get hold of any Viagra."

"I'm sure Natalia and the girls will soon wear them all out. Make yourself scarce when the action starts," she tells Jade, laughing.

"That's impossible if they have got their eyes on you. We will do as we always do. Lay back and take what comes. I suppose the other girls will be laid back thinking of Russia," Jade says, having a giggle.

"I'll phone you when I can Jade. Give the girls my love."


Rosie has all the time in the world to visit her father. She sits for hours on end talking to him, knowing full well he cannot hear or understand what she is saying. She has been so lonely, spending a lot of time in her apartment alone, watching television or occasionally going on a shopping trip. Jade has not been in touch either. She finds taking a couple of downers helps her to sleep but she knows she cannot keep taking the different types of drugs. She tells herself this all the time but she is still taking more than she should. Trouble is, she can get hold of anything with one phone call.

Drugs aside, she still manages to keep herself looking good for either Danny or the Amir.

One day she goes to see her father. As she enters the building she sees a young doctor with a clipboard in his hand, talking to a nurse outside her father's door. The nurse knows

Rosie and introduces Rosie to him.

"Doctor Lawson, this is Miss Lambert, Mr Lambert's daughter. Miss Lambert this is Doctor Lawson. Your father is one of his patients."

"Nice to meet you Doctor Lawson." She loves his smile.

"Likewise Miss Lambert," he says, giving her a very big smile.

"How's my father Doctor? Is everything okay?" Rosie asks.

"Yes, not a lot of change at all. We are thinking of trying a new drug on your father. I must emphasise, as I said, that it is new but it is worth a try. We will start over the next few days. Please don't build your hopes up, we'll see how it goes."

"Lets hope it helps my father, doctor."

She sees he has very deep blue eyes. She is watching how he is making eye contact with her and how occasionally he scans her body.

He opens the door to her father's suite for her to go in. She looks at him as she passes very close to him pausing.

"Thank you doctor," she says, looking right into his eyes.

"A pleasure Miss Lambert. Miss Lambert I should like to give you my card, just in case you need to ask me anything regarding your father's treatment."

He hands her his card. The nurse is just stood with a smile on her face. Rosie looks at the card. *Doctor Nathan Lawson.*

"Thank you again doctor. I appreciate what you are doing for my father."

He just nods his head as he walks away down the corridor in his white coat and with his stethoscope around his neck. He turns to take a last look at Rosie as she is closing the door. He sees she is looking at him he gives her a wink, and another very big smile, then he hurries off down the corridor.

As she is sat with her father she gives a little laugh to herself thinking the doctor was coming on to her. She thinks he is a very good-looking young man. She wonders if she will see Doctor Nathan Lawson again in the near future. Who knows?

When she gets home she gets a call from May. When she answers the phone May is very upset.

"Rosie... Rosie, that bastard."

"What's wrong May? What's happened?" she asks.

"That fucking Paul. He was after getting me to Soho. I overheard him talking on the phone. I remembered what you said about Jayne and I wasn't having any of that so I've done a bunk. They will never find me," May tells Rosie, crying; upset but sounding very mad.

"Just what happened May?"

"I overheard Paul on the phone, like I said. I think he was talking to Danny. He was telling him I'm not up to the same standard as the other girls, and am now getting too fat. What does he think we are a, piece of bloody shit? Whatever you do Rosie don't tell anyone I have spoken to you."

"I won't. You must be very careful May; I won't ask where you are going. Best I don't know but give me a call later just so I know that you're alright?"

"Yes, Rosie... I'm really pissed off and I've told my parents not to say anything to anyone."

"Have you got money May?"

"Yes Rosie, I've got my own money, and some money I took from that shit Paul. He won't like that. Rosie, you look after yourself. Don't let them boss you about. You should get out while you can. I have to go now Rosie. Don't forget what I said, love you. Bye."

"Bye May." She puts the phone down wondering what the hell is happening.


Rosie cannot understand why she has not heard from anyone, Danny, the Amir or the girls over the past two or three weeks. She has been going to the hospital quite often and she has seen Doctor Lawson but he always seems to be very busy. Although when he has seen her he gives her that big lovely smile and a wink.

She is reluctant to telephone Danny, thinking if he wants to speak to her he will call. She goes to the hospital. When she gets to her father's room Doctor Lawson is with her father. As she enters the room the doctor looks up at her and smiles. She walks to her father and gives him a kiss, stroking his hair. She looks at the doctor waiting for him to say something. He realises she is waiting for him to speak.

"Well, I'm a little disappointed that we have not seen any response to the new drug and treatment we have given your father. I am very sorry Miss Lambert."

Rosie takes her father's hand. A little tear trickles down her cheek. The doctor sees she is upset.

"I really hoped we could give you some good news. The only good thing I can say is he is not getting any worse."

She thanks him as he leaves the room. She sits with her father most of the day until the nurse comes in and suggests she should go to the restaurant for something to eat while she and another nurse see to her father. Rosie agrees. She walks slowly to the restaurant but is not feeling hungry. She decides to go for a drink of coffee, and while she is walking there she takes a couple of pills from her bag and pops them down before anyone can see her.

She is sat on her own daydreaming. The tablets she took seem to have affected her a little more than she expected. She sees the doctor walking towards her with a drink and a meal in his hand.

"May I join you Miss Lambert?"

She smiles at him and just motions for him to take a seat.

"You're not eating Miss Lambert?"

"Please doctor, call me Rosie." Her speech is a little strange. The doctor looks at her and she feels embarrassed.

"I would call you by your first name if we were in a different environment but you know, the whole doctor patient thing. Maybe I could take you for a drink or a meal... Oh I'm sorry, I should not have asked you."

"No, it's okay doctor. I would like that."

A big smile comes over his face. "Shall we say tomorrow night? That is if you're free. It's just that I'm clear for tomorrow night."

She throws caution to the wind. "What time would you like to meet?"

The doctor is getting a bit flustered because she accepted his offer.

"Eight o'clock. Where shall we meet?"

"Let's say eight o'clock at the pub around the corner? The Black Swan," Rosie suggests.

"Fine, fine, yes."

He eats his meal while they talk, unable to wait for tomorrow night.

She goes to say goodnight to her father. He is laid in bed and the nurses are just leaving. She goes hugs him before leaving.

She gets back to her apartment. Susie is just leaving.

"You need anything, Miss Rosie?"

"No, it's okay Susie. Has anyone telephoned or are there any messages?"

Susie knows what she wants her to say.

"No Miss Rosie no one called."

"Okay Susie. Goodnight."

"Night Miss Rosie."


She is all alone. She wanders into her bedroom. She looks around then starts undressing. She opens a drawer and takes out some cocaine. She snorts a couple of lines then goes to take a hot bath.

She lays in the bath daydreaming, thinking if she had not got involved with Danny how would her life be going? She laughs to herself, remembering Kjell. And now the young doctor Nathan comes to mind. Nobody has ever interested her other than Danny. She feels something is not right between them. Has he really just used her? She knew of men, and what they do to get girls into sex. Grooming is the word comes to mind.

She thinks, '*Have I been really that naive?*'

She is not certain. But the more she thinks about it the more she believes she has been.


Danny has been seeing the Russian girl Christina quite a lot while waiting to see if Ramon does try something else to get money out of him. Up to now things have been running smoothly since he agreed to pay the money. Everyone in the last week or so has been doing what they need to be doing. He is hoping it stays the same.

Paul telephones Danny.

"Hi Dan. That slag May, Rosie's friend, has cleared off and taken some of my cash."

"How the hell has that happened?"

"She must have heard us talking about getting rid of her, and she left when she knew we were not around. She was not much use to us. I wouldn't care but it's what she knows. I found out where her parents lived but they say they have no idea where she is."

Danny thinks, *'what now?'*

"Let's hope she keeps her mouth closed. But if you can find her you know what to do?'

"I know what to do. She doesn't know what she has coming to her."

Danny thinks a while.

"Tell you what Paul, I bet she has been in touch with Rosie. I'll give her a ring and see if she has."

"Yes do that Dan. I'll let you know if I find her. She will be sat in one of them shitty cubicles playing with some dirty old man two minutes after I find her."

Danny knows he hasn't bothered to see Rosie for a long time now. He has heard nothing at all about the Amir coming to London. He has been thinking of giving Rosie a bit of work but he is reluctant that she may tell the Amir and then he really would be in the shit. He telephones Rosie.

"Rosie, how are you?"

Rosie does not answer immediately.

"I'm okay. I am surprised to hear from you."

"Surprised? Why, do I have to call you every day? Do I have to tell you what I am doing and where I am going?"

Rosie is feeling that she is about to cry. "I did not mean it that way, I thought..."

Danny interrupts her.

"You thought, you thought what? Just do what you expect me to do? What do you bloody want? You have everything you need. Money, a beautiful apartment, expensive jewellery. Now you want me to tell you what I have been doing every minute of the bloody day? Look Rosie, just do as you're told. I want to know if that slut May has been in contact with you, has she?"

Rosie thinks she might have been persuaded to tell him but not now. "No, I haven't seen or heard from her."

She thinks, 'I better not ask questions while he is in a mood like this.'

"Why should she contact me?"

"Because you are suppose to be her friend," Danny says getting really annoyed. "If she contacts you, you tell me immediately, do you hear?"

"Yes Danny, I will," she says, feeling a bit of defiance towards him.

He just puts the phone down. She is beginning to realise that Danny has no real feelings or serious thoughts about her. She is determined to meet with the doctor just to distance herself from the set up.

## 18

# Nathan

She prepares to meet the doctor and decides to dress down a little, not wanting to look out of place, but not knowing how the date will go.

She takes a taxi to the Black Swan. As she walks in it is full of people. She looks around and at the back of the room Nathan is stood waving to her. She manages to get through the crowd. Nathan leans forward, taking hold of her hand and kissing her on the cheek.

"Well Rosie, what do you want to drink?" Nathan asks her.

"Just a tonic water please," she says, trying to make herself heard over the crowd.

"Look, we could go somewhere a lot quieter what do you think?" he asks.

"No, it's okay here, for now." She likes to be among people for a change.

"How about just having a drink here and then going somewhere else for a meal?"

"Yes, that's okay with me." She smiles at him.

He goes to the bar for the drinks. Rosie is watching him. He is a very good-looking man. When he gets back they sit talking. Nathan can be so amusing at times and he makes her feel so relaxed.

Having to sit very close to hear each other talking because of the noise means that they are in each other's personal space. He gets a smell of her perfume, and looking into her eyes he cannot resist her. He leans closer to her, and she has a smile on her face as he gently kisses her. She closes her eyes, not resisting. Nathan whispers to her.

"You are so beautiful."

This makes Rosie blush. She likes him very much and there is something she has never seen in a man. Nathan has a calm and wonderful nature and gentleness about him. She has always thought of Danny as the one for her, but thinking of what has happened in the last couple of days, and what he said to her she realises there will be no future with him. He needs her a lot more than she needs him at the moment because of the Amir, but what will happen if the Amir dumps her?

"You're daydreaming Rosie. Shall we go for some dinner then?"

"Oh sorry Nathan. Yes, I would like that. I'm ready for something to eat."

They get up and leave. Once outside, Nathan takes her hand. He pulls her closer to him then gives her a kiss on the cheek; putting his arm around her waist he tells her the restaurant is not too far and asks if she would like to walk there to get some fresh air. She agrees.

They walk slowly to the restaurant, chatting to one another. She tells him she has very few relations and her father is the only one she really cares about now. She is glad that he has not asked too many questions about what she does or anything about her apart from her parents. She does not want him to know anything about why and when she left uni.

In the restaurant Nathan just looks at her while she is eating.

"Nathan will you stop that, you are embarrassing me."

"Stop what?" He says, with a grin.

"You know, looking at me." she says playfully.

"How can I stop looking at such a beautiful woman like you?"

She laughs and taps his hand, "You're a very handsome young man but I don't keep looking at you."

They are both laughing, and through the meal they continue to flirt with each other. Nathan looks at her and asks, "Could I take you home?"

"I would say yes but that would be difficult for me at this time."

Seeing he looks so disappointed she adds, "Maybe another time."

Before they get up to leave she asks someone to call a taxi for her. Nathan, still looking disappointed, tells her, "We'll share the cab. How far do you have to go as I'm close by?'

"Oh, I have quite away to go so I'll drop you off."

His smile reappears. "Great," he says. They get up to leave and she puts her arm in his.


The cab is waiting. They get into the cab and Nathan tells the driver, "Stanton House, Sherburn Street."

She is just sat looking out of the window when Nathan pulls her closer, kissing her passionately. She responds and they get rather passionate in the back seat. The driver looks through his rear mirror and smiles to himself.

The taxi pulls up. The driver has to tell them that they have arrived. She tidies herself up.

"Rosie, please come in for a drink."

She thinks for a moment, and then looking at his face she relents.

"Just a drink. I can't stay too long."

Nathan is happy. He pays the driver and they make their way to his flat. It is very modest and he is a little embarrassed, trying to tidy things up as they enter.

"It's not always like this," he says, looking embarrassed as he is picking clothes and papers up from the floor.

She just laughs and says, "Don't make excuses. Typical man." She tidies the settee then sits down.

"Right Rosie, what would you like to drink? Tea, coffee, whiskey, rum?" he says, laughing.

"I'll have tea with just a little milk and no sugar."

"Your wish is my command. I'll just go to my kitchen."

He walks two steps to a small unit where the kettle is.

He puts some music on, and when the tea is made he sits next to her.

"I don't know too much about you Rosie. Can I ask what you do for a living?"

She was worrying this would come.

"I work for a modelling agency."

"Is that in London?"

"What's this, the third degree?" She asks, not wanting him asking any more questions. She is about to say she better go when he talks again.

"Sorry Rosie. I was just making conversation."

Things go quiet for a while. Nathan takes Rosie's cup from her then, as he walks back towards her, he has a serious look on his face. He sits down facing her and he strokes her face before kissing her. It is not just a kiss it is so full of passion, he is so gentle with her.

She is so relaxed and they soon start to undress. She is laid back on the settee now, nearly naked. He kisses her body. His hands are squeezing her breasts, he kisses her nipples and she can feel them hardening as he sucks them into his mouth. Using his tongue, he gently bites her nipples, making her squeal with delight. She is so aroused and she feels him knowing he is ready to take her. She arches her back inviting him to penetrate her. She gasps as he does and their bodies are moving together and her breathing is heavy. He grasps her bottom as he pushes inside her.

There is no thought of Danny, like when she had had sex with the others before. She is enjoying Nathan's lovemaking to the full again, and again she nearly reaches climax then Nathan withdraws to prolong the pleasure they are both having, until they have to let go when their bodies shudder together. They both cry out as they simultaneously climax. They lay still and are quiet. No words are spoken; there is just the sound of heavy breathing for a few minutes before Nathan kisses her again.

He takes her by the hand and leads her to his small bed. He lays her down and then lies beside her. She looks at him, encouraging him to make love to her again. He does so with a gentleness that she has never experienced before. He whispers in her ear, telling her how to move her body. She lies on her stomach and he is biting the back of her neck as she feels him enter her again. She is on fire and wants all he can give her, again and again.

In the morning Nathan is up and showered before she wakes. He is stood over her smiling when she opens her eyes. She sees him and holds her hand out to him.

"No my love, I must go. You stay if you want but I have a twelve-hour shift now. I will look in on your father."

"No I can't stay. I have your number so I'll call you later. I'll have a shower then get a taxi home. I may come to the hospital later to see dad."

She starts to get out of the bed.

"Don't let me see that beautiful body of yours, I might be tempted." He bends down to kiss her then leaves.

She takes a shower and wanders around his flat, looking at photos. There is one photo of a little girl on a beach, and a photo of a very beautiful girl. She thinks this could be Nathan's girlfriend but she is hoping that this one was just a quick jump in the hay. Before leaving she tidies up for him and takes a last look at the photo.

## 19

# Tying Up Loose Ends

Rosie arrives back at her apartment.

"Miss Rosie, Mr Danny telephoned me this morning. He ask where you where, and he said he as been telephoning you all night."

She thanks Susie. She knows he will want to know where she has been. She will have to come up with some excuses as to why she was not at home. She waits a while a little afraid before deciding to telephone Danny. She is really worried. When she picks up her phone she takes a deep breath before dialling his number.

"Hello," his voice shouts a response down the phone.

"It's me Danny."

"Rosie, where the hell have you been? I have been trying to get hold of you all night."

"I stayed at the hospital with my dad. I'm sorry; I forgot to take my phone with me. He wasn't too well."

There is no sound for what seems to be forever, until Danny decides to break the silence.

"Oh, at the hospital were you? In the future you let me know where you are do you hear?"

"Yes Danny. I'm sorry."

"Now listen, the Amir wants to see you but he is not coming here. You have to fly to Qatar tomorrow to see him. You must be ready for around lunchtime when you will be taken to the airport and to the Amir's jet. Make sure you have your phone with you all the time in the future."

"Yes Danny. I'll be ready to go tomorrow lunch time."

She feels relieved that he has accepted her story.

"Okay. If I don't see you before you go call me immediately when you get back. I was not told how long you would be there."

"I'll call you when I get back," she says.

She wonders what she can tell Nathan. She decides to call him.

"Nathan, I am very sorry but I have to go away for a while, so I'm afraid our date will have to be postponed for now."

"I'm sorry that you cannot make it. How long will you be away?" Nathan is disappointed,

"Not certain. I hope it's not too long. Please take care of my father and I'll be in touch."

"Okay Rosie. By the way the other night was great and I hope we can repeat it," he says, laughing.

She smiles to herself. "I hope so too. Bye for now Nathan."

"Bye Rosie."

She sits a while, thinking of the night they spent together. She realises how different Danny and Nathan are.

The next day she calls Jade to tell her where she is going and to remind her to keep in touch. She tells her she will call her when she gets back. Soon, she is on her way to the airport.

As they arrive at the small jet her luggage is taken on board. She feels like some celebrity the way everyone runs around after her.

She sits looking out of the window as the plane takes off and she wonders how long this will last.

As she exits the plane the heat hits her and she is led to a very large Rolls Royce.

Once inside and into the air-conditioned vehicle she feels a lot better. They have to go through a couple of checks but are not delayed and soon are able to proceed on their journey.

They arrive at the same place she had been to before with the other girls. Only this time everyone is making a fuss of her, and seeing to her every need. Once she is settled into her room Mia enters.

"Miss Rosie. I will come this evening and help you bathe and dress, ready to see the Amir."

She notices Mia is not her usual self. "Yes, fine Mia."
Mia just gives a faint smile as she leaves her.

She takes a nap and it seems like only a short time before Mia is back. Over the next hour or so Rosie is bathed and pampered by Mia, using her oils and gentle erotic massaging to relax her.

Mia doesn't talk a lot at the best of times but this time she has said very little.

She is ready to see the Amir and is dressed in the usual white silk robe. She looks so beautiful; her hair is shining, she needs very little make up but what she has on just enhances her beautiful features.

"Come on Miss Rosie, the Amir wants to see you now."
Mia walks slowly through the marble hallways with Rosie following her; she opens the door of one of the rooms and tells Rosie to go in. As she enters the room there is a large four-poster bed with a man dressed in white alongside the bed. Seeing her, he motions for her to come forward and then he leaves the room.

She thinks, how strange. As she gets close to the bed she sees the Amir propped up with large pillows around him. He smiles at her, holding out his hand to her. She sees he is pale. He seems to have lost a lot of weight, and as she stands alongside him she senses all is not well. In a kind of a whisper he tells her to sit on the bed alongside him.

"Rosie. My white rose. You can see I am not in good health. I have sent for you because it is unlikely I will ever get to see you in London again."
She now knows something is seriously wrong. She just sits looking at him.

"I am seriously ill. I have not long left but I wanted to see your beautiful face once more before I leave this place."

She cannot believe what he is saying. The tears run down her face. She does not know what to say and she is lost for words. Then, with great emotion, she cries out, "Oh no." She falls on to his chest.
He runs his hands through her hair, and then kisses her head.

"Come now little one, don't cry."
"But your highness, oh why…"

Rosie is sobbing. She has always had a great respect for him, as he has always been kind and considerate towards her.

"Why my dear it is the will of Allah. I want you to know that you will be taken care of. You will never want for anything and I am setting everything in place. The apartment will be yours and an allowance will be paid to you each year for the rest of your life."

She takes his hand.

"Why would you do that for me, I am not worth it?" she says, still crying.

"To me my dear you are worth more than I can ever give you. You gave me warmth and tenderness, you let me see your beauty, you showed me affection and that is why I would like to give something to repay you. Happiness I cannot give you of course, because wealth never guarantees happiness."

Again she is crying. She lays her head on his chest and can feel his heart racing. Other than the heartbeat, all is quiet as she lay with him. The same thoughts are coming back to her again. She asks herself why does everyone she has any feelings for leave her with a broken heart? The next thing she hears is a voice and someone is pulling on her arm. She had fallen asleep, laid with her head on the Amir's chest, and as she is helped up she looks at the Amir. He has his eyes open, but is very pale and not moving. Rosie realises that he has passed away.

There are two men there; one looks like the doctor and he is looking closely at the Amir as she is led away by the other man. As she is leaving she is crying and she takes a last look at him and breaks down. Mia comes to her and takes her to her room, trying to console her.

"Miss Rosie, my orders are you should dress and leave as soon as possible. Everything has been organised for you to return to London."

She cannot believe what has just happened, and so quickly. His passing is a big shock to her.

Everything is rushed. She is dressed and her baggage taken to the vehicle she came in. Soon she is being taken back to the airport where only yesterday she had arrived.

It seemed as though no one wanted anyone to see her. Apart

from Mia nobody had spoken to her and Mia had said very little to her. Back on the plane she is sad and still upset about what has happened but she is more concerned with what will happen now. The Amir has promised she could keep the apartment and she would have an annual income paid into her bank for the rest of her life. She cannot believe just what a wonderful position she is in now. Her thoughts go to Danny. She smiles to herself, realising she does not need him anymore.

Back in the UK, as she arrives back at her apartment, Rosie is wondering whether she should call Danny. She is very reluctant to do so, thinking why should she? She is independent now and she can make a break from Danny and his set up.

Nathan comes to mind. She does not want to contact him either until she has seen Danny. She does, however, want to see her father as soon as she can but decides to wait until the morning when she will call Danny.

The next morning she reluctantly calls Danny.

"Hello."

"Its me, Rosie, I'm back home." She is anxiously waiting for him to answer her.

"Bloody hell that was quick. Why? What's happened?" Danny is worried now, thinking maybe the Amir has got tired of her.

"The Amir passed away."

There is a deathly silence. Then, in an astonished voice, he says, "You're joking. He hasn't?"

"No, Danny I'm not joking. I was with him when he passed away."

There is a pause then he says, "I'm coming round. I'll be there in 30 minutes." Before she can answer the phone cuts off.

Now she is really worried. *'What do I say do I tell him about the arrangement that    has been made as he to know? I have to be strong.'* Impatiently she waits for him to arrive.

The apartment door bursts open and his face is like thunder.

"What the hell happened then?" he shouts.

"He had been very ill. He wanted to see me. He knew he was dying but I don't think they expected him to pass away that quickly."

"Well that's fucked that then. When do you have to move out of here, did anyone tell you?" he says, banging the table and showing his anger at knowing a good source of revenue has finished.

"I don't." She can see his face calming a little.

"What do you mean you don't? I don't understand."

"The Amir said that he was organising everything. He told me the apartment would be mine and I would get a yearly allowance for life."

He stands up in front of her. He is looking down at her as he laughs and throws his head back.

"Oh, so Miss Rosie sits on her arse with this very nice apartment and a very nice allowance. And what about me then? I just say goodbye then let you benefit from the generosities of the person I and, I emphasise, I got you? Well listen, I will make sure I get what is coming to me. This apartment must be worth a million or more. It will be sold, and your very generous allowance will be paid into a joint account and you will be given a very small share. And in the meantime you will be working with the girls."

She is mad and shouts back.

"No I won't and you cannot make me."

Danny pulls her up by her hair.

"You listen to me you drug taking slut. You will finish up like your girlfriend Jayne in a Soho shit hall."

She tries to break loose by pulling at his hands that are holding her hair. They struggle and he pushes her down on to the settee.

"I'm telling you for the last time. What will happen is that you will suffer the same consequences if you are going to be awkward. It is your decision. You have 48 hours to decide." His face is contorted with rage as he walks to the door.

He turns as he goes out of the door and shouts again.

"48 hours."

Then he slams the door behind him.

She is on the sofa, crying. Susie has overheard them arguing. When she hears Danny leave she runs into the lounge.

"Miss Rosie you okay? Please don't cry. Are you all

right? Can I help?"

"No you cannot help Susie. Leave me alone for a while please."

Susie leaves the room. She gets up and goes to her bedroom, takes some cocaine from her drawer and, still crying, puts a couple of lines on the bedside table and sniffs it up her nostrils. She keeps going like this for hours, as she no longer cares.

Danny goes back to his flat. He is furious knowing that the gravy train has finished with the Amir dying, and most of all thinking Rosie will probably get everything and he will get nothing. That will be very hard for him to take and he is determined to take from Rosie all he can, regardless of the consequences.

When he arrives back at his flat the Russian girl Christina is sprawled on the settee watching television with a black see-through gown on, and very little underneath. She is holding a drink in her hand as she stands up and walks to him, putting her arm around his neck and kissing him. He pushes her off then walks across to a small bar and pours a drink for himself. She stands watching him, then asks, "What wrong my darling? Why you mad?"

He just looks at her, takes a drink and picks his phone up.

"Paul. Got some bad news. The Amir is dead and, listen to this; our little Rosie is filling her boots. The old shit has left her his apartment and, get this, an annual allowance for life. Well if she tries to take the lot she will join her friend in Soho and she'll get absolutely nothing."

"Danny, does she think we will let her take the sodding apartment for herself? It must be worth over a million. What have you said to her?"

"I fucking threatened her. I told her any money paid to her will go into a joint account between her and myself and I will manage it. The apartment will be sold and we will take that. I told her she would be working with the girls. She didn't like that either."

"Will she consent to selling the apartment?" Paul asks, hoping he is going to say yes.

"The little slut at first said it was all hers. I have given her 48 hours to agree or else it will be Soho for her. We'll fill her up with you-know-what and then she will do as we say."

Paul tells Danny, "I have tried my hardest to find that other girl May but she seems to have disappeared into thin air. We even had a person watching her parent's place but there has been no sign of her."

"We have more to worry about at the moment than her, Paul," he shouts.

"Don't fucking shout at me Danny. I can see what is happening. We have to make sure it doesn't all fall apart. You get that apartment sold and we will be in the money."

"Don't worry, I will make sure she sells. Ramon seems to be keeping a low profile but at least he is off our back for a while."

"Danny, if you need me I'll come to London. Just let me know."

"I will manage. I will call you again when things are sorted out. See you."

"Okay Dan, see you."

Christina is listening to what he has been saying. She goes to him again and wraps herself around him,

"Come to bed. I need you."

Although Danny is worried he cannot help himself. He follows her to the bedroom.


The following morning Susie tries to wake Rosie up.

"Miss Rosie..."

She opens her eyes but cannot focus. All she sees is Susie's blurred face.

"What... do... you want Susie?"

"Please Miss Susie, there is a man to see you. A Mr Mustafa Rafi. He insists he must speak with you."

She sits up.

"Just give me a moment or two."

She goes to her bathroom and tidies herself up before going to see whom it is that needs to speak to her. *'Maybe it's someone the Amir has got to finalise things.'*

As she walks into the lounge a very well dressed Arab

225

man is sat waiting. He stands up holding his hand out to her.

"Miss Lambert, my name is Mustafa Rafi. I am acting on behalf of the brother to the late Amir. I am afraid I have some bad news for you. You must vacate this apartment as soon as possible."

"I don't understand. The Amir told me it would be signed over to me."

She is hoping there has been some mistake.

"I am sorry. I don't know anything about that. I am doing what I have been told to do," he says, shaking his head.

"That cannot be. I was told this apartment would be mine just before the Amir passed away."

"If that had been so I would have been informed as I represent the whole Royal family."

She is devastated.

"What about the allowance?"

"I take it you mean what has been paid to you in the past? I'm afraid that will stop along with any other payments for credit cards and anything else the Amir was paying for. The Amir gave me instructions to pay you a nominal sum of £20,000 when you agree to signing a document saying your acquaintance with the Amir will remain private and never be made public."

She is devastated. All that she thought she would get has gone and... how will she pay for her father's care? Her money will be gone in no time and another £20,000 won't go far.

She thinks for a moment then she has an idea.

"I will sign only if the £20,000 is per month for the next four years. And my father's care is paid for another four years."

She waits for his reply.

"Miss Lambert, I don't think the Amir will accept ultimatums."

"Well, I'm sorry then but I won't sign," she says stubbornly.

Mr Mustafa Rafi stands up.

"I cannot give you an answer now. I will call you tomorrow."

"Oh and another thing. I need a two or three weeks or so to move," she says, knowing she has the upper hand. She knows they will be worried, thinking she may go public and tell the media about the Amir and herself.

Mr Mustafa Rafi leaves her. She is proud of herself and thinks that she may get some, if not all, of what she has asked for. Now for Danny. How will she get out of that mess?

She thinks about the jewellery the Amir gave her, and the money she has in her account. If Danny gets his hands on that it would be a disaster. She decides to collect up everything that is of value, along with her money, and get it into a safety deposit box as soon as possible. She gets herself ready to go to the bank to sort things out. She tells Susie to telephone her on her mobile if anyone calls at all.


Coming out of the bank she smiles to herself and thinks, *'There Mr Franklin-Smith, get your hands on that if you can.'*

She leaves to see her father at the hospital. It hasn't been that long since she last saw him so she doesn't expect any change in him. On her way there she calls Jade.

Jade answers the phone. "Is that you Rosie? Where are you?"

"I'm here back in London."

"God, that was fast. Was it a quick jump and leave?"

"Jade, he passed away."

"Get away. Not while he was doing it was it?'

"No," she laughs. "I can't speak now. I'll tell you later what has happened, is everything okay with you?"

"Yes, nothing's changed. Call me when you can."

"Will do."


As she arrives at the hospital Nathan is on the steps and talking to a very nice looking woman. He kisses her on the cheek and waves to her as she gets into a car and drives away. She sits in the taxi until he has gone back into the hospital. When she walks into the hospital he is nowhere to be seen, so she goes straight to her father's room. He is sat by the window and he neither looks at her nor responds when she walks up to him.

She pulls up a chair and sits close to him, holding his hand occasionally, brushing his hair back then wiping his chin. He is still a good-looking man. You would never think anything was wrong with him at first sight. If the money stops she knows she is in trouble; she will have to shift him. If she does get what she wants then after four years she will try her hardest to get something in place to make sure he will always be taken care of.

While she is sat, she thinks of the woman she saw Nathan kissing. Was it the same woman she saw in the photograph at his flat? Maybe it is his girlfriend? The door opens and in walks Nathan. He is taken aback.

"Rosie, I thought you had gone away for a while. Is everything okay?"

"Yes, fine. It didn't take as long as I thought. Dad looks the same. No problems then?"

"No problems. He's just the same." Nathan senses coldness in her voice, as though she doesn't want to talk.

"Are you sure everything is alright Rosie? Maybe we could get together later, what do you say?"

"No, I'm afraid I'm busy."

"Come on Rosie. Why are you being like that with me?"

"Well if you want to know I saw you kissing a young woman on the steps outside as I arrived. It was the same woman you have a photo of in your flat. And is that little girl in the other photograph yours too?"

He laughs out loud.

"That beautiful young woman is my sister Martha and the little girl is my niece Lucy."

Again he laughs. "You can meet them before they go back to Canada."

Rosie is embarrassed about behaving like a jealous schoolgirl.

"Oh I'm sorry Nathan for acting so silly."

"I have not told you before but I have no other relatives apart from my sister. My mum and dad have both passed away. Right, now that is settled when can we get together?"

"I am rather tied up at the minute but give it a day or so and then we can."

"Oh well, beggars can't be choosers," he says, looking disappointed.

He examines her father and then they sit and talk for a while. He keeps trying to find out a little more about her but she always changes the subject.

"Rosie, you look a bit unwell. Are you sure you're alright?"

*'It's the drugs. He can probably see I've been taking them.'*

"I'm okay. Just had a bad night after all the traveling."

Nathan is looking into her eyes. He knows the signs as he has seen them many times. He feels that he should say something but he bides his time for the right time to confront her. He doesn't know just what the extent is of her drug taking but he has noticed her slurred speech before, and other tell tale signs.

He leaves her, with her promising to get in touch with him soon; she is tired and she kisses her father before leaving.

## 20
# The Net Closes In

She walks into her apartment. Susie is there to take her coat.

"No calls Miss Rosie. Can I get you anything?"

"No, no Susie. I just want to relax." She is on the settee. She is shattered due to the last couple of days and the drugs are taking their toll.

All is quiet the next day. She is waiting for Danny to come, and she is saying over and over again to herself what she plans to say to Danny. She knows Danny can get quite violent when angered, and she is now seeing what she didn't want to see in him before. She is still waiting for Mr Rafi too. She hopes her demands will be met, and there is no way that she will tell Danny about that deal, whatever the outcome.

She hears his voice. It's the moment she has been dreading.

"Rosie, Rosie where are you?"

She is hesitant.

"Coming."

As she enters the lounge he is sat down, tapping his knee. He looks up at her.

"Well?"

She wants to show him she is not afraid of him.

"Well what?" she says.

"I take it you agree with what I have suggested?" he says, looking straight at her.

"I have some bad news for you," she says, although she knows he will blow his top.

Before she can say another word he jumps up.

"Don't you dare?"

Before he can speak again she shouts back at him.

"The apartment is not mine."

"What do you mean it's not yours? You said…"

"I know what I said. I thought it had been sorted but the legal representative for the royal family paid me a visit telling me I have to move out and that the Amir had not made any official request to give me anything."

Danny sits back down, falling back in the chair. He is perspiring.

"The money, the allowance for life? What about that?"

She shakes her head. "Nothing. I have a couple of months to leave. First he said I would have to move immediately but I persuaded him to give me a month or two."

Danny is very quiet. He looks fidgety, as though he is thinking what to say next.

"Sit down."

She sits in the chair opposite him.

"You can move in with the girls. We can see if we can come up with someone else for you. Yes, that's it. "

"No."

"What do you mean no? Do you think you can pick and choose? Well my girl, you can't. What about your father? Who's going to pay for his care? You need me more than ever now," he says with a smirk on his face.

"I'll sort something out." She is not giving anything away.

"You'll sort something out? How are you going to pay? With fairy dust? Or are you going to get a job in Tesco or somewhere? Wake up girl, there is only one thing you can do and that is lay on your back."

She is upset at the way he is talking to her but she is trying not to show it.

"What about me and you?" she asks.

"You and me together is like saying the Amir has come back from the dead. To me you are just like the others. You are there to make the clients happy."

He has the same smirk on his face.

Susie comes in.

"Would you like a drink?"

"Get out," Danny shouts at Susie. She turns and scurries out of the room.

Things are quiet and nothing is being said. Danny gets up and walks across to Rosie. He takes hold of her arm and pulls her up, pulling her only inches from his face.

"Listen to me. You will be ready to move back in with the girls in two weeks. I would take you now but we will wait a while until I have spoken to my contact that I had with the Amir. That dead old bastard owes me money."

He pushes her back into the chair then starts to walk out. He leaves without saying another word, slamming the door behind him.

She is relieved. She is hoping that Mr Rafi doesn't know anything about Danny and that she can do the deal with him about the payments.

She is in her flat when she gets a call.

"Rosie. It's me, May." She sounds anxious.

"What is it May? Where are you?"

"Look Rosie, it's not that I don't trust you. The less you know about me the better. I'm leaving the UK. No way am I letting them bastards get anywhere near me so they can throw me in one of those shit holes in Soho."

"I understand May. I am sick of it all myself, but what can I do?"

"You will not have any trouble when I do what I'm planning to do. I'm going to telephone the police anonymously and spill the beans. And I mean really spill the beans. I will tell them about the whole operation. The girls, the clients - that will shock them, the Eastern Europeans involved and the two brothers. I will really stitch the bastards up."

"May, you have to be careful. And be careful not to drop us in it too. Get yourself away somewhere safe straight after you have spoken to the police."

"Rosie, I think you should just stay put, and wait for the outcome. I will say goodbye for now Rosie. You never know, when all this shit has passed over we may meet again. You take care. Love you, bye Rosie."

Before she can say goodbye May has gone. She doesn't

know how she feels about what she has just heard. If it helps her make a break from Danny and the set up it will be wonderful. But she is worried about what the future holds. These people cannot be messed with without repercussions.

Danny is thinking that things are not looking too good, with the very lucrative business with the Amir coming to an end, and the pressures of Ramon and his friends demanding more and more money.

He is in his apartment with the Russian girl Christina. He is trying to relax and forget his troubles; Christina knows just how to do that. They are in bed when there is a lot of shouting and a loud noise. The bedroom door bursts open, a lot of police enter the bedroom shouting at them, then tell Danny and the girl to get out of the bed. Danny gets out of the bed asking if he can get his clothes on, as he is naked. Christina has no inhibitions or showing any modesty. She just casually gets out of bed, picking up a dressing gown and putting it on slowly with the police officers just stood watching her. Danny decides to get on the offensive and question the police.

"What the hell's going on? What is this all about?"

The police officer in charge tells him.

"Mr Daniel Franklin-Smith, you are under arrest. You have the right to remain silent..."

They continue to read him his rights.

"I don't know what you're talking about. I want to speak to my solicitor."

The officer completes reading him his rights then tells him to finish getting dressed, as they will be taking them to the police station.

Both Danny and Christina are rushed away in police cars. Meanwhile other officers search the apartment, obviously finding drugs and money.

After some time being questioned Danny is informed that all the places involved in the trafficking of the girls have been simultaneously raided, and a lot of arrests have been made. The circle is closing in.

The police, through information they found and

connections through the mobile phones that were confiscated, have been able to arrest Ramon and his associates.

A couple of days pass. Rosie has heard from no one, not even Danny or Mr Rafi. Later that evening she is watching the evening news when she hears the news. A number of people have been arrested in London, Leeds, Birmingham and Brighton for trafficking women for sex; they are mostly girls from Eastern Europe. The people arrested are announced as four English men and several Romanians. They have all been held without bail. Some of the girls have been sent to a safe house, to receive counselling. They will be returned to their own country or will be given the option of staying in the UK, if there is any fear of them being targeted if they return to their own countries.

Rosie is in shock. '*She's done it, May's actually done it. I can't see Natalia and Monika needing counselling; as soon as they can they will be on their backs again.*'

She is feeling free at last; now all she as to do is settle with Mr Rafi. There have been stories in the newspapers about some of the clients that were at the sex parties; no names mentioned only hints about who they are. It is obvious that the establishment is in it up to their necks.

Rosie has not left her flat since the news broke. She gets a call from Mr Rafi. He wants to meet her at some hotel; she must be on her own and not tell anyone. This frightens her. Why won't he come to meet her in her flat? She is in a quandary not knowing what to do; she has a good think about it, and then agrees to meet him the next day.

She wants to see her father and Nathan but decides to see what Rafi has to say first, as this might make a difference to her plans and future life. She meets him at the agreed place. He is sat at a table waiting for her,

"Please sit down Miss Lambert."

She sits, not knowing what he will say.

"Miss Lambert, I am sure you know there is a lot of publicity about certain people we both know, and this could make things very difficult."

"For who Mr Rafi?" she asks sarcastically.

"For all of us. What we discussed about the money, the flat, and other things. My employers have informed me to negotiate with you a settlement. Because of the recent exposure of certain people you will never disclose your involvement with the late Amir. For this, my client is offering you half a million pounds. You can use the apartment until you feel you can move on. We think it would be best if you did this before certain people are released from prison. You understand what I mean don't you?"

She has just taken in everything he said, and now feels she can squeeze a little more out of him.

"I will never ever give anyone any information with regard to the Amir, I can promise you that."

"Ha, that is good Miss Lambert." His face lights up thinking the deal has been struck.

"Just one more thing Mr Rafi. My father's care will have to be included, over and above the £500,000. And, yes, I will leave London if we come to an agreement."

"Miss Lambert, you drive a hard bargain but I think I can agree to your terms providing there is nothing else."

"Just one thing," she says, smiling.

"Oh no Miss Lambert, you have squeezed all you can out of my client, nothing else."

"Mr Rafi, all I ask is for you to pay the housekeeper a small amount of money so she doesn't have to worry about her job. Shall we say £20,000?"

Mr Rafi smiles and holds his hand out to shake hands with her.

"Just one little thing more."

"No, no Miss Lambert."

She starts laughing while shaking his hand.

"Just joking, Mr Rafi."

He tells Rosie that certain papers will be drawn up and the money agreed will be paid into whatever bank she states. Any monies regarding her father's care will be paid to her in yearly amounts.

She takes a taxi back to her apartment. She watches the people in the cars and, walking around, she smiles thinking, *'I'm free.*

*Free and rich.'*
She looks up to the heavens puts her hands together, saying aloud, *"Thank you god, thank you."*

Later that evening she goes to visit her father. She sits with him in his room, and the nurse comes in now and again to see to his needs. Rosie asks if doctor Nathan is on duty. The nurse shakes her head.

"No. He should be on duty tomorrow. He is at home after doing a long shift."

She is wondering what to say to him. She is thinking of telling Nathan everything but that would probably finish their relationship. She says goodnight to her father and returns to her apartment.

She calls Susie, who comes into the room with the usual big smile on her face.

"Sit down near me Susie."

She sits down, wondering what Rosie is going to tell her.

Rosie takes her hand.

"Susie, you have taken good care of me while I have lived here. I have some bad news for you. I will be leaving very soon but I don't know when exactly."

She feels Susie's hand tighten on hers, and a small tear runs down her cheek.

"Oh Miss Rosie, I will miss you very much."

"I don't know what will happen with the apartment but don't worry you will be taken care of. I have seen to it that you will receive £20,000."

Susie smiles.

"£20,000? Oh Miss Rosie thank you, thank you."

"Don't thank me. You deserve it. As I said, I don't know how much longer I will be here but you will be with me until I leave."

"I will miss you very much Miss Rosie."

Susie wipes the tears from her face and gets up; as she is walking away she turns.

"May I say, I see news. I know it is Mr Danny. Excuse me Miss Rosie but I must say he no good for you. He cruel man sometimes."

"I know Susie, don't worry. Mr Danny will go away for a long time and I won't be seeing him again."

Susie has a big smile on her face.

"Miss Rosie is very happy now."

"Yes, Miss Rosie very happy."

She turns on the news just in time to hear about Danny and the rest of the people who were arrested. They have all been charged and will remain in custody, awaiting trial. The police say they are making more inquiries into the dignitaries that have been involved with the prostitution of the Eastern European girls. Apparently two Slovakian girls have already asked for leave to stay in the UK. They said it would be very dangerous if they were sent back to Slovakia. They were brought to the UK and forced into having sex with numerous men; some very important men.

Rosie thinks, *'If that is Natalia and Monika they must be having a laugh. Forced to have sex? What a joke.'*

Maybe the police will connect her to them if they find her telephone number on Danny's mobile. She is worried about this.

She calls Nathan.

"Hello."

"It's me Nathan. Rosie. I visited dad but I think you were not at the hospital."

"I'm sorry Rosie, you know what it's like when I'm there. It can be so very busy. I'm pleased you telephoned me because I've missed you. I would love to see you soon."

"I've missed you too Nathan. I would love to meet up with you. When and where will you be free?"

"Tomorrow night after six o'clock," he says.

"Yes, that's fine. Seven at the Pelican restaurant?" she says.

"Can't wait to see your sweet face, Rosie."

She laughs.

"Sweet face, have I? You have a beautiful face."

"Let's not keep praising one another. I just want get you in my bed," he says, breaking out in laughter.

"Love you. See you then Nathan, bye for now."
"Bye Rosie."


She walks to her bedroom, smiling. Then she opens the drawer where her stash of different drugs is. She takes out the small packet of powder, and looks at it. She is fighting with herself trying to resist it. Then, after standing there for some time she gives in and takes something that will help her sleep. The next thing she knows Susie is calling her.

"Miss Rosie, two gentlemen want to speak with you."
She tries to wake herself up.
"Coming Susie."
She gets out of bed wondering who it could be; as she walks into the lounge the two men introduce themselves.

"Miss Lambert, my name is DI Dickinson and this is Inspector Raymond. We would like to ask you a few questions."
"A few questions? What about?"
Everything is running through Rosie's mind. What does she tell them? She's guessing that all this is about Danny.

"Miss Lambert, could you tell me how you come to know or be connected to Daniel Franklin-Smith?"
"How do you mean, connected? Yes, I know him."
"Have you any knowledge of his friends or business associates?"
"No, not really."
"Come, Miss Lambert. We seem to know otherwise."
Before the inspector can say another word his mobile rings.
"Excuse me one moment."
He walks over to the other side of the room. Rosie can hear him.
"Yes, I'm with her now sir, but sir..."
There is a pause as a look of frustration comes over his face.
"I can." Again there is a silence. "Yes sir I understand. We are leaving now."
He puts the mobile in his pocket. He looks at his partner, shaking his head.

"I'm sorry for disturbing you Miss Lambert. Please forgive us, we don't need to ask you any more questions, and are very sorry for bothering you."

He and the other officer walk towards the door.

She wonders why they don't need to ask her any more questions, but she is happy and relieved she doesn't have to give any responses.

When the officers leave and are on their own DI Dickinson explains the call to his partner.

"That was the chief commissioner. He told me that we should leave Miss Lambert's apartment immediately, and forget about her as she is not relevant to the case."

Dickinson, an old fashioned copper keen to bang everyone that deserves it to rights, is far from happy.

"Bloody forget her? Talk about friends in high places. Come on Dave, let's get the hell out of here."

Rosie is hoping she sees no more of them. Maybe the Amir's family have friends in high places.

She cannot wait to see Nathan again; they meet up at the Pelican restaurant. Nathan cannot help showing how pleased he is seeing her.

"You look lovely as always Rosie."

He pulls the chair out for her to sit down.

"You don't look too bad yourself, Doctor Lawson."

They sit down. Nathan takes her hand and looks into Rosie's eyes. He looks concerned.

"Rosie, are you okay?"

"What do you mean Nathan? Course I'm okay." She realises he has an idea about her drug taking.

"Rosie my sweet, I'm a doctor. You can talk me."

She is quiet and does not answer immediately; Nathan just sits waiting for her to answer.

She bites her lip, she tries her hardest not to cry. She feels she must tell him, as she knows she needs help.

"I have a lot to tell you which is not pleasant. I think a lot about you but I know we cannot be together without you knowing the truth about me."

All is quiet. Nathan is wondering what she is about to tell him. He sits quite close to her, waiting for her to speak. Rosie's face is pale. She takes a deep breath.

"I'm not a model and I can't say I'm a nice person. I have done what a lot of people would describe as..." She stops, unable to say the word. "...Prostitution."

She begins to cry. Nathan, far from being disgusted or shocked, takes her hand again.

"Tell me Rosie, tell me everything. I can see you are a good person, no matter what your past has been."

"Yes it is my past Nathan. It's all finished now, finished for good. Look, I will understand if you don't want to see me anymore."

"Well, let me hear the whole story. And I mean the whole story."

She pulls no punches. She tells him everything from the very beginning; she tells him about meeting Danny at uni and right up to the present day. She tells him about the drugs and about the meetings with VIPs and a very important foreign dignitary, not disclosing just who he was. She watches his face. He is not looking shocked - he just listens intently.

She seems to have been talking for ages but he does not stop her, only pausing when ordering drinks for them both. Occasionally she cries but he always shows her compassion.

After what seems like hours Rosie sits quietly, not daring to look at him and thinking he will be disgusted at what she has told him.

"Rosie, I think we need to get you some help with the drug taking. If that's what you really want?"

"Oh yes, I do. I do."

"Regarding our relationship. Well, we should talk about that later."

"Nathan I don't want anything to eat, I don't think I can. Can we leave?"

Nathan can see she wants to go. He pays the bill for the drinks, helps her with her coat and they leave the restaurant.

"I'll go home now Nathan. I'm sorry, I'll understand if you don't want to see me again."

She is so ashamed and afraid that she will lose him. She starts to cry.

"You are a good man and I'm sure you can meet someone a lot better than me."

"Why do you think I want to meet someone else?" he asks.

"Why? Because of what I have told you."

She lowers her head again.

"Rosie, I have always suspected there was something that you did not want to tell me. Well now I know. I want to ask you one question, if I may?"

Rosie has tears running down her cheeks.

"What?"

"Do you want to be with me?"

Rosie throws her arms around him. "More than ever Nathan. I know I love you more than I have ever loved any man."

"Rosie, please come to my place. Please?" He puts his arm around her, pulling her close.

Rosie's face is close to his. She lays her head on his chest and he kisses her head.

"Yes, please take me home with you Nathan. I need you."

They take a cab to Nathan's place. They are quiet in the back of the cab, Rosie holding on to him as though to let go would result in him leaving her.

As they arrive at Nathan's place he takes her hand and leads her into his flat. Once inside he pulls her close to him. He takes her face in his hands, wipes away the tears and gently kisses her.

She puts her arms around him. He can feel her sobbing. He picks her up and carries her to his bed and lays her down, and then he lies beside her. There is no sex, no talking; they just lay together holding one another. They are both fully clothed and that's how they fall asleep.

When Rosie wakes up it is daylight and she can smell bacon. Nathan is stood in the small kitchen. He notices that she has woken up.

"Drink of coffee, darling?"

She cannot believe Nathan is like he is after she has told him everything.

She is embarrassed because she feels that she is not looking her best. She scurries to the little bathroom trying to make herself look better. When she comes out of the bathroom he is sat at the small table, smiling. He points to her plate.

"Sit down, eat your breakfast and do as the doctor tells you," he laughs.

"Nathan."

"Shush! Eat your breakfast."

She smiles at him, so relieved that he is being like he is; she knows they must talk more but at this moment nothing more needs to be said.


Nathan's sister Martha and little Lucy come to see him at his flat. She smiles at Rosie.

"So, you're Rosie. He has never stopped talking about you."

Nathan didn't expect her to visit this morning and he can see Rosie is a little embarrassed due to not really having the time to smarten herself up.

"Hi sis. Yes, this is Rosie. And this is my lovely big sister Martha, Rosie."

Rosie and Martha shake hands, with little Lucy looking on.

"Nice to meet you Martha. Nathan told me all about you."

"The reason I called to see you Nathan is that we leave for Canada tomorrow. I cannot convince you to come to Canada, can I? You could have a great career over there."

"No Martha, I prefer staying in the UK. In fact I have one big reason." He looks at Rosie smiling.

"He needs a good woman to look after him," she says to Rosie, laughing.

They talk for a while before Martha has to leave. Nathan picks Lucy up and gives her a hug, and then goes to his sister and kisses her.

"Give my brother-in-law Bob my regards."

When they have left he can see Rosie is a little uncomfortable.

"Look Rosie, don't worry. We'll sort things out when I get back."

Rosie goes to him and holds him.

"Your sister seems a very nice person," she says.

"She's great. She whispered to me before she left that she liked you. I have to leave now darling."

## 21
# Their Future

He leaves for the hospital. Rosie is also leaving to go to her apartment. Nathan tells her when he has finished his shift that they will have to get together to discuss their future, and to sort out Rosie's problems. She agrees and they make arrangements to meet at her apartment. She is not afraid to let Nathan see where she is living now that he knows everything.

Rosie is home and making herself look her best for Nathan. She is resisting taking any drugs but she is finding it very difficult as the day wears on. She is getting very fidgety and again and again goes to her drawer, looks at what she has, then tries her hardest to walk away.

Nathan telephones Rosie to tell her he is on his way and asks if she is all right.

"Please hurry, Nathan."

He notices there is a sense of urgency in her voice.

"I'm coming right away darling."


The doorbell rings and Susie goes to answer the door.

"No Susie, I'll get it."

She opens the door. Nathan is stood there; Rosie throws her arms around him.

"What is it Rosie?" he asks.

She shakes her head.

"Come in Nathan."

They go into the lounge. Nathan is looking around; unable to believe where she lives. They sit down and Rosie looks at him.

"I need something, I know I do. I have had a hell of a day

although I have not taken anything. I know sooner or later I will give in. Oh Nathan, help me."

"Rosie, I can make arrangements for you to enter a clinic but you must want to otherwise it will just be a waste of time."

"Yes I'll go, anything. Nathan, if you feel you don't want to be with me I will understand."

"I do want to be with you, and I know that you will beat this if you really want to. I'm going to make a couple of calls, okay?"

"Yes," she says, and starts crying.

After some time on the phone he takes her hand.

"Right darling, pack a few things, whatever you need and I'm taking you to one of the best drug rehabilitation clinics there is. Are you sure you want to go?"

"Yes Nathan, I'll pack a few things."

They go to Nathan's old banger, parked out front. He smiles at her.

"Not really the best but it goes alright, I hope. A bit different to what you're probably used to."

It starts up after a couple of turns of the ignition. A look of relief comes over his face, and then they are on their way.

"Don't be afraid. It will be difficult Rosie but I have faith in you. I know you can do it."

"I won't let you down, I promise," she says, clinging on to Nathan.

"I know you won't darling.'

As they arrive she sees a very large country house. She is a little nervous as they pull up outside and Nathan takes her bag and then Rosie's hand. They enter the building and a nurse and a doctor are there to greet them. Nathan introduces Rosie to them. Nathan knows the doctor.

"We'll take good care of her Nathan," he says, motioning to the nurse to show her where to go.

Nathan kisses Rosie, and holds on to her as he whispers in her ear.

"I'll come and see you darling. You have to be brave."

"I'll try," she says. She holds him for some time before Nathan persuades her to go with the nurse.

The nurse tells her to follow her. Nathan watches as she walks up the long corridor with the nurse before entering one of the rooms. She looks back at him and gives him a little wave.

Over the next month or so she finds things very difficult but somehow gets over that and is feeling a lot better. The cravings have almost gone through determination on her part and the excellent care she has received.

Nathan visits her regularly and each time he visits her he sees how she is looking better and better. She seems to be happier within herself. Being a doctor he understands just how with some people it can be the answer, and they go on in life never, ever touching drugs again. With others they can soon relapse and start taking drugs again. He is hoping that she is not the latter because he loves her very much. He has known from the very first day he saw her that she was for him.

After several weeks she is as good as she will ever be. She feels like a new woman, and cannot wait to go home. Everyone is happy at the way she has progressed. They tell her she can go home. She is told that, if at anytime she does not feel right or feels the need to take any drug, she should return immediately. She hopes that will never happen.

She gets herself looking her very best. She is expecting Nathan anytime to take her home. She is so pleased with herself, there is no more worrying about her past, and she is looking to her future at last. Her father is much the same; Nathan has been keeping her informed about his wellbeing.

Time passes and soon, after some very difficult times, she is now ready to face the world again. She has regained the confidence lost during her time with Danny. She cannot wait to be close to Nathan again. She is so excited knowing that she will be with Nathan soon.

He phones to tell her he is on his way; she panics a little looking in the mirror and straightening her dress, seeing to her hair.

A knock comes at the door. She rushes to open it; Nathan is stood with a beautiful bouquet of red roses.

"Roses for my favourite Rosie," he says, as he hands her the bouquet and holds out his arms. She throws her arms around him, kissing him and nearly crushing her roses.

"Rosie you look lovely. I am so pleased for you, you have been so brave."

"Thanks to you darling. "

She takes the roses from him. He picks up her bags and she puts her arm in his, clinging on to him. As they leave they say goodbye to everyone. Nathan's old banger is stood outside and she gets in while he throws her bags into the boot.

"Are we ready then?" he says to her, turning the ignition. Nothing happens.

"A bit temperamental," he says, turning the key again.

"A bit old and temperamental," she says laughing, kissing him on the cheek. A lot of black smoke comes out of the exhaust and the engine starts up. The car jumps about with a stop and start motion. They are both laughing as the car finally moves off.

They get to Rosie's apartment and as they enter Susie comes running to her.

"Miss Rosie, Miss Rosie." Susie is so happy to see her.

They get settled and Susie brings them a drink. They are sat kissing and cuddling on the settee.

"Oh sorry Miss Rosie."

"It's okay Susie," she says and they are both laughing.

"Anything else Miss Rosie?"

"No thanks Susie, you can go now."

Susie leaves, giggling.

Nathan suddenly looks serious.

"Rosie," he says, looking her in the eye.

"Yes Nathan?" she says, wondering why he is looking so serious.

"I love you and I want us to be together always. Rosie, we cannot stay here it doesn't feel right. Maybe we could get a place together, somewhere a little smaller?" he says, looking around.

"Darling whatever you want to do. Maybe we could move away, somewhere else in the country? Of course, that is if you agree?"

"I suppose in view of what you told me it might be the

247

best thing. I could look for another post."

"Nathan, could we forget everything for now?" she says, standing up and taking his hand.

"Come with me," she says, smiling seductively.

He follows her to the bedroom. Rosie doesn't want to seem forward and lets Nathan make all the moves. He holds her in his arms, kissing her, and then lays her gently on the bed. She watches him undress. He has a wonderful physique, and she is more than ready for him; she has not been near a man for quite some time. He slowly undresses Rosie, stopping and kissing her body as he takes each garment off. She wants him more and more, and soon she is completely naked. He leans back and looks at her.

"You're beautiful."

He lays down on top of her, kissing her face and her neck before slowly moving down her body. She is holding on to his hair. His every movement is setting her on fire and she feels she is about to explode as he moves to her thighs. She's pushing his head deeper into her and she is crying out with pleasure. He moves to lay on her; he kisses her, and finally he penetrates her. She is in ecstasy and she realises that Nathan is the one for her. She thought Danny was the one until he showed her just what a bad person he was. She knows she has never really felt like this about anyone, not even Danny.

Now she is being fulfilled, and she knows just what her friends talked about a long time ago when they said how wonderful sex was.


Nathan leaves the apartment with renewed energy, determined to try for a position away from London with the hope that Rosie will go with him. After looking around he finds a vacancy in Edinburgh, which he thinks would be ideal for him. He could be accepted for the position after visiting the hospital and attending a personal interview in a week's time.

He cannot wait to tell her. He telephones her.

"Rosie, I think I have got a position in a hospital in Edinburgh. I have to go up there for an interview."

"Oh Nathan, that's great. When will you be going?"

"In a week or so. They will email me."

Rosie can see he is happy and seems enthusiastic. She has a surprise for him and tells him.

"I will meet you at the hospital when you finish. I'll go and see dad."

"Okay darling. Should be around seven thirty unless anything comes up."

"See you later darling."

Rosie has had a call from Mr Rafi, who has seen to all her demands and the money has been put into her bank. She has been paid the money for Susie, and the money for her father's care has been seen to. She has heard nothing of the trial for Danny and his friends but she is not worried at all.

She wants to spoil Nathan so she goes to the garage near to where she lives. She looks at various cars, wondering just what he would like and then she sees this very nice sports car. Without bothering to ask the price she tells the salesman that she wants it. The salesman cannot believe his luck.

She buys him the new car. She is afraid he may not like her doing this but she loves him and can't wait to spoil him.

She asks for the car to be delivered to the hospital and that she will take the keys from the driver. She tells them the time that she will be there. The garage is only too pleased to oblige.

She goes in the evening to see her father and is sat with him when the keys are delivered to her.

She waits for Nathan to come to her. She is so excited, one about his new job and two, to see his face when she shows him the car. He enters the room. Rosie's face lights up and she runs to him, kissing him.

"Dad's okay, shall we go?"

"Sure, can we go to my place?"

"Anywhere you want darling."

She kisses her father then puts her arm in Nathan's.

As they leave the hospital she asks, "Where's your car?"

"Just around the corner in the car park," he says.

They walk towards his car. There is a very nice new car alongside his. He laughs.

"Somebody wants to show me up," he says, as he is about to open his car door.

Rosie turns him to face her. She is holding the keys up for the new car. At first he doesn't understand, then Rose is swinging the keys and smiling.

"Darling, it's yours," she says excitedly.

His face changes. First he looks at the car, and then at Rosie.

"I can't accept this from you. It wouldn't be right. No, I can't accept it Rosie."

She is upset.

"Why? Is it because of my past? Do you think the money has come from that?"

She starts crying and turns to walk away. He runs after her.

"Rosie, Rosie, I'm sorry. Please forgive me."

She still carries on walking while he is trying to stop her.

"Rosie! Please, I love you. Give me a chance and I'll explain."

She stops and turns to face him.

"It won't work, will it? You will never forget my past no matter what. It will always haunt us."

"It's nothing to do with your past. I have feelings. I'm a man and I should have to provide for you and buy you presents." He says all this while trying to show her he loves her. "You can buy me presents, and provide for me, but all I want is you and I want to make you happy." Nathan smiles at her and he holds his right hand out.

"Okay, you win. Give me the keys," he says, shrugging his shoulders.

A smile comes back onto her face as she gives him the keys. They walk back to the new car.

"What's wrong with that?" Nathan asks, pointing to his old car.

"It won't get us to Scotland, will it? We would finish up walking."

He is laughing now.

"You are not just beautiful. You know how to handle a stubborn man."

He takes her in his arms and kisses her.

A few days pass. Rosie has practically lived at Nathan's small flat but she has enjoyed every minute of it. Taking care of him and looking after the place has been simple but amazingly good fun. She thinks this is life as it should be. Yes she has money but she realises money or no money, this is what she wants.

Nathan has received an email inviting him to go for the interview. He tells Rosie as he arrives at the flat. He picks her up, kissing her.

"We're going to Scotland darling," he says, swinging her round.

"When?"

"Day after tomorrow. Pack your bag my love."

"I have an idea Nathan, if you agree?"

"What's that?"

"If we buy a place big enough to put in an annex for dad, would you mind?"

"Rosie that's no problem for me. We could get some private help for him."

She goes to him and kisses him. "You are so kind Nathan. Thank you."

She goes back to her apartment to see Susie.

"Oh Miss Rosie. I miss you."

"Sit down Susie."

She takes an envelope from her bag and gives her it.

"Susie, this is yours. I am going away soon so we won't be seeing each other."

She wipes a tear from her face. Susie opens the envelope and sees the cheque.

"Oh thank you Miss Rosie. I will always remember you."

Rosie gives her a hug, they hold each other for a while, and then she has an idea.

"Susie, do you have any family in the UK?"

"No Miss Rosie. No family."

"Give me your telephone number and address. How would you like to go to Scotland?"

"On holiday you mean Miss Rosie?"

"No Susie, to live with me and Mr Nathan."

Susie's face lights up. She has never had anyone care for her for a long time and she is so happy.

"Oh yes, yes. I give you money back?"

"No that money is yours. I would want you to look after my father. He needs a lot of help. Could you cope? I'll always be there."

"Yes, Susie can manage, no problem."

"We will be away a few days then I will call you."
She gets up to leave. They hold one another.

"You make Susie very happy."

"You take care and I'll be in touch."
When she leaves Susie sits down, unable to hold back the tears. She had wondered what she would do when Miss Rosie left. Now she knows that everything will be fine.


Rosie feels really pleased with herself and everything is falling into place. She tells Nathan about her plans for her father. He agrees and tells her she can do what she thinks best.

They are on their way to Edinburgh and happy to be with one another. The journey seems to last forever and when they finally get to Edinburgh they book into a hotel very close to the hospital. They have hardly been able to wait to be alone together and now, in their hotel room, Nathan is laying on the bed waiting for her to come from the bathroom.

The bathroom door opens and there is his beautiful woman. She walks slowly over to him; he reaches out but she pushes him away. She is teasing him; he wants to touch her but she pushes his hands above his head before climbing on him. She reaches behind her to take hold of him, and he is so ready for her. Her perfume is driving him crazy as she moves her hand slowly.

She releases him and stands up with one leg either side of him on the bed. Slowly, she takes her bra off. He is looking up at her then she encourages him to take off her stockings, and last of all her panties. He cannot stand any more. He pulls her down on him, his hands are all over her, and then they make frantic love until their bodies are spent, exhausted and unable to carry on making love. They fall asleep, holding one another close.

The next morning they go down for breakfast. Nathan is eager to get to the hospital and he is constantly looking at his watch,

"Nathan, it's nearly time. You may as well go otherwise you'll get high blood pressure."

"Right darling, wish me luck." He gives her a kiss. "I'll phone you when I come out."

They kiss and she wishes him luck.

She has asked the staff at the hotel where the nearest estate agents are. She nips out and gets a list of as many properties as she can before going to her room to look through them.

It seems a long time since Nathan left. She is wondering how he is getting on. Around three o'clock her mobile rings. She sees it is Nathan calling.

"Hi darling, how did it go?" There is a silence. Rosie fears the worst, and then a loud shout comes down the phone.

"I got it Rosie," he says laughing. "I like the hospital, the staff are great, and I can't wait Rosie. I start in six weeks time."

"Hurry back darling." She says. Nathan knows what she has waiting for him.

They have enjoyed making love, and are now relaxing, Rosie gets out the brochures. She had picked a few properties out but there was one that she really liked.

"Look Nathan, it has everything we need and it is not too far from the hospital."

"Darling we can look around. I'm sure there are plenty just like this."

"I know Nathan but I just know this is what we want. This is our future home I know it is."

He laughs and kisses her.

"Who could refuse you anything?" He grabs hold of her, playfully kissing her and playing around.

"Nathan I might give you a special treat if you come with me to look at that property tomorrow."

"Rosie, Rosie you can wrap me around your little finger. Come on then, give it to me."

She lays on him, kissing him, giggling and starts undoing his shirt.

The next day they make an appointment to see the property. They are both very impressed with it and its large bay windows at the front, high ceilings with ornate covings in all rooms. A large drive that opens up to a beautiful large garden also impresses them. Once at the back of the property they are amazed at just how big the annex is.

Rosie is already planning where to put things. They go from room to room. Rosie is so exited.

Nathan says, "We could negotiate the price."

"Oh Nathan, could we? The annex off is ideal for dad and there is enough room in there for Susie too. I have the money and you can use it if you want to."

"Rosie, I have some money. We will make an offer and see how it goes."

"Thank you darling."

She kisses him.

Nathan puts an offer in. Rosie and Nathan go and look around Edinburgh. At the same time, Rosie is doing a bit of shopping, looking for certain things to furnish the property if they get it.

She is thinking about the jewellery and money she has in the safety deposit box. She knows she has to get rid of it to rid her of her past. She is thinking of selling it all apart from the last present the Amir gave her. She knows it is worth a substantial amount of money and, along with her money in the bank, could make Nathan and herself very comfortable for the rest of their lives.

They are back at the hotel when Nathan receives a call from the estate agent. Rosie is watching his face.

"Yes I understand. Yes okay then, thank you."

He puts the phone down not looking too happy.

She is waiting patiently.

"Well Nathan?"

"I'm sorry, Rosie."

Her face changes, then Nathan tells her.

"Well, we got it. They will complete in five to six weeks time."

"Nathan Lawson, I could kill you keeping me in

suspense."

She picks a pillow off the sofa and throws it at him. She is laughing as she walks towards him and kisses him.

They go back to London to settle things up. Nathan has to inform the hospital where he is working now that he has the new job and will be leaving shortly, although this is not unusual for doctors. Rosie has to move all her belongings from the apartment with the help of Susie.

One evening at Nathan's place they are watching the news on television when they see an item about the trial for the girl traffickers. It has started and they have all put in pleas of not guilty. Nathan looks at her. She doesn't say anything for a moment or two then she puts her head in her hands and starts crying.

"What is it darling? Don't cry."

"Oh Nathan, I just want it all to be finished, so we can get on with our lives."

"I read it in the paper. Not guilty? It's a joke. They are all expected to get long prison sentences," he says.

"Please Nathan, I don't want to talk about them."

During the next few days she is able to sell her jewellery. She is amazed just how much it was worth. She is happy that part of her life has been sorted out.

The arrangements for her father have been made for him to join them when they have everything ready for him. She has had a word with Susie who will be coming with them to Edinburgh. Nathan has nothing in his flat that is worth taking and Rosie has told him only his personal things must go and the rest needs to be sent to the tip.

"Rosie, I love that chair. I can't part with that."

"Nathan that chair, what can I say, looks like something has been eating away at it?"

"That was probably me when I thought you had dumped me."

"Dumped you? I'm lucky you didn't dump me."

Nathan picks her up and kisses her.

"The only place I will dump you my girl is on my bed,"

he says, as he carries her over to the bed.

"Oh yes, that would be nice," she says, ruffling his hair.


They have completed on their new property and are both very excited. Nathan has finished at the hospital and they are ready to move to Edinburgh.

Rosie has had to travel up to Edinburgh by plane to purchase furnishings for the new house. She has bought some of the most beautiful things, wanting it to be a great surprise for Nathan. She insisted she should do everything. The annex is nearing completion also.

When the house is ready she returns to the flat, and tells Nathan how beautiful it is. He is so proud of her seeing the enthusiasm she has had for the project.


They say their goodbyes to Nathan's old flat. They are soon on their way with Susie. Her father will be brought up to join them in two days.

Leaving London seems to give Rosie a new lease of life. She feels she is free from her past; she cannot wait to get to their new home.

They arrive at the house and Nathan gets out of the car with Rosie and Susie following.

"Rosie, oh Rosie, it looks beautiful." He walks to the front door and opens it. He cannot believe what he sees and how it has changed.

"Rosie it's marvellous," he says, with a big grin on his face. He walks round the house with her following him. He looks in each room and finally he opens their bedroom door.

"Oh wow. Is this our lo...ve room?" he jokes.

"Do you really like it darling?" she says, feeling proud of herself.

"Rosie, everything you have done is fantastic. Absolutely fantastic."

He kisses her. They are stood in the bedroom just holding one another.

He takes hold of her hand. He goes down on one knee, takes a small box from his pocket. She is waiting for him to say the words.

"Rosie Lambert, I want you to be my wife. I love you so much."

She puts on her serious face as he looks up at her.

"Go on then, I guess it's a yes." She starts laughing then she tells him how she feels. "Darling. I do love you. And of course I will marry you."

Nathan takes the ring box. She is smiling as he takes the ring from the box and puts it on her finger. She sheds tears of happiness looking down at this wonderful man.

She doesn't care how much the ring cost. Even if it cost ten pence she tells herself, *'It will be on my finger until I die.'*

Nathan stands up and looks at her.

"Rosie, I promise you I am, and always will be, yours."

She kisses him again.

"I love you so much Nathan. Shall we get Susie settled in the annex? And come back to the lo...ve room.

"How could I say no?"


The End.